VALORIA
SEAT OF THE VALORIAN KINGDOM
PLAINS
SILENT MOUNTAINS
SEAT OF THE ELDWAIN KINGDOM
ELDWAIN
SERELUNE RIVER
OBSIDIAN OCEAN
SAPPHIRE DEPTHS

BLOOD WEAVER

BLOOD WEAVER TRILOGY

KARINA ESPINOSA

Copyright © 2024 by Karina Espinosa

All rights reserved.

No part of this book may be reproduced in any form or by any electronic or mechanical means, including information storage and retrieval systems, without written permission from the author, except for the use of brief quotations in a book review.

Cover design by © Christian Bentulan
Edited by Stacy Sanford
Map by Cartographybird Maps

Copyright 2024 by Karina Espinosa

ISBN-13: 979-8-218-35142-7
ASIN: B0CGN457HZ

To my closest friends and family.
(Too many to list)
You put up with all of my mood swings when it comes to writing.
Thank you for sticking around!

1

The fragrant aroma of brewing tea filled the air, intermingled with soft notes of cinnamon and jasmine. A delicate dance of light and shadow played through the intricate wooden lattices, making the polished mahogany tables gleam. Soft murmurs and chuckles filled the Tea House, setting a backdrop for the storyteller on the main floor. He was in the midst of a gripping tale, his voice rising and falling in a melodious cadence that captivated the crowd.

Suddenly, he was interrupted by the shrill voice of a young boy. "The lost princess has been found! The lost princess has been found!" The boy, Henry, no older than eight, stood out among the patrons. His sun-kissed skin was smeared with the dust and sweat of a hard day's work. His hair, the color of rich cocoa, was tousled and streaked with sweat. His eyes, big and almond-shaped, sparkled with mischief and enthusiasm. They reflected the innocence of his age, yet held the weight of the important news he carried.

As he wound through the Tea House, weaving in and out of the crowd, the light fabrics of his loosely draped clothing fluttered about him. His worn-out sandals slapped the wooden floors, creating a staccato rhythm that drew more and more attention. The storyteller's tale was all but forgotten as gasps and murmurs filled the space.

I watched from the top floor as the young boy continued his animated proclamation, heading straight toward my table. Not wanting to miss an opportunity, I discreetly flashed a shiny gold coin between my fingers to catch his attention.

When he finally reached me, his cheeks were flushed and his breathing was heavy. "Yes, Miss Leila?" he managed to pant.

"The lost princess ..." I started. "Where was she found?"

The young boy cleared his throat, clearly parched. I slid a cup of tea in his direction, which he accepted graciously.

"In the Grasslands," he said, catching his breath.

I raised a brow in surprise. "Is that so?" I murmured. "And who found the lost princess?"

"The Crimson Clan!" he offered animatedly. "They're holding her hostage. If the King and Queen of Valoria don't meet their demands, they're going to marry her off to the clan chief's son."

I couldn't stop myself from laughing. Me? Marry the chief's son? In their dreams. After all these years I'd hidden undetected, I wondered who the Crimson Clan actually captured.

"Do you know what their demands are?" I asked once I regained my composure.

He shook his head. "No, but they sent an envoy to Valoria with the terms."

"Very well." I tossed the gold in his direction. Henry caught the coin with ease, his eyes widening in surprise. Before I could change my mind, the boy, now richer by a gold coin, sprinted away, his joyous shouts continuing to echo in the Tea House.

My spirits took a nosedive with the sudden news, making the heady atmosphere of the Tea House suffocating. I swiftly made my way downstairs, hoping some fresh air would clear my mind. But just as I stepped onto the street, Selene, in a blur of motion, was already rushing toward me. We almost collided, saved only by my quick reflexes.

"Whoa, slow down there. Is the Rose Petal on fire?" I teased, my hands steadying her by the shoulders.

She took a moment to catch her breath, her relief palpable. "By the gods, you're safe!" she breathed out, pulling me into a heartfelt embrace.

I laughed again. "I'm guessing you heard the news."

She pulled back. "Of course I heard! Everyone in the Central Plains has heard." Selene looked both ways around the street before she whispered, "I really thought they had captured you this time."

I scoffed. "I've been hiding in the Central Plains almost five years, and I've been gone for ten. No one knows where I am or if I still breathe. Whatever the Crimson Clan is planning, it's most definitely a bluff."

"Are you sure? Don't be so confident, Leila."

"Positive." I smiled brightly. "Come on, I'll walk you back to the Rose Petal."

We walked side by side, arm in arm, down Lomewood's cobbled streets. Selene drew many admiring glances from passersby, and it wasn't hard to see why. With her statuesque figure, her skin a shade of deep olive and her raven-black hair flowing like an inky river down her back, she was dazzling. Her vibrant green eyes mirrored the deep forests of Valoria, always searching, always seeing beyond the surface. The silver adornments on her fingers and wrists added a touch of opulence to her otherwise muted attire.

But her captivating beauty was both a gift and a curse. Sold into servitude by her own father to a pleasure house, she'd been striving to reclaim her freedom for years.

Selene leaned in closer to whisper, "The Crimson Clan will arrive in the Central Plains tonight."

I raised a brow. "And you know this how?"

"Madam Rose is prepping all the girls for their arrival."

I clenched my jaw at the mere mention of the madam. That cunning woman had rejected every single one of my offers to free Selene. Due to Selene's rare merfolk heritage, Madam Rose set her price exorbitantly high, keeping Selene's freedom just out of grasp.

"If they start trouble, you know what to do," I began, my tone cautionary.

Selene sighed heavily and nodded. "Yes, yes," she muttered, revealing the whistle that hung around her neck on a supple leather cord. "I will call on you."

It wasn't just any whistle. Carved from a unique wood found only in the depths of Valoria, its sound was audible exclusively to those of Valorian lineage. A silent, secret alarm.

My mind wandered back to a time, four years prior, when the alleys and squares of Lomewood were still foreign to me. An epidemic had swept through the region, and Madam Rose, ever the opportunist, sought me out, knowing of my abilities, and asked me to treat the girls under her employ. Among them, Selene was in a particularly dire state, her merfolk heritage making her more susceptible to the virulent strain.

Being a blood mage, I secretly used a rare method whereby I transfused her with my blood to purge the ailment. I hadn't anticipated her semi-conscious state during the process, which inadvertently unmasked my identity. Only one female in all of Asteria was known to have the gifts of a blood mage—the lost princess. When she recognized me, Selene promised to safeguard my secret, a pact that forged an unbreakable bond between us.

Handing her the Valorian whistle was a gesture of protection, a silent call she could make should she ever find herself in peril. Yet, over the years, its song remained silent. But with whispers of the Crimson Clan's impending arrival in the

Central Plains, I couldn't shake the nagging feeling that its call might soon pierce the quiet night of Lomewood.

The Lomewood streets were a tapestry of history and culture, painted in cobblestones and framed by ancient buildings. Gas lamps lined the pathways, casting a soft amber hue that reflected off the wet stones. Vendors peddled their goods from wooden stalls, their voices weaving in and out of the murmur of conversations. The town had grown organically over the years, resulting in a maze of intertwining alleys and courtyards. Towering oaks and elms occasionally broke the monotony of brick and mortar, their leaves rustling softly in the evening breeze. Each turn of the street unveiled a new scent, from fresh bread to fragrant flowers.

As we navigated this labyrinth, the Rose Petal Lounge loomed ahead of us. Dominating its surroundings, the three-story building was an architectural marvel. Rich, velvety maroon bricks were interspersed with white, intricate stonework, creating a design that evoked its namesake. Elegant wrought iron balconies jutted out from each floor, draped with cascading tendrils of ivy and climbing roses. Large bay windows tinted in a rosy hue gave subtle glimpses of the luxurious interiors. The entrance was framed by two massive rosewood doors, above which an ornate sign read, *Rose Petal Lounge* in swirling golden script.

Already, a brass placard hung on the entrance, etched with words that indicated the lounge's closure for a private event tonight. It was a testament to the establishment's exclusivity that it could shut its doors to the general public for the elite and privileged—the privileged tonight being the Crimson Clan of the Grasslands.

"Selene," I started. "Be careful. Don't put yourself in any dangerous situations tonight."

"I know, I know." She nodded with a slight roll of her eyes.

"This isn't my first time dealing with those from the Grasslands. I'll be careful," she added with a wink.

I snorted. "Yes, yes, you're quite the siren," I chuckled. "Even so, be careful."

"Will do!" With a charming grin thrown over her shoulder, she jogged up to the rosewood doors and let herself inside the pleasure house.

2

In the vast realm of medicine, I'm convinced there's no potion more elusive than the one that persuades villagers to actually pay for it.

"It costs a single glint," I declared, lifting the sachet filled with medicinal herbs. "You know there's no one better and cheaper than me throughout the Central Plains. If you want to be cured ..." I left the statement hanging as I beckoned to the next person in line.

"Fine, fine. Just one glint, and not a spark or gleam more," the butcher grumbled as he slammed the golden coin down and snatched the sachet from me.

I flashed him a cheeky smile as he stood. "Pleasure doing business with you as always. And I promise that wart on your bum will be healed in no time."

He grunted something unintelligible as he turned on his heel. The usually buoyant town butcher departed my clinic with a dark cloud over his mood. His bartering skills were commendable, but I was resolute. My treks into the mountainsides to gather the finest herbs justified the hefty price tag. No need for bargaining, especially when I already undercut most physicians.

The Central Plains were vast, and in the small town of Lomewood, we were free from the surrounding kingdoms and clans. We were the only neutral location in all of Asteria. Many refugees flocked to the Central Plains for this very reason after dealing with the fallout at the conclusion of the war between Keldara and Valoria. Even so, people mostly lived peacefully here without troubles or worrying about social status and everything else that came from the surrounding lands.

My clinic was a harmonious blend of functionality and tradition. From the outside, it was a modest two-story structure built with aged wooden planks that bore witness to countless seasons. Moss had taken residence between the wood and ivy draped the façade, lending a touch of nature's elegance. A sign hanging by the entrance displayed the emblem of two intertwined herbs – a nod to my profession as the local physician.

It was well past midnight in the dimly lit room of my clinic, and the only sound was the mortar and pestle rhythmically crushing fresh herbs into a fine powder. Each turn, each grind, was precise and measured. Suddenly, the room's serenity was violently shattered by a haunting whistle, clear and persistent. My heart raced as I recognized the sound—it was Selene.

Leaving the herbs scattered on the scarred wooden table, I sprinted outside, the back door banging shut behind me. The usually quiet alleys of Lomewood were filled with the echo of my frantic footsteps. The Rose Petal Lounge wasn't far, but each second felt agonizingly long.

Upon reaching the lounge, I barely acknowledged the heavy rosewood doors, pushing them aside with a burst of adrenaline. The sight that greeted me was a cacophony of colors, noises, and tension.

The Rose Petal Lounge was typically the embodiment of

opulence and seduction. Deep burgundy velvet curtains draped the large windows, filtering the outside light to a soft, ambient glow that bathed the entire room. Crystal chandeliers dripping with garnets and amethysts hung from the ceilings, their soft illumination casting shimmering reflections that danced on the walls. The lounge's name was evident in its decor, with rose petals scattered on the marble floors and floating in ornate bowls of water placed strategically around the room.

Tall, carved wooden pillars painted in gold leaf supported the ceiling, their shadows creating intimate nooks and corners for would-be lovers to occupy. Along the walls, plush chaise lounges and settees upholstered in luxurious fabrics of deep purples and reds beckoned guests to sit and relax. Each seating area was separated by intricate gilded screens, offering a semblance of privacy even though dozens of eyes were watching.

Girls from the lounge, dressed in flowing silks and satins that accentuated their figures, moved gracefully among the Crimson Clan members. Their outfits were in varying shades of red, pink, and gold to complement the room's decor and add to its allure. Their laughter, flirtatious glances, and gentle touches were all part of the lounge's entertainment, expertly catering to the clan members' whims and fancies.

Everywhere one looked, the elements of the room were designed to entice the senses. The subtle scent of roses and jasmine wafted in the air, while the soft strains of a lute played from a hidden corner set a melodious background score. Exotic fruits and decanters of the finest wines adorned the tables, each bite and sip a testament to the Rose Petal Lounge's commitment to decadence.

Yet, amidst the allure and enchantment, there was unmistakable tension. The presence of the Crimson Clan members added a dangerous edge to the room's seductive aura, an unmistakable reminder of their power and the unpredictability of the night.

The opulent interior of the Rose Petal Lounge was dominated by members of the Crimson Clan. Their signature long hair with tightly woven braids on the sides of their heads cascaded down to their behinds. Their skin was covered in crimson tattoos across their bodies. These tattoos were not mere adornments, but narrated the stories of their lineage, feats, and status within the clan. They were a symbol of their identity, pride, and unity. But the most unsettling part of their demeanor was their uniquely colored eyes. Their irises, ranging from a light rust color to a deep blood-red, reflected their namesake and were often associated with their reputed demon blood.

I scanned the room, searching for Selene amongst the sea of red. Every second counted, and I had to find her before it was too late.

The whistle blew louder now that I was near, and my ears popped from the frequency. When I didn't find Selene in all the chaos around me, I hurried to the second floor where the girls entertained privately, taking the stairs two at a time. Running and pushing my way past Crimson Clan members and pleasure house girls, I kicked open Selene's door and stormed inside. My stomach dropped when I found her pinned down by three Crimson Clan members.

Selene wasn't the type to cry. Her unfortunate life was already filled with so many horrors, she was practically a stone wall. But in that moment, her eyes glistened with unshed tears and fear.

Her vulnerable state kicked me into action as I ran toward them, drawing upon the energy within me. The room grew cold and the candles flickered out as darkness closed in. A force, invisible but palpable, radiated from me, pushing against everything in the room. The heavy wooden furniture groaned and slid, and the ornate tapestries flapped wildly in a turbulent wind. The three men pinning Selene were forced back, their grip releasing her as they struggled to maintain their footing.

The room was a maelstrom of raw power and chaos, and the very air seemed to shimmer and warp. I stood in the eye of this storm, my gaze locked onto Selene, ensuring her safety. As quickly as it started, the tempestuous energy receded, leaving the room in disarray.

Three men lay sprawled across the room, dazed and panting heavily. Selene, looking disheveled but otherwise unharmed, pushed herself up to a sitting position, her green eyes wide with a mix of relief and awe.

The energy that had surged through the room provided a momentary advantage, but it wouldn't last long. As Selene pushed to her feet, I positioned myself between her and the three Crimson Clan members who were regaining their senses and getting up.

The first one lunged at me, swinging a dagger. Relying on years of training and instinct, I sidestepped his assault, catching his wrist and using his momentum to send him crashing into a nearby wall. The impact was violent, causing plaster and wood to crack.

The second assailant was more cautious, circling me with a wary look in his crimson eyes. He was sizing me up, gauging my abilities. With a swift kick, I knocked the weapon from his hand, then closed the distance between us and delivered a series of strikes targeting his vulnerable points: the neck, kidneys, and knees. He stumbled back and gasped for breath.

The third, however, was the most skilled of them all. He advanced slowly, his eyes darting and analyzing my every move. We danced around the room, trading blows, each trying to find an opening in the other's defense. His movements were precise and calculated.

The size of Selene's room was considerable, which allowed

for this dance of death. Suddenly, with a feigned misstep, he lunged, trying to catch me off guard. But I saw through his ruse. Ducking under his swing, I grabbed his arm and pivoted on my heel, then used his own momentum to throw him to the ground. I quickly followed up with a swift kick to the head, rendering him unconscious.

I turned to Selene and sized her up and down to make sure she wasn't hurt. Though bruises were starting to form on her wrists and neck, she seemed fine. "Are you okay?"

She nodded shakily but didn't answer, still trying to compose herself. I was about to grab her and drag her out of this hell hole when Madam Rose waltzed in, looking furious.

Madam Rose was an imposing figure despite her middle-aged stature. Her raven-black hair, streaked with lines of silver, was pulled back into a severe bun, giving prominence to her sharp, hawk-like eyes. Every line and wrinkle on her face told a story of battles fought and won in the underbelly of Lomewood. Her lips, painted a deep shade of maroon, were set in a tight line of disapproval. Her silk robe, adorned with embroidered roses, flowed elegantly as she moved, barely making a whisper against the ornate rug. A thick gold necklace encircled her neck, reflecting the dim light and lending an almost regal aura.

She scanned the room silently, taking in the aftermath of the struggle. Her eyes settled on the unconscious Crimson Clan members before shifting to me, then to Selene. "What have you done?" she hissed, her voice dripping with venom.

"Protecting my friend," I responded defiantly, standing between her and Selene. "It's more than what you've been doing. Isn't she your most prized possession? Shouldn't *you* be protecting her?"

She narrowed her eyes and took a threatening step closer. "You've always been a thorn in my side, Leila. But this time, you've really outdone yourself."

"Perhaps you should be more selective about the company you keep!" I shot back.

If Madam Rose had powers and wasn't just a measly human, she would have killed me on the spot. I knew she wanted to. She probably dreamed about it every night. But alas, she couldn't.

"Watch your words," she gritted between her teeth, glancing slightly behind her back in case any of the Crimson Clan members overheard us.

I gently gripped Selene's wrist without hurting her already bruised skin and dragged her behind me. "I'm taking her out of here," I said. "You obviously don't care what happens to your girls."

"You'll take her over my dead body!" she threatened.

"What seems to be the problem here?" a male voice boomed as he entered the room. His long hair, tattooed skin, and crimson eyes made it obvious he was a Crimson Clan member.

Madam Rose's gaze swung to the newcomer and her body stiffened visibly. The room's energy intensified further as the weight of the situation pressed down on all of us.

The man was imposing, standing over six feet tall with a physique that was lean, but muscular. His presence filled the room with an undeniable aura. He was strikingly handsome, almost unfairly so. His strong jawline and sharp cheekbones lent him an aristocratic, regal look. Waves of jet-black hair cascaded back from his forehead, braided at the sides, stopping just short of his hips. Those crimson eyes, which would have been menacing on any other face, possessed a mischievous glint that hinted at a playful side, or perhaps a dangerous one, hidden beneath the surface.

His lips, full and shapely, curled into a smirk that could make anyone's heart flutter, albeit with a mixture of attraction and trepidation. Every feature of his face seemed perfectly crafted, as if he was the very embodiment of allure. The scars and tattoos that adorned his skin spoke of battles, wisdom, and experiences that only added depth to his beauty.

Even his posture was one of confident ease. The way he held himself, his every movement, suggested a deadly grace, like a predatory cat. When he spoke, his voice was deep and resonant, sending chills down the spine, not solely out of fear but also an inexplicable pull. There was something about him, an almost magnetic charm, that could draw someone in, despite the clear and evident danger that came with his affiliation to the Crimson Clan.

In any other situation, one could almost mistake him for a charming rogue or a misfit prince from a far-off land. But given the current circumstances, his beauty came with a foreboding sense of peril.

"Nothing you need to concern yourself with," Madam Rose said hastily, waving off his concern. "Merely a personnel matter."

The male looked from Madam Rose to his unconscious men on the floor, then to Selene, then me.

"That doesn't seem to be the case, Madam. Why are my men unconscious?" He stepped further into the room to inspect the men on the floor.

Madam Rose cleared her throat. "I was handling it. I won't let her get away with it, I promise you." Madam Rose snapped her fingers and called out for the servants in the Rose Petal Lounge. "Take Selene out back and dispense forty floggings!" she commanded.

"Like hell you will!" I shouted and stood in front of my friend. "I don't care who these people are. They deserved what they got!"

The Crimson Clan member looked up at me before he stood and gave me a once over. "*You* did this?" he asked in surprise.

Proudly lifting my chin, I didn't deign to respond.

He laughed. "A little thing like you took down three of my men?"

I was far from little, but compared to his men, I guess I could be described that way. "They were going to violate her," I replied unflinchingly.

"And?" he questioned with a raised brow. "This is a pleasure house; they've merely come to claim what they paid for. Or are we not in a pleasure house?" He glanced around pointedly to confirm he was indeed in the Rose Petal Lounge.

"Leila," Selene whispered from behind me, pulling at my arm to stop me. "There's no use arguing," she whispered so they couldn't hear.

I scoffed and ignored her plea. "I doubt Selene agreed to entertain three at a time, no matter who paid for what. Get a handle on your men, or I will," I threatened.

The clan member laughed again as he turned back to Madam Rose. "Am I hearing this correctly?" he chuckled. "*You* will get a handle on *my* men? Well, this is a first. I don't get a lot of females threatening me."

"I'm so sorry, Ronan," Madam Rose apologized. "I will have her escorted off the premises at once."

"No." He held up a hand to stop her. "I'm intrigued. Tell me, what's your name?"

I didn't want to answer, but I knew if I didn't, Madam Rose would surely tell him. "Leila," I answered through gritted teeth.

"Leila what?"

I shook my head. "No family name. I'm an orphan," I lied ... somewhat.

"Leila," he sang my name a couple of times. "What a lovely name. Tell me, Leila, could I pay for your time?"

I scoffed and rolled my eyes. "Do I look like one of the girls who works here?" I pointed to my blouse and trousers.

He smirked. "No, but you could for the night."

"I'd rather choke to death," I deadpanned.

Ronan's smirk grew wider and the mischief in his crimson eyes became even more pronounced. "Such fire," he mused, taking a step closer to me. "It's not often that I meet someone like you."

"Keep your distance," I warned him, raising a hand in caution.

He halted but continued to observe me with an almost predatory gaze, as if sizing up a worthy opponent. "It's unfortunate. We could have had quite a delightful evening."

"I'm sure we would have," I retorted.

Madam Rose, visibly flustered, tried to regain control of the situation. "Sir, I assure you, I'll handle this."

He waved her off, his focus entirely on me. "I've got it from here," he said calmly, though there was a dangerous undertone to his voice that I didn't miss. "Leave us."

"Madam Rose, don't you dare leave us alone with him!" I snapped, but she quickly retreated, leaving me and Selene alone with Ronan and his still-unconscious men.

Selene's grip on my arm tightened, a silent plea for caution. "Leila," she whispered, "this is not the time for your foolhardy bravery. We need to be smart about this."

Ronan crossed his muscled arms over his thick chest and cocked his head slightly. "Now that we're alone, maybe we can have a civilized conversation, hmm?"

"I doubt anything involving the Crimson Clan could be civilized. You're all a bunch of savages!" I spat, my eyes darting to the fallen men on the floor.

He chuckled, seemingly taking pleasure in our banter. "You have a sharp tongue, Leila. I respect that. But remember, I'm not your enemy ... not yet."

His implication hung heavily in the air. For all his attractiveness and charisma, Ronan was a force to be reckoned with. But what he didn't know was that he and his people were already my enemy, whether they knew it or not. Not just for their presumptive announcement that they held the lost princess hostage, but also for their part in Valoria's attack ten years ago that prompted me to flee my homeland.

For many centuries, the Kingdom of Keldara was at odds with Valoria, their temporary truce teetering on the verge of snapping at any moment, until the day it did. Ten years ago, Keldara invaded Valoria, forcing my parents, the King and Queen, to smuggle me out of Valoria for my own safety. My guard, Sir Edric acted as my guardian as we roamed Asteria. I was meant to return after the dust settled, but Sir Edric told me it wasn't safe. He claimed Valoria would *never* be safe for me. He knew he was going against my parents' wishes, but he was adamant that even though Keldara lost and had to retreat, I would never be safe at home. Sir Edric was like another father to me growing up. And even though I knew my parents wanted me to return, I believed him without an ounce of evidence. He said he'd tell me the truth once I was of age, but unfortunately, he died before he could make good on his promise. He took that truth to the grave.

Ronan's eyes lingered on me as he tried to read my thoughts, unaware of the flood of memories swirling in my mind. Every time I thought of the Crimson Clan, I was filled with a deep, festering rage. To the world, they were a separate entity from Keldara, but to me, they were synonymous with pain and loss.

"Once an enemy, always an enemy," I muttered.

In four quick strides, Ronan was upon me. He grabbed my face, gripping my cheeks tightly as he forced my face up to look at him. "I have patience, but not much of it." He glared down at me as he looked at my forehead. "You don't bear the crescent moon of the Valorians, so what is your strife with my people?"

I tried to pull out of his grasp, but he only squeezed tighter.

"Please, sir!" Selene pleaded as she came out from behind me. "She meant no harm! Please!"

I glared at him and tried to ignore the pain in Selene's cries. "Don't bother, Selene. They're all a bunch of barbarians."

His crimson eyes turned blood red and his jaw locked. If he could snap my neck in this moment, he would.

I was about to spit on his face when I noticed a rash creeping out of his collar and up his neck. He'd been poisoned. And recently, too.

"You don't know a thing about the Crimson Clan," he growled.

I grunted. "Possibly not, but what I *do* know is that someone hates you enough to poison you," I gritted out and pointed to his neck. "If you're not treated within the hour, you'll die. I guess I have nothing to worry about." I attempted a smirk as he squeezed my face even harder.

He narrowed his eyes. "Poisoned? Impossible."

"Leila can treat you!" Selene chimed in. "She's the best physician in all of the Central Plains, possibly even Asteria."

His gaze went from Selene back to me.

"Does your mouth feel as dry as a cotton ball? Are your hands beginning to sweat?" I asked knowingly.

He released me as if I'd burned him, his hand reaching for his neck. "What did you do to me?" he demanded.

I snorted. "Nothing at all. But someone else did something roughly an hour ago, so you don't have long."

"Help him, Leila," Selene urged.

I scoffed. "Why should I? If he dies, it's just one less brute roaming Asteria."

Ronan took a menacing step toward me and placed his face inches from my own. "Heal me. *Now.*"

3

My clinic was surrounded by Crimson Clan members as they waited for Ronan to be treated. Ronan stormed in like he owned the place, then snapped his fingers at me to hurry and treat him. Before he could speak, I grabbed a handful of herbs and stuffed them in his mouth with a smirk.

"Your throat is about to close up, and I need time to make an antidote," I said when he glared daggers my way.

He chewed on the bitter herbs and coughed from the unpleasant taste. His reaction brought one of his men inside my clinic.

"Are you okay?" the newcomer asked as he surveyed my clinic. "Did she do something to you?"

Ronan shook his head. "I'm fine, Silas," he choked out, waving him away.

Silas growled. "You don't *look* fine. For all we know, this Central Plain whore is the one who poisoned you!"

I paused what I was doing and looked up at Silas. "Central Plain whore?" I repeated icily. "If you want me to save him, I suggest you watch your words. I'll happily let him die."

"If he dies, you die with him!" Silas threatened.

I smirked. "I'd like to see you try."

Silas started to take a step toward me when Ronan stopped him. "Enough! She didn't poison me, but I want you to find out who did. It must be one of the girls at the Rose Petal Lounge. Find out which one of them was recently hired."

Silas bowed with a fist placed over his heart, accepting the mission, and hurried outside. I frowned and wondered what rank Ronan possessed to deserve that much respect.

"What are you, a general?" I questioned as I grinded some herbs together.

Ronan shrugged. "Something like that."

I snorted. "Such loyalty. I wonder how many people you had to kill to gain it."

Ronan lazily trailed his red eyes toward me. "As if you've never killed anyone."

"I haven't," I answered sincerely.

He rolled his eyes. "I find that hard to believe, considering how easily you took down my men."

I stopped grinding the herbs for a moment and met his eyes. "Training and self-defense are one thing. Taking a life is another entirely."

He smirked. "A moral compass. How quaint."

"Something you obviously lack," I retorted with a scowl, turning my attention back to the herbs and grinding them with more force than necessary.

He was silent for a moment. "Don't be so quick to judge, Healer. We all do what we must to survive."

"Yes, well, I survive without spilling innocent blood," I shot back.

Ronan chuckled. "*Innocent* is a rather subjective term, don't you think? And just so you know, not every person I've killed was innocent. Some were monsters. Worse than you could ever imagine."

I paused to consider his words. "That doesn't justify murder. Every life is precious."

Ronan leaned closer and his crimson eyes drilled into mine. "Not all lives are equal. Some are venomous, waiting to strike when you least expect it."

Despite myself, a chill wormed down my spine. His eyes held a dark intensity I hadn't seen before. A depth of pain and experience that spoke of countless battles, betrayals, and hard-won victories.

I finished grinding the herbs, then mixed them with a few drops of water to make a thick paste. Carefully, I applied the paste to the rash spreading across Ronan's neck. His steely gaze never left mine.

"Take off your leathers," I ordered.

Without a second thought, he swiftly took them off and I couldn't help but scan his bare body. Olive skin covered in crimson tattoos covered his well sculpted body. Every inch of him was hard as my fingers gingerly applied the paste to the infected areas. I gulped loudly at his warm touch. I tried to avert my eyes, but they were glued to his beautiful body. A beautiful body that I truly wanted to hate.

"And what are those blue eyes looking at?" he inquired with a smirk.

I averted my gaze. "Nothing." I continued to apply the paste, my hand rubbing the warmth of his skin sending shivers through me.

He chuckled. "It's okay. Look and touch all you want. I don't mind."

I rolled my eyes. "Asshole," I mumbled.

"You should be careful, Healer," he whispered. "Intriguing as you are, you've already made plenty of enemies tonight."

I met his gaze head-on. "I've survived this long. I can handle a few more threats."

He smirked. "We'll see."

I finished applying the antidote and stepped back. "There. That should stop the spread. But you'll need to rest and avoid any strenuous activities for a few days."

Ronan nodded and stood slowly. "Thank you," he said as he reapplied his leathers.

I snuck one last gaze before he covered himself up again, then realized what he said. Surprised, I raised an eyebrow. "You're welcome. Now get out of my clinic."

But instead of leaving, Ronan plopped down on one of the cots I had for my patients and laid down, interlocking his hands behind his head. "I don't know, Healer. I feel like I might need to spend the night here ... You know, just in case something goes wrong." He grinned.

"Nothing is going to go wrong," I gritted between my teeth. "Now get out!"

He chuckled. "Is that really how you treat a paying patient?"

I rolled my eyes. "Oh, so you're a paying customer now?"

He dug inside the pouch at his waist and produced three glints, then carefully placed them on my wooden table. "Now I am."

"That's more than necessary."

"Think of the extra as me paying for your time."

I blew out a breath. This whole situation was utterly ridiculous and dangerous. If he found out who I really was, I would be in hot water. I could take down three of his men, but I couldn't take down the army of Crimson Clan members that currently surrounded my clinic.

"Fine," I muttered, folding my arms. "One night. Then you're gone. And if you or your men even *think* about causing any more trouble around here, you'll regret it."

Ronan arched an eyebrow, amusement dancing in his eyes. "I believe you, Healer. But I assure you, no harm will come to this place tonight."

I took a deep breath and tried to calm my racing heart. "What's your game, Ronan? Why are you really here?"

He looked thoughtful for a moment as he scrutinized me. "I've heard rumors of a healer who could cure any ailment, someone skilled beyond her years. Imagine my surprise when I find that same healer isn't just talented with herbs, but also has some moves."

My pulse kicked up a notch. "That doesn't explain why you want to stay the night."

He sighed and turned to face the ceiling. "Perhaps I'm just curious. Curious about you, curious why someone with your skills lives in such a place. Or maybe I'm just trying to put the pieces together."

I felt uneasy. He was getting too close and asking too many questions. I needed to divert his attention. "All you need to know is that I'm here to help people. That's it. Nothing more, nothing less."

He chuckled and closed his eyes. "For now, that's enough."

"And I'm sure you didn't come to the Central Plains to simply see this miraculous healer. I know what you're truly after."

He smirked. "Is that so? And what's that?"

"The lost princess," I said hesitantly.

He froze, then opened his eyes slowly and turned to face me. "And what do you know about the lost princess?"

I shrugged. "Nothing at all. But Lomewood is abuzz with rumors that the Crimson Clan is holding her hostage and the chief plans to marry her off to his son if his demands aren't met."

Ronan nodded. "Very accurate information, Healer."

I thought about what Henry told me and the pieces started falling together.

"You're the envoy, aren't you?" I whispered.

He smiled broadly. "That I am."

I tensed. "I thought you were supposed to be heading to Valoria to meet with the King and Queen?"

He shook his head. "The King and Queen of Valoria are extremely careful about who enters their lands. They're sending an envoy of their own to the Central Plains to deal with this on neutral territory."

It made sense, but I couldn't believe he was divulging all this information to someone he just met. There had to be a catch. Or possibly it was a trap. For now, I'd asked enough questions and it was best to remain ignorant.

"You can stay the night. There are blankets and pillows over there." I pointed to a closet. "I'll be upstairs in my residence."

He nodded. "Thank you, Leila."

I paused at the door and glanced back at him. There was something about his demeanor that suggested he wasn't simply a ruthless member of the Crimson Clan. Perhaps, somewhere deep down, he had a sense of honor or some fragment of a moral compass. But I couldn't let my guard down.

I fixed him with a stern look. "Don't make me regret this decision, Ronan."

He met my gaze, his crimson eyes softer than I'd seen them before. "I have no intentions to, Leila."

With one last wary look, I made my way upstairs. The wooden floorboards creaked underfoot, echoing the uncertainty that filled my mind. As I settled onto my bed, I couldn't shake the feeling that allowing Ronan to stay, even just for one night, would have consequences that reached far beyond this moment.

4

When I woke up the next morning, Ronan was gone and so were his men who had surrounded my clinic all night. On top of the folded blanket and pillow he used, there was a note that simply said, *See you soon*. I crumpled it up and threw it in the wastebasket. He was the last person I wanted to see again after last night.

I prepared the clinic for my first appointment of the day, then stepped outside to flip the sign around to *Open*. At the rap of knuckles on my door, I glanced up to see Anna, the town's baker. My first client of the day was seven months pregnant and here for a check-up.

"Hello, Anna, how are you feeling?" I asked as I ushered her inside to sit.

"Hello, Leila," Anna replied, her cheeks rosy from her walk. "Feeling the weight of this little one more and more each day," she chuckled as she affectionately rubbed her baby bump.

"Any discomfort or unusual feelings?" I questioned as I checked her pulse. Once I confirmed that her's and her baby's pulses were steady and strong, I started to prepare a tea that would help with any swelling or cramps.

"A bit of back pain and some swelling in my feet by the end of the day," Anna admitted with a wry glance at her feet. "But other than that, everything seems normal."

"That's pretty common," I said, handing her a warm cup of tea. "This should help. Make sure to elevate your feet when resting and consider wearing more supportive shoes."

Anna took a sip and smiled. "This is lovely, thank you. Make sure to stop by the bakery today, Leila. I just made a fresh batch of mooncakes. I know those are your favorite."

I beamed. "Yes, thank you. You certainly know the way to my heart. I'll stop by later today."

She nodded as she took another sip of tea, then glanced around the clinic and back at me as she cleared her throat. "I heard there was quite a ruckus last night with those Crimson Clan men."

I sighed and hesitated for a moment before replying. "It was an eventful evening, to say the least. But everything is fine now."

Anna's eyes widened slightly in curiosity. "Did one of them stay here? Alberta said she saw one of them leaving your clinic early this morning with a whole army."

I raised an eyebrow. "Alberta always was observant," I murmured, a hint of sarcasm in my tone. "Yes, he needed a place to rest for the night, but he's gone now."

Anna looked concerned. "You must be careful, Leila. You know the stories about them."

I nodded. "I do, but he wasn't here to cause harm. At least not last night."

"Very well," she murmured, not completely convinced. She dug into her purse and pulled out a pouch full of coins. "Fifty gleams," she said as she handed them over.

Fifty gleams equaled half a glint. Because she often paid me in baked goods, I always gave her a discount for her check-ups.

"Thank you, Anna," I offered graciously.

"No, thank *you*, Leila. I don't know what this town would do without you."

I smiled, touched by her words. "Thank you, Anna. And remember, anytime you feel off or need a check-up, come see me."

She gave a nod with a smile that was both warm and genuine. "I will. Thank you, Leila."

As the day progressed, a steady stream of patients visited my clinic, each with their unique ailments and stories. Yet, despite the busy hours, the events of the previous night continued to linger in my thoughts. Ronan's cryptic words – *See you soon* – seemed to echo endlessly, an unsettling reminder of our unexpected encounter.

It was past noon and I was just wrapping up a late lunch when someone barged into my clinic. I looked up from my meal to find the Governor of Lomewood at my doorstep.

"Leila, please, I need your help!" he wailed, sweat beads dripping from his round face.

Governor Theodore Otto of Lomewood was a rotund man, aging but still possessing a vitality that hinted at a more youthful and robust past. His full beard was salt-and-pepper, each strand meticulously groomed, portraying a man who cared deeply about his appearance. His round spectacles sat low on his nose and magnified his hazel eyes, which usually held a calculating, yet discerning gaze. Today, however, they were wild with fear.

He was dressed, as always, in the finest robes tailored just for him — a deep blue shade embroidered with intricate silver patterns that reflected his elevated rank. His fingers, pudgy and short, were adorned with multiple rings, each signifying a different accomplishment or title. In Lomewood, his word was law, and while he was often known for his strategic mind and diplomatic skills, he was not beyond showing his temper when provoked.

His sudden, unannounced appearance was unusual. Governor Theodore never went anywhere without at least two guards by his side, yet today, he was alone. The desperation in his voice was palpable.

"What's the matter, Governor?" I inquired, trying to mask my surprise. His presence in my clinic was unprecedented, and the urgency in his demeanor piqued my concern.

"An envoy from Valoria is here and he's extremely ill!"

My brows shot up. If it was an envoy from Valoria, I couldn't show my face. They might recognize me.

"What happened?" I asked hesitantly.

"We were having lunch when he suddenly collapsed. Please, hurry!"

I didn't move. "Tell me what he ate, and I can come up with an antidote."

"No, no! You need to come see him now!"

I sighed. "Governor, just tell me what he ate."

Clearly exasperated, he began to recall their dinner. "Lamb, duck, vegetables ... oh, and some fae fruit."

The mention of fruit sparked my interest. "By any chance was this envoy from Eldwain?" Eldwain was another kingdom south of the Central Plains, whose people were of half fae ancestry. They were allies with Valoria, so it wouldn't be a surprise if they were the ones who sent the envoy.

The governor's eyes widened in shock. "Yes ... yes, he is. How did you know?"

I sighed. "The people of Eldwain might be half fae, but fae food from Ellyndor is extremely poisonous to them."

Governor Theo gasped, and his eyes rolled back as he stumbled backward a bit. "Dear gods, I've poisoned the young prince."

I shot up to my feet in shock. "*The envoy is Prince Caelan of Eldwain?*" I nearly screamed.

"Shhh!" he quieted me. "No one is supposed to know!"

Prince Caelan wasn't just the Prince of Eldwain ... he used to be my best friend. Growing up, we were inseparable. It was always Caelan, me, and my brother Marcellus. If the prince was here as an envoy ... that meant Marcellus was as well. Unless they had a falling out, which was entirely possible with both their fiery tempers. In any event, I couldn't imagine my brother assigning this task to Caelan alone.

Unfortunately, I didn't have the herbs necessary to treat him. It would take days of travel into the mountains to find it, and by then he would already be dead. My only option was to feed him my blood. My blood could cure just about anything. While Marcellus was a blood mage, his blood didn't possess healing properties like mine did.

I was about to follow the governor out when it dawned on me. If I healed Caelan with my blood, my identity would be revealed. I couldn't afford that to happen. It wasn't that I didn't trust my brother or Caelan, but I was still unsure if it was safe to return to Valoria. Until I found out the truth Sir Edric kept hidden from me, I wouldn't step foot back home, much less let anyone know who I was.

But I couldn't let Caelan die.

"Governor, I need some time to prepare an antidote. I'll meet you at your residence in thirty minutes."

He nodded quickly. "Yes, yes, I'll give you one hundred glint. Just heal the prince!"

One hundred glint was far more than I could ever ask for, but I wasn't about to squabble. "I'll be there soon."

As soon as the governor left, I darted to my shelf of herbs and pulled out the ones most similar to the cure. After grinding them into a fine powder, I boiled water and dumped the herbs inside. Once it had boiled for exactly ten minutes, I poured the tincture into a small vial. Before sealing it, I pricked my finger and let a few drops of blood fall into the vial as the final ingredient. Grabbing my satchel of medicine and slipping the vial inside, I ran to the governor's residence.

The governor lived in one of Lomewood's most prestigious architectural marvels. Positioned at the heart of town, it was a three-story stone mansion surrounded by a high, ivy-covered wall. The entrance featured a grand wooden door with intricate carvings that depicted the history of Lomewood, flanked by two tall torches that lit the entrance at night.

The grounds were extensive and flawlessly manicured. Rare flowers and exotic trees imported from distant lands dotted the landscape. Gravel pathways weaved around serene fountains and quiet reflection ponds, providing the townsfolk a glimpse of the opulence inside.

Upon entering the mansion, one was greeted by a magnificent hallway adorned with marble floors and golden chandeliers suspended from high ceiling beams. Artworks from famed artists all over the realm hung on the walls, each telling a different story. A majestic staircase spiraled upwards to the private quarters and guest rooms, an area off-limits to most.

To the left was the opulent dining hall that was large enough to comfortably seat fifty guests. Tall windows provided ample natural light during the day and magnificent views of glittering stars at night. The walls were decorated with tapestries showcasing the various achievements of past governors.

To the right, a more intimate drawing room was furnished with plush velvet seating, a wide fireplace, and shelves filled with rare books and artifacts. This was where the governor usually held his meetings and entertained important guests.

Deep within the mansion, I'd heard that the governor had a private study, a sanctuary filled with maps, scrolls, and tomes detailing Lomewood's history and the neighboring regions. A small hidden door led to the wine cellar, which boasted vintages from the best vineyards across the continent. The governor's residence was not just a symbol of his status, but also a testament to Lomewood's prosperity and the town's significance in the region.

Upon reaching the front door, I was hastily ushered inside with a sense of urgency that belied the tension in the air.

Prince Caelan had been moved to the drawing room. His unconscious body was lying on the plush velvet couch with the governor, Marcellus, and another person hovering over him.

Adjusting my wrinkled blouse, I cleared my throat to announce my presence and stepped inside.

"Oh, thank the gods!" the governor exclaimed. "Prince Marcellus, this is Leila, our town's, and perhaps the Central Plains' most talented healer. She knew what was wrong with him almost immediately."

My brother turned to face me, his blue eyes a mirror of my own but now lined with worry and fatigue. A cascade of wavy brown hair framed a rugged face that had grown more mature since I'd last seen him. A crescent moon on his forehead signaled his Valorian heritage. The jaw was sharper with a faint shadow of stubble, and his lips were pressed into a tight line of concern. Time had added lines of responsibility to his forehead, and the boyish mischief I remembered from our childhood had been replaced by the stern expression of a prince. His attire was rich, fitting for his royal status, with a cloak clasped by a golden emblem representing Valoria.

His gaze met mine, searching, but there was no flicker of recognition. I had changed a lot over the years, and the innocence of our childhood was now hidden behind the mask I wore as Leila, the healer. My brown hair, once long and flowing, was cut to my mid back and my attire was simple, unlike the elaborate dresses I used to wear.

"Leila," he acknowledged with a curt nod, his voice deep and commanding. "I've been told you can help him," he said cautiously.

I nodded and managed a smile. "Of course, Your Highness." It hurt, the formal address between us, but I had to keep my identity concealed. I couldn't risk being recognized, not even by my own brother.

As I moved towards Caelan, I couldn't help but glance occasionally at Marcellus. Even amidst the dire situation, the heartache of being so close and yet so distant from my brother was overwhelming. I had to remind myself to focus on the task at hand and save Caelan.

Prince Caelan of Eldwain was a stark contrast to Marcellus, yet they shared the camaraderie of brothers. Whereas Marcellus was the very embodiment of night with his dark hair and intense gaze, Caelan seemed to embody the day with a head of tousled silver hair. Even in his unconscious state, his face retained an air of regality and serenity, a testament to the innate grace that came with his half-fae heritage.

His skin, though paler now due to his condition, usually boasted a healthy, sun-kissed glow, a testament to the many days spent outdoors, exploring the terrains of Eldwain. High cheekbones framed a straight nose, and his full lips, now slightly parted in distress, had a natural rosy tint.

Resting on his chest was an ornate silver pendant of a phoenix poised mid-flight – the symbol of Eldwain. It was encrusted with sparkling gems, each signifying a region in his kingdom. The pendant was a familiar sight. It was gifted to him by his mother on his eighth birthday.

His attire was elegant, yet less ostentatious than Marcellus's. He wore a finely tailored tunic in a shade of forest green, embroidered with silver threads that shimmered with every breath. Over the tunic he wore a leather vest, showcasing the blend of royalty and adventurer in him. But what was most captivating about Caelan were his eyes. Even closed, one could envision them – a mesmerizing shade of hazel that seemed to shift between green and brown, holding depths of wisdom, humor, and kindness. I had always found solace in those eyes during our childhood escapades.

As I prepared to administer the antidote, I felt a tug at my heartstrings. The boy I once knew had grown into this magnificent prince, and it was imperative that I save him, not just for Eldwain's sake, but for the fond memories that bound us together.

I was about to tilt his head back when a hand wrapped around my wrist.

"What are you giving him?" Marcellus asked tersely.

"The cure. He needs it soon or he *will* die," I replied adamantly.

My brother narrowed his eyes at me. "I don't know who you are. How do I know you can be trusted? There don't happen to be a lot of cures for fae lying around."

He was right about that. The people from Eldwain and Ellyndor were rarely seen in the Central Plains.

"You'll just have to trust me." I ripped my wrist out of his hand. "I'm his only chance at survival. Now, will you let me help him, or are you going to let him die?"

"Your Highness, she is trustworthy," the governor chimed in. "You may or may not have heard of her, but she's the best healer in all the Central Plains. Possibly all of Asteria. I would only get the best for the prince."

Marcellus looked wary, and rightfully so. But eventually, he nodded in acceptance.

I tilted Caelan's head back and poured the liquid from the small vial into his mouth. After a few seconds, I released him and waited with bated breath as the color in his face returned and he started to breathe normally. I placed three fingers on the pulse point at his wrist to confirm the antidote actually worked. I released a breath and turned to Marcellus and the governor.

"He's fine. He's going to be fine," I said, relieved.

They both exhaled loudly and thanked me as if I'd just saved one of the gods.

The governor reached into his pocket and pulled out a pouch filled to the brim with glints. "As promised," he said, exhaling a relieved sigh.

I brushed off the governor's generosity. "Oh, don't worry. You don't have to pay me. Especially not this much."

The governor placed it in my hand. "Take it, Leila. It is much deserved."

I hesitated until Marcellus spoke. "Please, Leila," he said awkwardly. "We really appreciate your aid. This is the least we could do."

With no other choice, I accepted the money and dropped it into my satchel. "He'll wake momentarily. It won't be long." My heart pounded as I looked at Marcellus and wondered if he recognized me beneath the disguise of age and years apart. His blue eyes studied me with a keen interest that made me uncomfortable. It felt like he was trying to pierce through the façade, to find some familiar feature or semblance of the girl he once knew.

"I can't thank you enough," he finally said, his voice a rich baritone that had deepened over the years. Genuine gratitude shone in his eyes, but there was something else – a hint of curiosity, maybe even recognition.

"You're welcome," I replied, doing my best to maintain a calm exterior. "Just ensure that he doesn't consume any more fae fruit. It can have severe consequences."

He nodded, a faint smile playing on his lips. "We'll ensure it. Your expertise has been invaluable."

The governor, relieved and grateful, added, "Lomewood owes you a debt, Leila."

Feeling an overwhelming mix of emotions, I simply nodded. "Please let me know if there are any changes in Prince Caelan's condition. Otherwise, I'll take my leave." I gathered my things and headed for the door when I heard my brother speak.

"Thank the gods you're fine. Lyanna would skin me alive if I let you die," he whispered.

The sound of my real name sent tingles down my spine.

As I stepped outside the governor's manor, the weight of the encounter, the closeness to my past, and the realization that my identity was still safe washed over me, leaving me both relieved and melancholy.

5

I walked back to my clinic in a daze of memories as I thought about Marcellus and Caelan. They were here. For me. Except the Crimson Clan didn't actually have me. I needed to figure out a way to let them know about the ruse without giving myself away. If only I could discover the secret Sir Edric kept from me so I could return home.

I opened the door to my clinic and found Selene waiting for me with baked goods from Anna's bakery.

She beamed at me. "I took it upon myself to pick up your order."

"Ah, and this is why you're the best, Sel." With a spring in my step, I walked over to the table to dig in on some fresh pastries.

"Where were you? I've been waiting for a while," she commented as she nibbled on a mooncake.

I sighed and reluctantly answered, "I was at the governor's residence."

Her perfectly shaped brows shot up. "How come?"

"Prince Caelan was ill and needed a physician," I answered, hoping it would go over her head.

She nodded and continued to eat until the words finally settled in and she realized who I was talking about. "Prince Caelan from Eldwain?" she nearly shrieked.

I nodded. "The one and only."

"Was your brother with him?" she asked nervously. I'd told her my secret long ago, and she knew they were inseparable.

"He was ... and he didn't recognize me."

She frowned. "How? You're his sister. You couldn't have changed *that* much."

"True, but it's also been ten years, Selene. The last time he saw me I was eleven years old. A child. I would have been surprised if he recognized me," I said, slightly disappointed but relieved at the same time. "Either way, they're here for me ... to rescue me."

Selene looked at me with a mixture of sympathy and confusion. "You must be feeling so many things right now," she whispered.

I took a deep breath. "It's complicated. On one hand, I want to wrap my arms around them and let them know I'm okay. But on the other, I don't know if it's safe yet. Until I find out what Sir Edric hid from me, I can't risk revealing myself."

"But Leila," Selene said gently, her eyes filled with concern, "how much longer do you plan on hiding? You can't run forever. And from the way you talk about them, it seems they care as deeply for you as you do about them."

A pang of longing hit me. "They do, but the circumstances of my disappearance ..." I shook my head. "I still don't have all the answers. I need to know why I was sent away, what dangers may still be lurking for me in Valoria, and most importantly, why Sir Edric never told me what was going on."

Selene hesitated for a moment, then said, "What if I help you find out? You know I can uncover just about anything at the Rose Petal Lounge."

I shook my head. "It's too dangerous. If you ask too many

questions, especially if they're the *right* questions, you might risk exposing me before we learn anything."

Selene bit her bottom lip. "There must be something we can do."

"Let's just wait and see."

Selene sighed. "Well, in other news, tonight is the lantern festival. This year, I don't want you to spend it with me at the pleasure house. You should go out and enjoy it. At least one of us has the freedom to do so."

"No," I said adamantly. "If you can't spend it with me, I won't go. You know that."

She sighed again. "I don't want to tie you down, Leila."

I reached out for her hand. "You're not. You're my friend. Tonight, I'll keep you company."

∼

THE STREETS WERE BUSTLING with people getting ready for the lantern festival. Children's laughter rang out as they ran through the streets playing, trying to release their excited energy for the night's festivities. I was closing my shop after treating my last patient for the day when there was a knock at my door. I opened it and without looking to see who it was, said, "We're closed for to—" I stopped talking mid-sentence when I looked up into Caelan's hazel eyes. Behind him stood the governor. Remembering who I was supposed to be, I bowed slightly in greeting. "Your Highness."

"May I come in?" Caelan asked.

"Of course you can!" the governor blustered, answering for me and pushing the door wider to give them enough space to enter. "The prince wanted to meet his savior."

I tensed. "It was nothing. I was just lucky to have the right ingredients on hand."

"And what *were* those ingredients?" the prince asked suspiciously.

"A mixture of milk thistle, licorice root, and ginger," I replied without hesitation. He was testing me, but fortunately, I was a knowledgeable healer.

He narrowed his gaze as if to intimidate me, but I didn't waver. Suddenly, he said, "I see you know how to cure fae poisoning."

I nodded. "I lived for a while in Eldwain. My father was a traveling merchant, so I learned a lot growing up," I lied smoothly. My father obviously wasn't a merchant, but I did travel all over Asteria with Sir Edric.

"Ah, so you know our customs, too." He glanced around my clinic.

"Yes, Your Highness."

"From what the governor told me, your healing abilities are well known throughout the Central Plains."

"I wouldn't go that far, but I'm quite talented," I admitted without a shred of modesty.

"Whatever you need, Your Highness, Leila would be more than willing to help," the governor volunteered. I sent him a glare, which he pointedly ignored.

"Unless she can help me get Princess Lyanna back from the Crimson Clan, I don't believe there's anything she can do," he muttered as he finished scanning my clinic, his hazel eyes landing on me again. "Thank you ... for healing me." He started to leave, his sudden icy demeanor taking me by surprise. The governor quickly followed him as if he was afraid of messing up again.

"Wait!" I called after them. "There's something I need to report to the prince."

He stopped at my door and peered over his shoulder. "Which is?"

"Princess Lyanna ... she's not in the custody of the Crimson Clan," I said quietly.

Caelan whirled around to face me. "How do you know this?"

"I have a reliable source," I lied. "Don't fall into their trap ... because it *is* a trap."

Caelan narrowed his eyes on me. "I don't know you. Why should I risk the princess's safety on nothing more than your word?"

The governor cut in between us. "Leila's best friend works at the Rose Petal Lounge. She must have heard this from her. You know as well as I do that all information travels through there, and the Crimson Clan has spent almost every night since their arrival at the pleasure house," he supplied nervously.

Caelan's eyes widened at the governor's explanation. He took a step toward me, pushing the governor out of the way. "Can you guarantee this?"

"Yes."

"If you're wrong, will you take responsibility?"

"Yes," I answered confidently. "I'm not wrong. And if you have any qualms, you know where to find me." I pointed to the ceiling. "I live on the second floor."

He stared at me unblinking. "Very well. I hope for your sake that you're correct." With that, Caelan spun on his heels and left, leaving the governor running behind him to catch up.

∽

ONCE THE EXCITEMENT of the day passed, I finally had a moment to get ready to spend the evening of the lantern festival at the Rose Petal Lounge. Jogging upstairs to my room, I picked out my clothes, which were a stark contrast to what I usually wore every day.

I chose a flowing dress of deep indigo, which shimmered with silver embroidery that depicted crescent moons and delicate willow branches. The fabric was soft and it swayed effortlessly with every step, echoing the ethereal beauty of the night. Around my waist, I donned a sash of pale silver, which was tied into a loose bow at my back. My dark hair was pulled up into a graceful chignon, adorned with tiny silver pins that gleamed like stars. Tiny droplets of moonstones hung from my ears, catching the faint light.

Once dressed, I stepped out the front door and was immediately engulfed in the mesmerizing charm of the lantern festival. The streets of Lomewood had transformed into an ethereal realm. Countless lanterns floated above, illuminating the night with their warm, soft glow. They ranged in size from tiny orbs to large balloons and were painted with intricate patterns and designs, each telling a unique story or symbolizing a special wish.

The cobblestone streets were lined with vibrant stalls, each decorated with strings of colorful lights and glimmering ornaments. Merchants showcased their best wares, from delicious street foods to handcrafted trinkets. Musicians played soft, enchanting melodies, filling the air with a magical ambiance as horse drawn carriages bustled down the streets to reach their destinations.

People from all over the Central Plains had gathered, dressed in their festive best. Children ran around with sparklers, their laughter echoing through the streets, while couples and families released lanterns into the sky, each carrying a silent wish.

As I walked to the Rose Petal Lounge, I quickly became lost in the mesmerizing beauty of the festival. The very air seemed to hum with energy and hope. Nights like these made me fall in love with Lomewood all over again.

The only thing that could make this night better was if Selene had the freedom to leave the lounge and enjoy the festival. But Madam Rose wasn't going to miss out on one of the most popular days of the year. Selene was one of her most popular courtesans, and this would be one of the busiest nights … which brought me to the doorstep of the Rose Petal Lounge. If Selene couldn't enjoy the festival, then neither could I.

A tap on my shoulder pulled me out of my morose thoughts. When I looked beside me, my mood plummeted. "What do you want, Orion?" I asked the fae walking beside me.

I'd met Orion years ago when Sir Edric and I did a stint in Ellyndor. He just happened to show up in the Central Plains a year after we arrived.

Orion, with his silvery hair, striking emerald eyes, and delicate, glowing skin, looked every bit the fae that he was. Tall and lean with pointed ears, there was a certain elegance to his movements that gave away his otherworldly origin. His pale lips turned upward in a teasing smile that I'd long ago learned not to trust.

"You act as though you're not happy to see me," Orion drawled, his voice dripping with faux hurt. His eyes twinkled with mischief, a trait all too common in his kind.

"Because I'm not," I replied sharply. "What are you doing here?"

He chuckled, the sound airy and carefree. "Can't I enjoy the lantern festival like everyone else?"

I eyed him suspiciously. With the fae, there was always an ulterior motive. "There are plenty of other places to enjoy the festival. Why here?"

Orion shrugged, his glimmering eyes never leaving mine. "Perhaps I wanted some company, and who better than you?"

I snorted. "We're not friends, Orion. And your definition of 'company' usually involves me getting into some sort of trouble."

He feigned shock. "Now, Leila, you wound me. After all the times I've helped you out of a tight spot? Granted, they were spots I might have gotten you into in the first place, but still."

Our relationship was, in one word, complicated. Orion had

an uncanny knack for showing up at the most inconvenient times. Yet, there were instances when he had genuinely assisted me, though those moments were few and far between. Despite his seemingly lighthearted and playful demeanor, there was always a hidden agenda with him, a riddle to be solved or a deal to be made. This unpredictability was why I didn't fully trust him. With Orion, nothing was ever as simple as it seemed.

"I don't have time for your games tonight," I said as I tried to move past him.

But he effortlessly matched my pace. "Who said anything about games? Maybe I genuinely want to spend time with you and, oh, what is that lovely girl's name …? Oh, right, Selene."

I growled. "Stay away from Selene. I've told you this on more than one occasion. She can't afford your trouble."

He grinned. "And *I've* told *you* plenty of times that I can free her. Why don't you let me?"

"Because with you, there are always conditions, and I'm not sure I can pay them."

He chuckled. "Always the smart one."

I glanced at him with naked skepticism evident on my face. "If I know anything about the fae, it's that you're rarely genuine."

His grin widened. "You're always so quick to judge. Maybe one day, you'll see the *real* me."

"The day that happens," I retorted, "will be the day the skies turn green."

"Ah, Lomewood's famous green skies," he mused. "But until that day, how about a dance? Just one. No tricks, no riddles."

I shook my head. "Some other time, maybe."

He bowed dramatically. "Until our paths cross again, dear Leila."

And just like that, he disappeared into the crowd, leaving me to wonder about the mysteries that surrounded him.

I opened the doors of the Rose Petal and stood at the

doorway a moment, surveying the scene. In the center of the lounge was a stage where musicians played a tantalizing melody. Dancers draped in gowns of deep reds, soft pinks, and shimmering golds moved gracefully to the rhythm, their every motion echoing the allure and mystique of the roses for which the lounge was named.

Around the stage were plush velvet seating areas. Each was like a private alcove surrounded by beaded curtains, offering patrons both a view of the entertainment and a degree of privacy. The men, mostly rich merchants and visiting nobles, reclined on the seats, their lidded eyes fixed on the performers and their glasses filled with the finest wines.

It was an opulent setting, designed to cater to the senses and provide an escape from the outside world. But beneath its glamorous veneer, the Rose Petal Lounge held stories of many women like Selene, bound by circumstances, dreams deferred, and hopes held close to their hearts. As much as the place was a testament to Lomewood's prosperity and luxury, it was also a reminder of the disparities and hidden stories that often went unnoticed in the glittering glow of the chandeliers.

I stopped one of the girls as she was making her way across the room and lightly touched her arm. "Can you please let Selene know I'm here?" Without a word, she nodded and headed in the direction I knew Selene to be.

Finding an empty table, I settled into a chair and watched the entertainment from afar. One of the girls recognized me and brought over a jug of wine and a cup. I accepted it graciously and poured myself a drink.

"Fancy meeting you here," a male voice said from behind me. I turned and looked up into Ronan's face. My mood, which had just started to recover from seeing Orion, plummeted to the pits of hell all over again.

"What do you want?" I grumbled and turned back around to face the performers.

Without waiting for an invitation, Ronan came around and sat in the empty chair at the table, setting his sheathed sword on top of it. He flagged down one of the girls and got an extra cup, then helped himself to my wine.

"I didn't peg you for the type to fancy these sorts of lounges." He drank the wine in one gulp. "But this is the second time I've met you here. It must be destiny," he smirked.

I rolled my eyes. "More like I'm being punished for something. Shouldn't you be somewhere else instead of hanging around me and *my* wine?"

He chuckled. "Don't worry, Leila. I'll buy you an even better wine. I heard the Rose Petal has a very expensive wine called A Thousand Roses. Consider it an olive branch?"

I ignored his offer. "Have you learned who poisoned you?"

His relaxed expression turned stony in a blink. "Yes."

I peered over at him. "And?"

"And it was handled. That's all you need to know."

I snorted. "Of course."

"You look beautiful, by the way. You should wear more dresses instead of those hideous trousers," he said, changing the subject. "If I didn't know any better, I would think you were one of the courtesans of the Rose Petal."

I glared at him. "I don't know whether that's a compliment or an insult."

"Definitely a compliment." He grinned, his crimson eyes full of mischief, and opened his mouth to say something else when one of the girls slithered over to him and began to dance between his legs.

The dancer, a young woman with blonde hair cascading down her back and gold hoop earrings that shimmered in the dim lounge light, moved sinuously, drawing the attention of those seated at nearby tables. But it was apparent that she was putting on a show for Ronan's benefit. Her hands trailed up his chest as she continued her sultry dance.

Ronan's eyes momentarily shifted to the dancer with a fleeting look of interest before he turned back to me. His eyes met mine, a challenging glint in them. "Jealous?" he teased.

"Hardly," I responded, taking a deep sip of my wine and looking away from his intense gaze.

From my peripheral vision, I secretly watched as he continued to stare at me while he trailed the girls' curves with his large hands, appreciating her without degrading her. He leaned back in his chair, opening himself up more for the girl to dance.

"Females are quite exquisite creatures," he murmured, his eyes never leaving mine. "The curves of their hips, the mounds of their breasts," he said as his hands traced every part he mentioned. "Their supple skin and the quiet sighs when one touches all the right places. It's enough to drive a man mad."

My face heated and I took another sip of my wine, feeling decidedly uncomfortable.

Ronan's eyes remained fixed on the profile of my face. Growing bold, I turned to face him, prepared to show him my disgust but found myself ensnared when his once crimson eyes appeared to grow a shade darker until they were nearly black. I shifted in my seat. Suddenly the room felt vast and empty, but the rolling energy cascaded all around me and I was unable to look away.

"I think you've had enough attention for one night," I snapped, the words slipping out before I could reel them back in. My annoyance wasn't really with the dancer. She was doing her job and doing it well. But something about Ronan's words, his proximity, and the charged energy that crackled between us made me edgy.

Ronan chuckled. "I thought you weren't jealous."

"I'm not!" I said defensively. "I just don't want to bear witness to your affair with her. If you want to be entertained, do it elsewhere."

Ronan smirked, then his fingers gently caressed the dancer's waist, signaling her to stop. He offered her a glint before she stepped away and cast me a curious glance before moving to another table.

I raised an eyebrow. "You seem popular here."

Ronan smirked and poured another cup of wine. "You could say I've made some acquaintances during my stay. But don't worry, my attention right now is solely on you."

"And what makes you think I want it?" I retorted.

He leaned in closer, his scent blending with the heady aroma of wine and incense. "Because, despite your protests, I can see it in your eyes. You're curious. And curiosity, my sweet Leila, can be a very dangerous thing."

I tossed back the rest of my wine in one gulp and slammed the cup down on the table angrily, ignoring his heated gaze. I refused to feed into his nonsense. The Crimson Clan was not to be trusted. If I got too close to Ronan, he would discover my identity in no time.

He threw his head back and laughed. "Fine, I won't persist. But I *am* curious: Why are you here, of all places? The lantern festival outside is quite lovely."

I sighed. "Because Selene is here. I'm going to spend it with her."

He snorted. "I assure you, Leila, the mermaid will be quite busy tonight. You should just accept my company instead."

I gritted my teeth but kept quiet. The merfolk were rarely seen on land, as they resided in the Luminar Sea located to the west of Keldara. The vast expanse of water was known for its bioluminescent waters and as the home of the merfolk. To be able to walk on land, some of the merfolk made deals with the fae. Selene never told me who her father made a deal with to get them on land, but she hasn't been back to the water since she was a child. She still missed it sometimes.

"I can't be *that* unpleasant," he persisted.

I rolled my eyes. "I would rather burn in the fiery pits of hell than spend another moment with you."

"Well ... that's one way to go."

"All of you from the Crimson Clan are barbarians. I would rather die than be with you!"

"Is that so?" he asked with a quirked brow. "And how are we such savages?"

I turned my gaze to him and met his crimson eyes unflinchingly. "Because your people decided to ally yourselves with Keldara. You can't get any lower than that."

Ronan tilted his head to get a good look at me. "I've said it before, but I'll say it again: you don't seem Valorian, so what's your problem with Keldara?" He sized me up once more, taking in my moon earrings and narrowing his gaze on them.

All Valorians had crescent moons on their foreheads, which indicated to all they encountered who they were. Valorians believed in the moon goddess who blessed our lands. Using magic, I'd covered my forehead to appear like a normal human from the Central Plains.

Feeling like my identity was at risk of being discovered, I shot to my feet so fast, I tipped over the jug of wine. Rich red liquid spilled over the edge of the table and dribbled onto the plush carpet. "I've had enough of this!" I stormed away, intent on finding Selene.

Without a care about the spilled wine or the company I left behind, I stomped toward the dark hallway that led to the courtesans' private chambers to see if Selene was in any of them. Before I reached the first closed door, someone grabbed my wrist and pulled me into a dark alcove, hidden from prying eyes. A hand covered my mouth to keep me from screaming. I whirled around to see Ronan's smirking face.

"Why the rush?" He slowly removed his hand and boxed me in against the wall. "I thought we were having a good time," he added with a sultry grin.

He was so close, I smelled the fruity wine on his lips. I dropped my gaze to his mouth and unconsciously licked my own before glancing away. "You're playing a dangerous game, Ronan," I managed to say, my voice quivering.

His eyes roamed over my face and lingered on my lips, which parted involuntarily under his intense scrutiny. "And yet," he whispered as he leaned in closer, his warm breath teasing my ear, "here you are, playing."

I shivered, a strange mix of anger and attraction. "Release me," I demanded, but the softness of my tone betrayed me.

He leaned in closer and the heat of his body radiated against mine, creating an intoxicating pull. His lips brushed against the sensitive shell of my ear. "You say one thing, Leila, but your body says another."

I realized then that my body was leaning in towards him and my hands had crept up to his warm torso, almost as if I wanted to push him away but didn't. I jerked back and pushed him away using all my strength. He stumbled back with a surprised look on his handsome face. Trying to regain my composure, I whispered, "You mistake my vulnerability for attraction. Tread carefully, Ronan."

He looked amused. "Is that a challenge?"

"Consider it a warning," I responded, my voice steady.

He smirked and leaned in again. "I've always been drawn to the dangerous ones."

The space between us dwindled as his face neared mine. Shrouded in the darkness of the alcove, every sensation was heightened. A poignant silence pulsed with unspoken words and tension, thick and suffocating as it seemed to suck all the breath from my lungs.

"Tell me, Leila," Ronan murmured, closing the small gap that I had created between us. His fingers traced a line from my wrist, up my forearm, making me shiver. "Why are you so afraid of me? Or are you afraid of what I make you feel?"

His words hit a nerve. "You presume too much," I countered. My eyes darted away to escape the intensity of his gaze, but he was not deterred.

He chuckled softly. Using his other hand to lift my chin, he forced me to meet his eyes. "I can feel your heartbeat, Leila. It's racing, just like mine."

I swallowed hard, trapped by his proximity and the truth of his words. "This," I waved between us, "can never be anything."

He arched an eyebrow and the corner of his lips curled into a teasing smile. "Who said I wanted it to be 'something'? Maybe I just enjoy the chase."

My eyes narrowed, even as my heart skipped a beat. "Or maybe you're just not used to being denied."

The challenge in my words seemed to ignite something in him. His hands found my waist and he pulled me flush against him until I felt every line and curve of his body mold against my own; air escaped my lungs at the movement. The realization of how perfectly we fit together made me dizzy.

Ronan leaned down, his lips hovering just above mine. "Maybe," he whispered, his breath warm against my skin. "But it makes me want to play with you even more."

The world seemed to spin and his heady presence was overwhelming. I felt intoxicated by the mix of danger and desire. Our lips were millimeters apart. All I had to do was lean forward a fraction. Anticipation toward the inevitable was building until someone knocked on one of the doors down the hall and our trance was broken. Taking full advantage of the distraction, I pushed him away and slid out of the dark corner.

As I turned to leave, Ronan caught my arm one more time. His voice was husky when he warned, "Know this, Leila ... this isn't over. I have a feeling our paths will cross again, and next time," his eyes darkened with promise, "I won't be so easily interrupted."

My resolve faltered for a brief moment, but I managed to

smile. "We'll see about that." Before I could second-guess myself, I left the intoxicating darkness of the alcove and Ronan's magnetic pull, quickly stepping back into the main area of the pleasure house. But to my horror, I stepped outside the alcove just as Caelan and Marcellus entered the Rose Petal.

What are they doing here? Pleasure houses were widely considered to be the province of those in the lower classes, not the playground of royalty. I certainly hadn't anticipated that our paths would cross here, of all places.

I was frozen in place as Madam Rose approached them. The odious woman practically vibrated in her excitement. It was rare for royalty to make an appearance here. Much less *two* princes.

"Hello, Your Highnesses! It's a pleasure to host you here tonight," Madam Rose blustered cheerily.

Caelan cleared his throat. "I want to see one of your girls ... Her name is Selene."

"Oh, I'm sorry!" Madam Rose raised her brows in faux shock. "The mermaid is currently entertaining another guest, but I'm sure I can find another suitable girl for your time here." Madam Rose snapped her fingers, catching the attention of a handful of girls standing close by. They glided toward the madam and stood in a line, bright eyed and hoping to be picked. No doubt they hoped one of the princes would fall in love with them and whisk them away from the shackles that bound them to the Rose Petal Lounge.

Caelan shook his head. "I don't want another girl. I want Selene," he said as he tossed a pouch filled with coins. "*And* a private room."

Madam Rose caught the pouch with one hand and took a quick glance inside. From her expression, she was pleased with what she saw. It must have been filled to the brim with glints.

"Of course, Your Highness," Madam Rose said eagerly.

Shooing the girls away with an imperial wave, she turned on her slippered foot and hurried to retrieve Selene.

I frowned as I watched the exchange, then it dawned on me why Caelan and Marcellus were here ... I told Caelan that the Crimson Clan didn't have the lost princess, and the governor hinted that it was due to my friend Selene's pillow talk connections. He was here to confirm it.

I couldn't let them talk to her. Not without giving her a heads-up. I started to stop them when a calloused hand encircled my arm and pulled me back against a firm chest.

"And where do you think you're going?" Ronan asked.

"I don't have time for your nonsense right now!" I gritted as I futilely attempted to rip my arm out of his firm grasp.

He looked between me and the two princes, then back to me. "How do you know the princes?" he asked with a quirked brow.

"Who said I did?"

He snorted and tightened his hold on my arm. "It looks like you're about to run right into one of their arms."

"Leila?" Caelan called out my name once he saw me. He looked at Ronan and the grip on my arm and back to Ronan. "Why am I not surprised to see you in this sort of establishment?"

Ronan smirked as he pulled me closer, then answered on my behalf. "Well, I'm more surprised to see you here ... in *this sort* of establishment. Looks like you're no different from the rest of us."

Caelan glared at him before turning his attention back to me. "I didn't know you two were so well acquainted."

"We're not," I answered quickly as I finally ripped my arm out of Ronan's grip.

"And what if we are?" Ronan countered, earning a glare from me.

Caelan chuckled. "Then it would confirm my suspicions."

"Which are?"

Caelan straightened and looked at Ronan unflinchingly. "That you and your people don't have the lost princess."

I peered over at Ronan, who maintained a carefully neutral expression. After a beat, he smiled. "And what gave you that crazy idea?"

Caelan nodded in my direction. "It's not a what, but a who. *She* told me."

I bit down the groan that threatened to escape. The last thing I needed was for Caelan to snitch on me to Ronan. He'd just put me in a deadly position.

Ronan glanced over at me in surprise. He sized me up and down, observing every inch of me, not caring that Caelan was standing right there. My neck and face flushed and I feared I'd unintentionally outed myself.

Ronan laughed and turned his attention back to Caelan. "I can assure you, Your Highness, that the lost princess is in our custody. And if Valoria doesn't meet our terms, she will soon be married ... *to me*," he said as he looked straight at me.

My eyes widened in surprise. I couldn't help but blurt, "*You're* the chief's son?"

Ronan smirked. "The one and only. Who else did you think I was?"

"I ... I just thought you were a regular Crimson Clan soldier ..."

He snorted. "Far from that, sweetness," he said with a wink.

Oh. My. Gods. I wasn't just getting close to one of my enemies; I was getting close to someone far worse. I barely had time to register the shock when Caelan's voice boomed across the parlor.

"You will *never* marry the princess!"

Marcellus, who had been standing off to the side waiting for Madam Rose, turned his attention our way and jogged over just as Caelan took a threatening step toward Ronan.

"I won't allow it!" Caelan gritted between his teeth.

Ronan looked unfazed. "Your approval matters little to me. Unless Valoria agrees to the terms, she and I will be married by the next full moon."

This was the spark that ignited Caelan's fury. Without hesitation, he unsheathed his sword, his intent clear. Ronan mirrored his movements and readied for battle. I instinctively darted aside as steel met steel. Seizing the chance, I attempted to discreetly exit the scene, but Marcellus swiftly intercepted me.

"And where do you think *you're* going?" he inquired as Ronan unleashed chaos by slicing a table asunder.

The pleasure house was filled with screams from courtesans as they ran away in fear, and the scuffle of men trying to leave as fast as possible, while Caelan and Ronan made a mess of things.

"This is none of my business," I blustered. When I tried to go around Marcellus, he cut off my path again.

"I think it has everything to do with you."

The last thing I wanted to do was fight my own brother, so I stayed put and hoped I could wait out this brawl. Feeling the weight of Marcellus's wary eyes on me, I turned around to watch the fight between Caelan and Ronan. The sound of clashing swords reverberated around the Rose Petal, creating a deadly symphony in the silence left by the musicians and patrons who had fled.

At a glance, I could tell Ronan was a stronger sword fighter than Caelan and Caelan relied too heavily on his fae magic. I watched in horror as Caelan spun out of the way of a deadly lunge, but Ronan was quick on his feet and aimed the sword straight at Caelan's heart.

Without thinking, I lunged between them and felt the sharp sting of steel piercing the back of my shoulder. Even as Ronan realized what happened and tried to halt the blade, the momentum caused the blade to sink even deeper.

Caelan stared at me with wide eyes, clearly bewildered as to why I would save his life. "What are you doing? Why?"

Breathing heavily, I managed a weak smirk. "Two life debts now ... you're in the red," I said, wincing as the blade was withdrawn.

"Leila!" Selene's voice was filled with dread as she dashed towards me. Though Caelan's arms were outstretched, she pushed him out of the way and caught me as I fell. Pain rocketed through my body and the world spun as the pain threatened to pull me under.

"Take me to my clinic," I whispered to Selene. She nodded and started to half-walk, half-carry me out of the pleasure house.

Madam Rose stomped down the stairs where she'd been hiding on the second floor. "And where do you think *you're* going?" she hissed. "I didn't give you permission to leave!"

Selene whirled on her. "What? Can't you see she's hurt? We need to treat the wound before—"

Madam Rose held up a hand. "If she dies, it might be for the best. Unless ... the princes or the Crimson Clan would like to save her?"

Sweat beaded on my forehead and upper lip, and my eyes were rolling back in my head. I fought to keep from passing out while the insufferable madam bargained for my fate.

Madam Rose glanced between the men with a calculating gleam and they yelled in unison, "Save her!" Irritated that they were on the same side for once, they glared at one another before swiveling their attention back to me.

Madam Rose grunted. "Very well. Take her, Selene, but do hurry back. You're still on the clock."

With a curt nod, Selene whisked me out of the Rose Petal.

6

Caelan ushered our unlikely group outside and into his waiting carriage. With the help of my brother, they gingerly picked me up and placed me inside. Once everyone was settled, Caelan yelled to the driver and gave him directions to my clinic.

Ronan leaned into the carriage and gave me a look, which even in my half delirious state struck me as odd. "I'll meet you there," he said. Then he jogged away and vaulted onto one of the horses tied to a post outside the brothel.

Blood seeped steadily, even as Selene applied pressure to the wound. With every sway and jostle of the carriage, a jolt of pain sliced through my shoulder.

"What do you need once we reach the clinic?" Selene asked, worry etched prominently on her lovely face.

I attempted a smile, but it probably came out as more of a grimace. "First, relax," I muttered. "I'm not dying. This is fixable. So don't stress yourself out."

Selene bit her bottom lip and nodded, but I knew she was on the verge of crying.

I looked over at Caelan, who stared at me with a million

questions written on his face, in stark contrast to Marcellus, who couldn't stop staring at Selene. Even in pain, I chuckled.

"What's so funny? This isn't funny, Leila!" Selene all but shrieked as she tightened her grip on the bandage.

I grimaced. "I know, I know."

Caelan cleared his throat. "While I appreciate your assistance, I'm curious as to why you did what you did, Leila."

I avoided his gaze. "No need to overthink it," I replied breezily. "Just didn't want the Prince of Eldwain to die in the Central Plains ... much less in a pleasure house. What would people say?"

Caelan narrowed his eyes. "Right ... the people."

He was unconvinced that my motives were purely altruistic, but right then, I was in too much pain to think of a better excuse. Although the wound wasn't deadly, it felt like my arm would fall off at any moment.

We reached my clinic in record time and the carriage ground to a halt. The driver jumped down from his bench seat and placed a stepping stool in front of the door so we could descend. As soon as we entered the familiar sanctuary of my clinic, I started listing out the ingredients I needed to treat my wound.

"The main ingredient is agrimony. There's a jar on the top shelf," I called out to Selene as I shuffled to the cot. "You're going to have to stitch me up."

Selene was on a ladder, reaching for the herbs. She turned and looked down at me. "I've never stitched flesh," she mumbled.

I chuckled. "You will today."

Just then, Ronan stormed into the clinic with wild eyes. When he saw me sitting on the cot, his glacial gaze stared me down. "Are you absolutely *insane*, or do you have a death wish?" he yelled as he stormed toward me.

"Death wish ... definitely a death wish," I joked.

He scoffed. "This isn't a joke, Leila. I could have killed you! All because of *him*!" He pointed at Caelan. "Who is absolutely *useless* in a fight, I might add."

Caelan shot to his feet and was about to start another brawl when Marcellus intercepted him.

"If you're going to fight again, take it outside. Not in my clinic," I said tersely.

Ronan continued to glare at me, but I ignored him as I watched Selene grind the ingredients. I'd taught her several basics over the years, and she was a good student. After making a paste, she bent down in front of me to apply it.

I cleared my throat. "You all can go now."

"I'm not leaving—" Ronan started.

"I have to undress, and I'm not doing that in front of three men!" I snapped.

"Oh," Ronan croaked out.

The three of them looked at one another sheepishly and slowly exited my clinic without another word.

"Thank the gods," Selene mumbled. "I thought they'd never leave."

I chuckled as I pulled down the top of my dress to expose my shoulder. "Don't forget that they're still outside," I whispered. "They're already suspicious."

Selene applied the paste and blew on it to dry the mixture. "I can understand why. You literally used your body as a shield to help someone who was supposedly a stranger! Why did you do it, Leila?"

I sighed heavily. "Ronan was going in for the kill. I couldn't just stand by and watch Caelan die!" I whispered. "He's my ... he's my best friend."

But Selene wasn't having it. "Correction— he was your best friend when you were *children*," she muttered. "You're no longer children. You don't have any idea what he's like now."

She wasn't wrong. Ten years had passed since Caelan and I

last saw each other. After all that time, we were strangers all over again, no matter how I felt about our shared history.

"Maybe it was stupid, but I don't regret it." I craned my neck to the side and glanced at the wound. "I don't think you need to stitch it. Just wrap it up."

Selene was hesitant. "Are you sure?"

I rolled my eyes. "Who's the healer here?"

She sighed. "You are." She stood and walked over to my cabinet where I kept a stack of fresh cloths. Once she'd bandaged me up, I slid my dress back up and stood, rotating my arm to gauge the range of motion in my shoulder. I could already feel the effects of the medicine working.

A loud bang on the door grabbed our attention. "Are you done yet?" Ronan yelled.

I exhaled loudly and called out, "Yes!" But before the word was out of my mouth, Ronan stormed back inside.

"Are you okay?" he asked as he tried to peer through my dress to the bandage underneath.

"I'm perfectly fine. You haven't killed me yet," I joked.

He grunted and crossed his muscular arms over his thick chest. "Yeah ... *yet*."

Caelan and Marcellus walked in. My brother's eyes were glued to Selene.

"I'm glad you're okay," Caelan offered. "If ... if you need anything, just let us know. We'll be at the governor's residence."

"Thank you," I said. "But I should be fine."

He nodded. "Thanks ... by the way."

"No problem."

I looked between Marcellus and Selene, noticing she wasn't paying attention to him whatsoever, and decided to play match-maker. "There *is* one thing you can do."

Caelan's eyes brightened, eager to be of service. "Of course, what is it?"

"Can you escort Selene back to the Rose Petal Lounge?"

"Yes!" Marcellus answered immediately. "Of course we can."

I bit back a laugh at his enthusiastic response.

"Leila!" Selene scolded. "You need someone to tend to you—"

"I'm fine," I cut her off and pushed her towards the door. "I don't plan on dying in my sleep, and you need to go back before Madam Rose has a hissy fit."

She groaned but did as she was told. Marcellus held her elbow gallantly and hurried to open the carriage door for her.

Just before Caelan stepped out of my clinic, he leaned in and gave me an earnest look. "Thanks again, Leila."

I nodded and watched them leave in silence. Once they were trotting down the street, I turned around and faced Ronan's steely-eyed gaze. "You can go now, too."

He walked toward me like he was about to leave, but instead of walking out the door, he closed it and turned the lock.

"We need to have a talk ... *Princess*."

7

I stood there in horror when Ronan said the one thing I'd carefully hidden for the last ten years. I kept quiet, hoping that no admission was a good enough answer.

Ronan laughed and stepped away from the door. "Ah, you almost fooled me ... almost. But too many things didn't add up," he said. "The simple fact that you knew without a doubt that the Crimson Clan didn't have the princess was my biggest clue, but saving Prince Caelan sealed the deal." His eyes scanned the length of my body and slid back up to my face. "Also, your crescent moon dress just screams Valoria."

"You don't know anything!" I denied hotly.

"I don't?" he said with a raised brow. "Please enlighten me. Where have I gone wrong?" he asked knowingly.

Taking a deep breath, I tried to hold onto the façade a little longer, but his piercing gaze saw right through me. I cursed myself for being careless and letting my emotions take control.

"Why are you here in the Central Plains? Shouldn't you be at the palace, surrounded by guards?" Ronan leaned in closer, his crimson eyes scrutinizing me.

"I can't go back," I whispered. "Not after what happened."

His eyes softened a bit. "What happened, Leila? Why did the Princess of Valoria vanish into thin air?"

I bit my lip and walked over to the window, where I gazed down onto a street filled with hundreds of revelers celebrating the lantern festival. "Honestly ... I don't know," I admitted. "Keldara invaded Valoria. The attack was sudden and unexpected. My parents snuck me out of Valoria with my guardian and I never looked back."

Ronan frowned. "I don't understand. Keldara's attack was sudden, but they weren't prepared to face down Valorian mages. They lost and had to retreat within three days. Why didn't you return after Valoria claimed victory?"

"I wish I knew ..." I looked away from the window and back at Ronan. "All I know is that my guardian told me it wasn't safe. He told me I shouldn't return and promised to tell me why when I was older."

Ronan stared at me for a quiet moment as if he wanted to say something, but then he seemed to change his mind. "Oh," was all he said. He glanced around my clinic. "Where is your guardian now?"

I shrugged one shoulder. "He died."

He frowned. "Then you should have returned!"

I shook my head. "Not until I find out why he was so adamant about me staying hidden." I walked over to the scarred wooden counter and started putting away the plants and herbs Selene pulled out to make my poultice. "So whatever it is that you want, just do it and get it over with. I'm tired of running and hiding."

Ronan sounded almost offended. "You think I'll take you to the Crimson Clan? To my father?" he guessed.

I nodded. "Isn't that your whole purpose here? To capture the long-lost Princess of Valoria? I mean, you've already told all of Asteria that she's your hostage."

He grimaced. "That was my father's plan ... not mine."

I snorted derisively. "You're the chief's son. Your plans are all the same."

He gazed at me intently. "No, Leila ... or should I say, Princess Lyanna. Our plans are *not* the same."

We stared at each other in silence; each weighing our options and assessing our trustworthiness. No matter what Ronan said, he was a Crimson Clan member. I could never trust him.

He sighed and ran a hand through his dark hair. "I know what you must think of the Crimson Clan, but you have to understand that I am *not* my father. I don't want war, bloodshed, or chaos."

My gaze hardened. "Yet, you've indulged in all three by siding with Keldara."

His face contorted with frustration. "I've been raised a certain way, with a certain mindset. But there are things you don't know—"

"I don't care if I'm the most ignorant person in the world, Ronan. Keldara invaded my home! I'll never forgive them for that, or anyone associated with them. So make your decision, whether you're taking me back to the Grasslands or not, because I'll warn you now, Ronan ... you won't take me alive."

His expression hardened. "I won't let you kill yourself, Leila. So you can forget about that notion."

"Try me," I threatened.

"Fine," he sighed. "You don't want to believe me and are dead set on making me the villain? Then that's what I'll be." He took a step toward me. "Don't even think about leaving the Central Plains, princess. I'll hunt you to the ends of Asteria," he growled. With that, he spun on his heels and stormed out of my clinic.

∽

AFTER RONAN LEFT LAST NIGHT, I hardly slept a wink. The simple fact that my decade-long secret had been exposed made me sick to my stomach. I didn't know what to do. I was torn between packing my things and running or staying put as Ronan said. The last thing I wanted was to be on the run for the rest of my life. Especially when I didn't know what was so dangerous in Valoria.

Deciding I wasn't up for seeing any clients today, I closed the clinic and walked to the Tea House, enjoying the respite of the early morning hour and the quiet streets it afforded. The pain in my shoulder was still there, but it was better since I changed the bandages.

The instant I crossed the Tea House's threshold, a delicate bouquet of floral aromas invaded my senses and imbued my body with instant relaxation. Coming here was the perfect remedy. I was still patting myself on the back for having such an enlightened notion as I made my way upstairs when I came face to face with Caelan, nearly bumping into him on the steps.

"Oh ... good morning." He looked down at me, surprised to see me up and about. "How are you feeling?"

"Better," I answered with a tight smile.

"Are you here for the storyteller?" he asked. I nodded. "They said he should be here in thirty minutes. Today's story is about the Nine Tailed Fox Demon of the Crimson Clan."

"Oh, okay," I said. "I'll uh ... see you—"

"Would you care to join me?" he interrupted. "I have a table right over there," he said as he pointed to a table with the best view of the stage.

Feeling unexplainably awkward, I replied, "Sure, thank you," and followed him to his table. We sat down and a pot of tea instantly appeared, alongside two delicate cups. "Wow, I've never had such great service here." I glanced around warily. "Not that the service is bad, but I usually have to wait."

"Well, I *am* the prince," he said with a chuckle. After an

uncomfortable silence that felt interminable, Caelan spoke again. "I still don't understand why you saved me last night," he muttered. "It doesn't make sense."

I nodded. "I know. Aside from the fact that you're the Prince of Eldwain, you, uh ... well, you remind me of someone I used to know. I guess I just—"

His brows shot up. "Oh! Is it someone from Eldwain?"

I bit my bottom lip nervously. "Yes."

"Are you still friends?"

It took me a moment to answer his question, since I wasn't sure. "Not really. We ... lost touch."

He leaned back in his chair, looking smug and with a renewed sense of purpose. "Well, if you'd like, when I return to Eldwain, I can look for him. I mean, you *are* my savior and all." His teasing grin reminded me so much of the boy I once knew.

I chuckled. "That is very true." I took a sip of my tea to give me time to gather my thoughts. "So ... you've been looking for the lost princess all this time?" I asked hesitantly.

He sipped his tea and nodded, then gently set the cup down. "I have."

"Why?" I blurted. The instant the word left my lips, I realized it probably came out wrong.

Caelan peered over at me. "Because she's my soulmate," he answered honestly.

His answer caught me off guard and I frowned. "Your soulmate? You look awfully young. Correct me if I'm wrong, but she's been gone ten years, which means you were just children when she disappeared."

He nodded. "Yes, we were. Eleven, to be precise. But I know what I know, and Lyanna was ..."

He paused and my hands trembled with nerves. To calm down, I reached for my cup again and took a restorative drink of tea. The warmth soothed my throat and distracted me from the conversation.

"Lyanna promised me," he continued. "She promised to marry me."

I choked on my tea and nearly spit it out. "What?"

He fixed me with a curious stare and handed me a handkerchief. "Here."

I took a moment to wipe my mouth and think of what to say. "She promised to marry you? I apologize for my frankness, Your Highness, but you can't be serious. The promise of a child is meaningless."

"Maybe to you, but not to me." His voice was soft and sounded far away. "It's why I can't let her marry Ronan. He'll ruin her."

I cleared my throat. "I'm sure she won't marry him," I said. "No one with an ounce of common sense would marry into the Crimson Clan."

Caelan shook his head. "You don't know Lyanna. She's ... delicate. She avoids confrontation at all costs. She won't be able to defend herself, especially if they're holding her captive."

I barely restrained an eyeroll of epic proportions. Sure, I was a bit fragile when I was a child, but I wouldn't necessarily claim to be *helpless*. Except Caelan didn't know that. He didn't know what I'd endured the last ten years. He was in love with the idea of the princess he once knew. Unfortunately, that wasn't who I was anymore.

Caelan's earnestness was touching, but at the same time, it was a stark reminder of how much had changed. I stared down at my cup. The steam rose in delicate swirls, mimicking my turbulent thoughts.

"Perhaps the Lyanna you knew was delicate," I began, choosing my words carefully. "But ten years can change a person. Shape them in ways you can't possibly imagine."

His eyes met mine, searching for something. "I just want her to be safe. And happy."

"Everyone deserves happiness," I replied softly. I hesitated for a moment, then plunged ahead. "But sometimes, happiness doesn't come from where or whom we expect."

A thoughtful look passed over his face and he took another sip of his tea. The Tea House had steadily filled with more patrons, and the murmurs of their conversations blended into a comforting background hum.

"Whether or not you find her, it's important to remember that she might not be the same person you remember. She might have her own path to follow."

Caelan nodded slowly. "I understand that. I just wish she was here so I could tell her how much she means to me."

A lump formed in my throat. "Perhaps she knows," I whispered. "Maybe she never forgot you."

A faraway look settled in his eyes. "I hope so. I just ... I want to be there for her, protect her. I can't stand the thought of her being with someone like Ronan." His upper lip curled in disgust.

"And what makes you think she can't protect herself?" I retorted, unable to curtail the touch of defensiveness that crept into my voice. "Like I said, people change. Maybe she learned to be strong. To defend herself and those she cares about. She is a blood mage, after all."

Caelan seemed taken aback by my sudden intensity. "I didn't mean to imply she's weak," he said gently. "I just care about her. A lot."

Just then, a server stopped by to refill our teapot. The atmosphere had gone from teasing to tense, and we were both lost in our thoughts. I regretted snapping at him. I knew his intentions were pure, but it was hard hearing someone else define who I was or used to be.

Finally breaking the silence, Caelan asked, "Do you plan to attend the festival tonight?"

I blinked in surprise, startled by the sudden change in topic. "I ... I hadn't planned on it."

"You should," he said, his voice soft. "It's beautiful, from what I saw last night. The lanterns, the music, the dancing. It's a night to forget all the burdens and simply enjoy the moment."

I smiled hesitantly. "Maybe I will."

He grinned. "I hope to see you there."

The storyteller stepped onto the stage and began his tale, but my mind was elsewhere. The weight of my identity, my past, and the uncertainty of my future pressed down upon me. But for now, I had a cup of tea, a potential friend, and a festival to look forward to.

8

That night, I considered attending the lantern festival on my own to see if I might bump into Caelan, even though I promised Selene I'd spend it with her. But after the draining experience I'd had earlier in the day, I just wasn't in the mood. After dispatching a messenger to deliver a message to Selene that I wouldn't be at the Rose Petal, I found myself at the tavern nursing my second bottle of wine.

The Twisted Oak Tavern was bursting with old-world charm. It was named after a large, gnarled oak tree that stood in the center of the tavern, which the proprietors claimed to be over five centuries old. The building was constructed with dark brown oak planks that had aged to a weathered gray over the years. The thatched roof kept the heat in as a stone chimney belched out comforting tendrils of smoke into the night.

Inside, the amber glow from strategically placed lanterns illuminated the cozy space, making the shadows dance in rhythm to the soft hum of conversation. At one end stood a grand hearth with a roaring fire, the flames licking at the dry wood and crackling merrily. Above the fireplace hung a large, hand-painted sign of the tavern's namesake – the twisted oak – with its roots and branches intertwined in a complicated dance.

The tavern was filled with long, sturdy wooden tables and benches, and a makeshift stage for live performances was situated on the opposite end of the room from the fireplace. The scent in the air was a comforting mix of roasted meat, freshly baked bread, and the unmistakable tinge of various ales and wines. The bar stretched along one entire wall. Crafted from polished cherry wood, gleaming bottles of all shapes and sizes were lined up behind it.

Patrons of the Twisted Oak were a diverse lot – from tired travelers seeking solace and rest, to local villagers catching up on the day's gossip. The general atmosphere was that of camaraderie and relaxation, with bursts of laughter echoing every so often.

I sat in a dimly lit corner away from the bustle, with a clear view of the entrance. Occasionally my eyes flicked to the dancing flames in the fireplace, which seemed to reflect my tumultuous emotions. The wine bottle in front of me was my solace for the night; a temporary means to escape the complexities life had thrown my way.

My heart was heavy. Even amidst the comforting hum and warmth of the tavern, I was encompassed by solitude. It wasn't just the revelation about my past with Ronan or my chance meeting with Caelan, it was the overwhelming weight of secrets, unspoken emotions, and uncharted paths that lay ahead.

Every sip of wine provided a temporary reprieve, a momentary pause from the myriad thoughts that threatened to overwhelm me. My fingers occasionally traced the rim of my glass as my mind played a melancholic tune on repeat.

The Twisted Oak was a refuge for many, a place to lose oneself in good company or a strong drink. But for me, tonight, it was a mirror to my soul: warm and inviting on the surface, yet concealing a depth of pain and introspection.

My cheeks were rosy and flushed from all the drinking and my head was woozy, but I wasn't ready to stop. I tossed back another cup of wine and stared at the ceiling for a beat or two before waving over a server and asking for a third bottle of wine.

"Leila, maybe you've had enough," Amelia, the server said as she collected the two empty jugs of wine I'd already polished off.

"I'm perfectly fine," I slurred as I continued to stare at the ceiling. "Bring me another."

"Leila, please," Amelia whispered. "I don't want to have to send a messenger to the Rose Petal."

I straightened and stared her down. "I said *bring me another!*"

She sighed and walked away, although she didn't confirm whether she would bring me more wine or not.

In my drunken haze, the weight of the tavern's surroundings seemed to bear down on me. Clinking mugs, the low hum of conversations, and the occasional burst of raucous laughter formed a cacophonous symphony around me. Each sound felt amplified, echoing my inner turmoil. The distant strumming of a lute from a bard in the corner added a somber melody to my already heavy heart.

Amelia returned shortly, but instead of another jug of wine, she set a pitcher of water down in front of me with an apologetic smile. "No more wine. I've sent a message to Selene to pick you up."

I scoffed and turned away from the water as Amelia walked away to another table. If I couldn't get more wine here, I'd go somewhere else.

I dropped coins onto the table and stood, wobbling on my

feet from the sudden movement. The world swayed and the bustling noise of the tavern grew louder, mounting on the edges of what promised to be a truly horrendous headache. Taking a deep breath, I gripped the table's edge to steady myself and cautiously waited for the room to come back into focus. I took a few tentative steps and tried to maneuver my way out, but the worn floorboards were unsteady beneath my feet, like a shifting labyrinth that made every step feel like a challenge.

A few patrons eyed me with a mix of concern and amusement. A pair of old men playing dice in the corner whispered something to each other and chuckled, no doubt commenting on my inebriated state. The smell of roasting meat from the tavern's kitchen wafted over and suddenly, my stomach lurched.

Stumbling the last few steps to the entrance, I pushed the wooden door open and felt instant relief when the chilled night air washed across my face, a stark contrast to the warm, heady atmosphere inside the Twisted Oak. The sensation sobered me up a little, but not enough for what was ahead.

I hesitated for a moment on the threshold, taking in the moonlit cobbled streets and distant chatter from the ongoing lantern festival.

"Well, isn't this a surprise!" a voice said. A man approached and took my elbow to steady me.

I turned and squinted, surprised to see Orion. I groaned. "What do *you* want?"

He laughed. "Nothing in particular, but you seem to be in need of aid."

I pulled away from him and stumbled. "I don't need your help!"

He snorted. "It looks like you do, dear. Come on, let's get you home."

Lacking the energy to fight him, I allowed him to lead me out of the Twisted Oak and guide me down the street towards my clinic. With every step we took the crowd dwindled, but the soft glow of an array of lanterns continued to illuminate our path. The festival was a kaleidoscope of colors, each lantern telling a story of wishes and dreams. But with my blurred vision and foggy mind, the beauty of the scene was lost on me.

Orion's grip was firm yet gentle as he ensured I didn't trip over the uneven cobblestones. There was a sense of security in his grasp, one I begrudgingly appreciated, though I would never admit it.

"You don't have to do this," I muttered, my words slightly slurred.

Orion chuckled softly. "I know. But it's not every day I get to rescue the fiercely independent Leila."

I rolled my eyes, even though the motion made the world spin. "I wasn't in need of rescuing, you know."

"You could barely stand," he pointed out, amusement evident in his voice.

"Technicalities," I huffed.

We continued in silence for a bit, with only the sounds of our footsteps and the distant murmur of festival goers. The cool breeze carried a mixture of fragrances—fresh flowers, burning candles, and spiced food from the stalls.

"As a healer, you should know better than to drink this much," Orion chided as we entered an area that was largely deserted. "Aren't you the most famous healer in all the Central Plains? I mean, imagine if they could see you now," he smirked.

"Very funny," I mumbled. "It's okay to let loose once in a while. Besides that, I needed it."

"Ah, trouble in paradise?"

I snorted. "Who said I lived in paradise? More like my own personal hell."

"Aw, come on, Leila. Things can't be *that* bad."

I laughed and threw my head back. "If you only knew …"

"I just might," he whispered.

Just as I was about to open my mouth and ask him what the hell he was talking about, something stopped us in our tracks. Up ahead a group of six men stood, all holding weapons of different sorts, as if they were waiting for us.

"Bandits," Orion murmured. "Are you good enough to fight?"

I shook my head to clear it of the cobwebs and nodded. "I'm good."

Orion gave me a sideways glance, clearly skeptical but impressed by my determination. "Alright, stay close. And try not to use any of your magic. It'll only drain you further."

I grinned as I pulled a concealed dagger from my boot. "Who said I only use magic?"

One of the bandits, probably the leader, given his larger build and the ornate weapon he held, boldly stepped forward. "Well, well, what have we here? A fae and a drunken healer. This should be fun."

"We don't want any trouble," Orion said calmly, positioning himself slightly in front of me. "Step aside and we'll be on our way."

The bandit leader let out a loud laugh that echoed harshly down the dimly lit street. "You're in *our* territory now. All we want is your coin and any other valuables you might be carrying. And maybe the healer can give us a little special treatment, eh?"

A surge of indignant anger and adrenaline momentarily cleared my mind. "You'd be wise to reconsider."

He sneered. "Is that a threat?"

"No," I replied, twirling the dagger in my hand. "A promise."

Before the man could react, Orion drew his own blade and lunged at him. The remaining bandits, seeing their leader engaged, charged at me.

Despite my inebriation, years of training and reflexes kicked in. I deftly parried an attack from a bandit wielding a rusty sword, countering with a swift kick to his midsection. He grunted and stumbled back. I used the momentary advantage to launch another attack, quickly disarming him with a jab to his throat.

On my right, Orion danced with two bandits, his blade flashing in the dim light. He moved with a grace and efficiency that would have been mesmerizing if I had the time to watch. The clash of steel against steel and the shouts and grunts created a chaotic symphony. And yet, Orion and I moved in perfect harmony, covering each other's backs and making quick work of the would-be robbers.

Just when we thought they were down, a group of another six or seven bandits emerged from the shadows and caught us off guard.

"Am I drunk and seeing double, or are there more?" I muttered to Orion.

"Oh no, my dear, you're definitely seeing more," he whispered back. "Looks like they were prepared. Either that, or this is all an elaborate trap."

"What? Are you some special kind of fae? Because I doubt they're here for me," I mumbled.

"Don't be so sure about that, Leila," he said.

We stood back-to-back and faced our oncoming threat with grim resolve. "Looks like I'm going to have to use magic." I lifted the hand that wasn't clutching my dagger and readied myself.

Right before we were about to launch an attack, a battle cry rang out in the distance and suddenly a group of twenty or so Crimson Clan members materialized from the shadows and roofs of the surrounding area with Ronan leading the charge.

"I don't like when others touch what's mine." Ronan approached the leader of the bandits while stretching his hands and wrists, preparing for a fight.

The leader of the bandits sneered and tried to mask his growing anxiety. "Who says she's yours?"

Ronan simply raised an eyebrow, the cold fire in his eyes doing more damage than words ever could. The Crimson Clan members fanned out and surrounded the remaining bandits. The numbers were now on our side.

"Back off," the leader growled, casting worried glances at his fellow bandits, who hesitated as they glanced between him and the overwhelming force before them.

Ronan laughed, a dark and foreboding sound that echoed eerily along the quiet street. "Do you truly think you can take on the Crimson Clan? You should've done your research before picking a fight here."

With just a snap of Ronan's fingers, the Crimson Clan attacked in sync, cutting the bandits down as if they were nothing but tree branches. The scene that unfolded was a well-choreographed dance of death. The Crimson Clan, known throughout the realm for their precision and ruthless efficiency, sprang into action with deadly grace. Each movement, each strike, was executed with the kind of expertise only years of training and experience could bring.

I watched in awe. The bandits were clearly outmatched. Their frantic movements and desperate cries stood in stark contrast to the silent, focused aggression of the Clan.

It was over in minutes. The bandits, including their leader, lay defeated, some unconscious, others nursing their wounds, and some ... dead. Ronan walked over to the bandit leader who was trying to crawl away, clutching a bleeding gash on his side. With one swift motion, Ronan pinned him to the ground with his foot, pressing just enough to cause discomfort but not enough to seriously harm.

"Now," Ronan said, his voice cold and steely, "you will tell your friends to spread the word. The Crimson Clan is not to be trifled with, and the healer is off limits. Do you understand?"

The bandit leader nodded frantically, his eyes wide with fear. "Yes, yes, I understand!"

Ronan removed his foot and glared down at the man. "Leave. And remember this night," he warned.

The bandit leader nodded, then crawled to his feet and gestured for his gang to retreat. They disappeared into the dark alleyway and left the street silent once again, save for the distant sounds of the festival.

With the threat eliminated, Ronan turned to me. "Are you alright?"

I sighed. "I'm fine. Everything would have been fine. I can handle things," I slurred and stumbled on my feet. Orion caught me before I fell.

Ronan frowned. "Are you ... are you drunk?"

"No," I scowled.

"Yes, she is," Orion answered. "Very."

Ronan sheathed his sword and walked toward me. "I'll take you home." He reached to grab me, but Orion stood in his way.

"No offense, *friend*, but I don't know you. It's best if I escort Miss Leila home myself."

Ronan scoffed. "Friend? I don't befriend the fae." He glared at Orion's pointed ears. "How do you know Leila?"

I could barely keep myself standing, much less follow the convoluted arc of their conversation. I wanted to say something to stop their verbal sparring match, but when my stomach lurched, all thoughts beyond self-preservation fled.

Orion laughed. "Does it matter how I know her? What I'm wondering is who *you* are?" He glanced around at the group of warriors. "I know Leila well enough to know she wouldn't befriend anyone from the Crimson Clan."

Ronan's hand edged to the hilt of his sword. "Is that so? Well maybe you don't know her as well as you *think* you do."

"Oh, I know her rather well."

Ronan reached for me and grabbed my other arm as Orion held the other. Stuck in a tug of war between them, I couldn't hold it in anymore. I gagged and emptied my stomach right between where they stood. They released me immediately and stepped out of the splash zone, wearing matching grimaces.

Orion gallantly handed me a handkerchief and pointed to his face, letting me know I was a mess. I accepted his handkerchief and wiped my mouth hurriedly. Even though I hated to throw up, I had to admit I felt clear headed for the first time in hours.

"Are ... are you okay?" Ronan asked hesitantly.

I nodded. "I'm fine. You can both stop the pissing match."

Ronan scowled. "That is *not* what was happening."

"Of course not," I said sarcastically. "I think I can take myself home from here on out."

Orion reached for me and took ahold of one arm, while Ronan gripped the other. "Let me escort you home, Leila," the fae declared.

Ronan pulled me toward him and I stumbled in his direction. "She's not going anywhere with you!"

Orion tugged on my arm and I lurched toward him. The motion was making me dizzy and my stomach threatened to make its displeasure known. "Enough!" I attempted a shout, but it came out as a hoarse whisper.

"I don't trust the Crimson Clan," Orion countered.

"You—" Ronan attempted to yell, but he was cut off by a shrill cry.

"Neither of you will be taking her home!" Selene yelled from down the street.

I sagged in relief at the sight of her. "Oh, thank the gods," I mumbled as I ripped myself free and stumbled toward my friend. "Have I told you how much I love you lately?"

She gave me a tight smile. "No, you haven't. Why would you do this to yourself?" she whispered the last part.

I shrugged and fell into her arms with a sigh. "I was ... in a mood."

"You can't risk falling into these moods, Leila," she chided.

I nodded in agreement but kept quiet. She didn't know about my conversation with Caelan earlier today, and she didn't know that Ronan had already blown my cover. I needed a break. A moment where I was free from all my troubles.

"*I'm* taking her home. And neither of you better follow," Selene said sternly. "She's had enough of you both." With more force than necessary, Selene dragged me down the street toward my clinic, leaving the others behind.

9

Selene eased me down on the cot downstairs in my clinic and started to pace. "Something is wrong. You wouldn't be this reckless, otherwise."

I nodded. "You're right ... something *is* wrong."

"Well?"

I sighed. "Ronan knows I'm the lost princess."

Selene's eyes widened in shock. "Excuse me? What did you say?"

"You heard me." I laid down on the cot to stop the world from spinning. There was nothing left in my stomach for me to vomit. Now all I felt was discomfort.

"Impossible!" she shouted as she continued to pace. "If he knew, he would have taken you straight to the Grasslands."

I rubbed my temples and shrugged. "I thought so too, but he has something up his sleeve. I just don't know what it is yet."

Selene dropped to her knees beside the cot and tugged on my sleeve. "Let's get out of here, Leila. The Central Plains are vast, and we can hide in the mountains. Let's just *go*."

I sighed, then sat up and pulled Selene onto the narrow cot to sit beside me. "Do you really think Madam Rose would let you leave? She'll send bounty hunters after you. You know I'm right."

"So?" she said. "That just means we'll both be on the run. We're better together than separated."

I reached for her hand and held it tightly. "I would love to, but it's useless. Ronan and his men know what I look like now. He'll hunt me down until he finds me, and so will Madam Rose. The idea of going on the run seems novel from where you sit now, but trust me when I tell you it's not. I've been doing it for ten years."

She shot to her feet. "Well we can't just sit around and wait until they capture you! We have to do something!"

"*We* don't have to do anything, Selene. This is my problem. I'll handle it."

"No. We're a team," she insisted stubbornly. "Since the day you saved my life, I vowed to serve you until my last breath."

I shook my head. "You know I don't want that. All I've ever wanted for you is freedom, not servitude," I argued. "You don't owe me anything, Selene. You've done more than enough in the last few years."

She dropped to her knees again in front of me and reached for my hands. "Please, Leila, *do* something!"

I wiped away her tears and smiled. "Don't worry. I'll be okay. I won't allow myself to be married off to the Crimson Clan."

Her eyes widened. "We'll tell the princes!" she exclaimed. "If they knew who you were, they would save you!"

"No. You know I can't tell them. Not yet," I said. "And I don't need saving. I'm powerful enough to take care of myself."

She rested her forehead on my knees and silently wept. I brushed her inky black hair away from her face and tried to reassure her that everything would be okay, even though it was far from it.

∽

Selene spent the night with me in the clinic to make sure I was okay. When I woke the next morning, she was still sleeping on the cot downstairs. I adjusted the blanket over her and silently stepped outside to grab breakfast for us both before Madam Rose sent someone to fetch her back.

Nursing a monster hangover, I walked down the street toward Anna's bakery, stepping around the remnants of the lantern festival. The town was quiet this morning since most people stayed up late last night.

The baker greeted me with a bright smile when I approached her stall. "Good morning, Leila!" she chirped.

"Good morning, Anna," I said, trying to soothe my roiling stomach. "What warm goods do you have?"

"I have fresh bread that I just took out of the oven," she offered. "Unfortunately, I sold out of mooncakes last night and haven't had time to make any more yet."

I smiled. "No worries. It's too early in the morning for sweets. Give me two loaves of bread, please."

She nodded and went to fetch the warm bread. As she packed them up, I waited on a stool sitting off to the side. Casting my eyes over the nearly empty streets, I was surprised to see Marcellus and Caelan. Just then, Anna came out with the bread.

"Here you go, Leila," she said warmly.

With a wave goodbye, I walked toward the princes and greeted them with a bow. "Good morning, Your Highnesses." I straightened and Caelan raised a brow.

"Are you okay?" he asked with concern in his voice.

I ran my fingers through the tangled mess of my hair, knowing I looked a fright. I chuckled awkwardly. "Yes, just suffering the effects of a long night of drinking."

He nodded and looked me up and down. "Ah, okay, that makes sense. I didn't see you at the lantern festival. I guess you were off having fun."

"Yeah, sorry. I sort of got carried away," I replied sheepishly. "Well, it was nice seeing you both." When I attempted to side-step them, Caelan stood in my way.

"Hold on," he said, stopping me.

Puzzled, I asked, "Do you need something, Your Highness?"

"Why don't we escort you home? You don't look well," he offered.

Marcellus groaned. "Come on, Cael," Marcellus complained. "I'm hungry. She can get home on her own."

Caelan glared at him and turned his attention back to me. "I heard there was a large group of bandits roaming the streets last night. It's not safe for you to be walking around alone."

I attempted to downplay the veracity of his claim. "It's fine. I can take care of myself," I urged.

He waved me off. "Please, allow me."

Marcellus looked like he was about to throw a tantrum, and I almost laughed. Some things never changed. He was still cranky when he was hungry.

"I have enough bread for all of us ..." I offered, then added, "including Selene, who's waiting for me at home." That certainly caught my brother's attention.

His eyes widened and he stepped toward me. "Selene is at your place?"

I nodded.

"Well, what are we waiting for? Let's hurry!" Without further prompting, Marcellus spun on his heels and rushed down the street toward my clinic.

I pressed my lips into a thin line to keep from laughing. Before I left home, he was barely ten and couldn't stand the sight of a girl. Now, he'd grown into a man.

While Marcellus raced ahead, Caelan and I walked together down the street in stilted silence.

He finally cleared his throat. "Did you ... spend last night at the pleasure house ...?" By the way he left the question hanging, he really wanted to ask if I was with Ronan.

I shook my head. "No. I was at the Twisted Oak ... *alone*."

"Oh ..." he murmured. "Is everything okay?"

I nodded. "Yeah, just a little stress relief," I laughed, and he did the same. "What did you do last night?"

"Marcel and I spent it along the riverfront where they were lighting lanterns and sending them down the river. It was quite a sight."

"I bet." I looked ahead. "Did you make a wish?"

He chuckled. "Yes."

"Care to share?" I pushed.

He sighed. "What do you think?" I shrugged. "To find Princess Lyanna, of course," he stated like it should have been obvious. Maybe it was.

"You'll find her," I promised. "One day you'll be reunited."

"I hope so," he said wistfully. "I just ... the thought of her in the clutches of the Crimson Clan makes me sick to my stomach."

I shook my head. "I told you, Your Highness, they don't have her."

Though he nodded, he was obviously unconvinced. "You mentioned that before, but Ronan seems so confident. I just – I'm not sure."

I faced him. "From my understanding, Princess Lyanna comes from a line of blood mages, which means she must be extremely powerful. I doubt she would allow herself to get captured so easily," I said to reassure him.

"That may be, but Lyanna was only ever taught defensive magic. She never learned offensive magic."

While that was true, in the years after I escaped the castle, Sir Edric taught me how to fight. He also managed to locate a mage trainer to teach me more about my magic while keeping my identity as a blood mage a secret. It wasn't easy, but he did his best to prepare me. But Caelan didn't know any of that.

"It might be different now," I muttered reluctantly.

"I hope so," he whispered. "I hope Lyanna is stronger and braver and can hold on until I find her."

"She will," I reassured him.

We arrived at my clinic and found Selene waiting outside with Ronan and his friend, Silas. I gave an inward groan, knowing this wouldn't be good. "What are *you* doing here?" I pushed past him to Selene and handed her the two loaves of fresh bread.

Ronan followed me inside. "What do you think? I'm making sure you're okay after last night."

"What happened last night?" Caelan asked as he followed us. I looked behind me and saw Selene and Marcellus standing together outside.

I walked to my mixing table to start working on prescriptions. "Nothing happened," I replied breezily.

"She was attacked by bandits. Probably *your* doing," Ronan accused.

Caelan looked taken aback. "I did no such thing!"

Ronan snorted. "Oh, pardon, Your Highness. I forgot. You would never lower yourself to such levels."

"Unlike *your* people," Caelan said under his breath. Silas charged across the room, already unsheathing his sword.

"No fighting in my clinic!" I shouted before they turned my place upside down.

Ronan motioned for Silas to put away the sword, which he did begrudgingly.

Caelan eyed me up and down. "You don't look hurt."

I scowled. "I'm perfectly fine. Just because I'm a healer doesn't mean I don't know how to fight!"

"If you know who they are, we can get the authorities involved," Caelan suggested.

Ronan snorted. "Oh, please. What can that governor do besides wave that fat finger around as if he runs things here?"

I stepped around my station and walked back outside. "Your Highness?" I called out to Marcellus. "Would you mind escorting Selene back to the pleasure house?"

His eyes brightened. "Of course!"

"Leila, no." Selene inched closer. "You can't be left alone with them," she whispered so only I could hear.

I waved off her concern. "I'll be fine. Now go, before Madam Rose sends bounty hunters to come after you."

She hesitated for a brief moment before nodding and turning to walk away with Marcellus.

I turned back around to find Caelan, Ronan, and Silas waiting impatiently. Getting rid of them would be a pain in the arse. I walked back inside and waved them away. "Can you all leave so I can nurse my headache in peace?" I groused.

"It's not safe to be left alone, Leila," Ronan chided. "Bandits are swarming the Central Plains."

"That's not news. They've always been in the Central Plains; it hasn't stopped me before. I'll be fine," I blustered.

"Like you were last night? You were very nearly overpowered," he warned.

"I was not! You just stepped in before I had a chance to do anything. There's a difference. Maybe next time you should mind your own business."

Ronan scoffed. "I won't allow anyone to touch what is mine," he growled.

Caelan studied the scene and silently watched us volley barbs and protests back and forth. It was unsettling.

"I don't belong to anyone! You better watch your words before others get the wrong idea," I gritted between my teeth. "You should know a woman's reputation is everything."

Ronan snorted and raised a brow. "And being with me would ruin yours?"

"Yes. It would." I stared at him without flinching. "So stop giving others the wrong impression. We are *nothing* to each other!"

Ronan burst into a throaty laugh as he prowled toward me, stopping when he reached the edge of my boots. "You. Are. Mine," he announced. "The faster you get that through your head, the easier things will be." He looked slightly over his shoulder to Caelan, who still watched us intently, then turned back to me and lowered his voice. "I'm sure you don't want others to learn the truth."

"I don't take kindly to threats," I whispered.

He smirked. "No threats, sweetness. Only promises."

I pushed him away and he stumbled back with a slight chuckle. "Remember my words, Leila."

I glared at him until Caelan stepped between us and faced me.

"Leila, you're more than welcome to stay with us at the governor's residence if ..." he peered over his shoulder at Ronan and then back at me, "if you don't feel safe here."

I looked between the prince and the clan chief's son. Ronan's eyes glinted dangerously in response to the prince's offer. The air between them crackled with unspoken threats and tension.

"I appreciate the offer, Your Highness, but I'll be fine," I replied, determined to stand my ground. "This is my home and my clinic. I won't be scared out of it."

Caelan studied my face for a moment, a hint of interest evident in his eyes. "Very well. If you change your mind, just send word."

Ronan, still bristling, grunted, "She won't need to."

The clan chief's son looked ready to attack at any moment. Right as I was about to step between them, the door to my clinic burst open and Henry, the young boy who hung around the Tea House barged in, holding his forearm.

"Miss Leila!" he called out. "I need your help."

I frowned as I approached him, then sucked in a startled gasp when I moved his hand off his forearm to reveal a nasty gash. "What happened?"

When he looked away guiltily, I didn't push any further. He was obviously doing something he shouldn't have done.

"Come on, let's get you cleaned up." I led him over to the cot and asked him to sit.

As I started cleaning his wound, he asked, "Do you want to hear any more information on the lost princess?"

I tensed and peered over my shoulder to find Caelan's eyes going wide. If he wasn't suspicious before, he definitely was now.

Ronan laughed. "Who *doesn't* want to hear about the lost princess? It's top-tier gossip nowadays," he cut in, trying to shift the attention to himself.

The young boy looked up at Ronan and his eyes went wide. "Crimson Clan," he whispered, belatedly realizing who Ronan and Silas were. The young boy shifted closer to me.

"Don't worry, they won't hurt you," I whispered. Turning to the men, I announced, "I think it's best if you all go now."

Silas, who had been quiet this whole time, finally spoke up. "Ronan, let's go. We have matters to attend to."

Sending one last possessive glare my way, Ronan nodded at his companion. "Remember what I said, Leila," he warned, then stepped outside.

With them gone, the atmosphere in the clinic lightened. I let out a sigh of relief. Caelan lingered, a curious expression on his face. "Leila, are you sure you don't want an escort or guard? The streets are dangerous these days," he added carefully.

I gave a wry smile. "I think I'm more afraid of the men trying to protect me than the actual threats out there."

He chuckled softly, but it sounded forced, as if there were a million questions running through his head—particularly why the local healer was so interested in learning more about the lost Valorian princess. "You're brave and headstrong. But don't be too stubborn to ask for help when you need it."

I offered a stiff smile. "Thank you. I'll keep that in mind."

He nodded, seemingly satisfied with my response. "Take care, Leila. I'll see you around." With a parting glance at the young boy, he left.

I hoped I hadn't placed a target on him like I had already done to Selene. Once it was just the two of us, I closed the door and turned back to Henry. "Now that they're all gone, want to tell me what happened?" I quirked a brow.

He sighed. "I was in the mountains following the Valorian army," he said. "I was running from them so I wouldn't get caught."

"The Valorian army?" I questioned. "Why would they be here?"

The young boy shrugged. "I don't know. I was trying to find out, but then I almost got caught by one of their generals."

Caelan and Marcellus were supposed to be here as envoys. When making deals, it was poor form to bring an army along to intimidate the other party. What did they have up their sleeves? Whatever it was, it was no good. If war ravaged the Central Plains, the people would be the ones who suffered.

"Do you know if they came with the princes?" I asked casually as I applied ointment to his wound, then blew on it gently to dry.

"They didn't. The army didn't arrive until yesterday," he said, then winced from the sting on his arm as the medicine started to work. "The princes only came with a handful of guards."

I nodded. "How do you get your information?"

He grinned. "Information is money, Miss Leila. It's the only way I can survive."

I snorted and ruffled his messy hair. "You need to stay out of trouble, is what you *need* to do. Where are your parents?"

"Dead," he answered. "The plague took them."

Unfortunately, stories like his were all too common. If only I could help him. But letting him get involved with me would only make things worse.

I bandaged him up and stood, dusting off my hands. "You're all set."

He started to dig through his pockets and pulled out a couple of sparks and gleam coins, jiggling them in his palm to count how much money he had. "I don't have much, but I'll give you all I have."

When he tried to hand the coins to me, I waved him off. "Don't worry about it, Henry. You can come to me anytime. Free of charge."

His eyes widened again and he froze. "Really?"

"Really. But do you think you can do me a favor?"

He pocketed the coins and nodded vigorously. "Anything, Miss Leila."

"If you hear anything about the lost princess, the Valorian army, or even the Crimson Clan, could you come tell me?"

"Of course!" He jumped to his feet.

"Just make sure I'm alone and no one is around when you tell me this information," I warned.

"Will do, Miss Leila."

I fished in my pocket for a glint and handed it to him. "For the information today."

He tried giving it back. "No, Miss Leila. You've helped me; I couldn't charge you—"

"Information is money, Henry, or did you forget saying that? Don't ever turn it down, even from me." I patted his shoulder. "If you ever need help, my clinic is always open."

10

The day passed in a blur of patients and treatments. My supply of herbs and plants was dwindling and I would have to make the laborious trip up the mountain soon to replenish. The trip took a couple days and I hated leaving Selene alone, especially with the Crimson Clan around.

Once I was done treating patients, I flipped my sign to closed and started toward the Rose Petal. I hadn't had a chance to check in with Selene since she left my place earlier that morning.

The instant I stepped into the pleasure house I was assaulted with a blockade of rose perfume. The sweet scent tickled my nose and I sneezed before glancing around the busy establishment filled with men and working girls. One person caught my attention, and I made my way over to his table.

"Your Highness." I bowed as I approached Marcellus, whose eyes were fixed on the stage where Selene danced. "Your Highness," I repeated a little louder, finally snapping him out of his daze.

He cleared his throat. "Oh, Leila, You're here."

I chuckled. "And you're *still* here. I figured you would have dropped her off and left."

He bit his lip guiltily. "I did ... but I returned."

I nodded and took a seat at his table, uninvited. "You like Selene, don't you?"

The blush that stained his cheeks told me all I wanted to know.

"It's okay if you do," I reassured him. "As one of the merfolk, she's obviously extremely beautiful."

"Yes ... but my parents," he murmured.

I realized where his train of thought was. I flagged down one of the girls and asked for two cups and a jug of wine. When she returned, I served us both and handed him a cup of wine.

"May I be frank, Your Highness?"

He accepted the wine and nodded. "Go ahead," he said, though he kept his eyes fixed on Selene.

"Selene has had a hard life," I started. "Harder than anyone could ever imagine. And while many of the girls here would kill for a chance at a prince taking interest in them in the hopes they would gain their freedom, the idea isn't as novel as it sounds."

That caught his attention, and he turned his gaze to me. "What are you trying to say?"

"What I'm saying, Your Highness, is that I'm pretty sure the King and Queen of Valoria would not accept a courtesan as the Crown Princess," I said straightforwardly.

I hated thinking like this. Selene more than deserved to be a Crown Princess, but I also knew our parents, and they would never allow it. Especially our mother. Marcellus might be able to persuade our father, but our mother would be next to impossible, and she had the final say on our marriages.

As the first son, Marcellus was next in line for the throne. His marriage in particular was of great importance.

His expression darkened and I watched his hands curl into tight fists. I'd angered him.

"How dare you?" he exclaimed, catching the attention of those around us when he slammed his cup of wine down on the table. "Do you think you know my parents' wishes more than I do? The prince?"

I sat back and calmly sipped my wine, taking no offense to his words. "Am I wrong?" I questioned with a raised brow.

He took a deep breath and then his eyes darted to Selene, then back to me. He seemed to be grappling with his feelings and the realities of his elevated life.

"No, you're not," he admitted begrudgingly, his tone deflated. "She may not be able to be my first wife, but I can take her as my second."

I glared at him. "No you can't. That's not fair to her."

He sighed. "You're right ... but that doesn't mean I have to like it."

"I understand," I replied softly. "Feelings don't abide by the rules and obligations of royalty. But there are consequences to your choices, especially when it involves the future of Valoria."

Marcellus took a long drink of his wine. "I just ... I've never felt this way before. Every time I see her, it's like my entire world is drawn to her."

I watched him with sympathy, torn between my desire to see my brother happy and the need to protect Selene from possible heartbreak. "Your Highness, if you truly care for her, you need to be careful. Falling for a prince, especially the heir to the throne, can be a dangerous game. She's vulnerable in ways you can't understand."

He looked at me with pain-filled eyes. "I would never hurt her."

"It's not just about you," I said gently. "It's about your family, the court, the politics. It's about the expectations of a kingdom. If rumors spread, Selene could be in grave danger from those who would seek to use her to gain power, or from those who would want to remove her as a threat."

Frustrated, he ran a hand through his hair. "It's so maddening. Why does it have to be this complicated?"

I shrugged one shoulder. "That's the price of royalty."

We sat in silence, each lost in our thoughts, while lilting music and the sounds of the pleasure house continued around us.

He turned his attention back to the stage. Selene danced gracefully, and her beauty and charm were evident to everyone present. "I need to think about this – truly consider what I want and what I'm willing to sacrifice."

I wanted to counter his comment, but from the fixed set of his chin, I'd already given him plenty to think about. If I said any more, I might push him too far. Even though I was talking to him as his sister, he didn't know who I was and only saw me as a commoner. In this guise, I couldn't overstep my bounds.

The prince was entranced by Selene's beauty, but he didn't know her well enough to be in love with her. Eventually he would get over his infatuation and move on. At least I hoped he would.

"Have you ever seen any of the merfolk?" I asked as he continued watching Selene.

He shook his head. "No. Since they reside in the Luminar Sea by Keldara, I've never had the opportunity."

I frowned and tilted my head. "Have you ever left Valoria?"

He shook his head again. "No. This is my first time venturing out of my homeland."

"But ... I thought the King and Queen sent both you and the princess out of Valoria during Keldara's invasion?"

"Only my sister," he confirmed. "I stayed in Valoria."

My head started to spin. I'd lived my life believing we were both sent out for our safety, but if what my brother said was true, it was only me. Why? It didn't make sense. In fact, it only introduced more questions to which I didn't have the answers.

I took a deep breath and tried to process this revelation. What could have possibly prompted such a decision from our parents? Was I in more danger than Marcellus during that time? It would lend credence to what Sir Edric warned me about. Maybe he was right, after all.

"The invasion was a dark time for Valoria," Marcellus continued, seemingly lost in memories. "Father believed it would be best if at least one of his children remained within the kingdom to show our people we were with them, standing in solidarity against our enemies."

Curiosity gnawed at me and I couldn't help but ask, "But why you? Why not keep the princess and send *you* away for safety, since you're next in line for the throne?"

Marcellus sipped his wine and took a moment to consider my question. "Hmm ... I never thought about it that way," he answered honestly.

"And since then, you've never left Valoria's borders?" I pressed.

He nodded. "Since my sister disappeared, our parents became stricter. I had to literally beg to be the envoy on this trip. The only way they allowed it was if Caelan accompanied me."

My brows shot up in surprise. "What? Why?"

He turned to me with a quizzical expression. "You know, you ask a lot of questions."

My mouth snapped shut. "Apologies, Your Highness."

He waved me off. "No need to apologize. It's not like you're asking anything confidential."

To him it felt like useless information, but to me, these were clues I'd sought for the last ten years.

I leaned back in my chair and took a moment to process what I'd just learned. Every bit of information was a fragment of a puzzle I was slowly starting to piece together. There was a bigger picture at play, one that had been hidden from me for years. I turned my attention to Marcellus, whose gaze had returned to Selene as if drawn by a magnet. Although he was now a man, my brother looked so ... *innocent*. He'd been sheltered his whole life, whereas I had traveled the world. Not by choice, but we'd taken different paths, nonetheless.

I was about to excuse myself when Selene approached the table with concern etched on her face. "Are you okay? I haven't heard from you all day. I've been worried."

I waved away her concern. "I'm perfectly fine. No need to worry."

"If there's anything I can help with, just let me know," Marcellus cut in.

I bit down on a laugh. He was desperate for Selene's attention, but she simply ignored him. "Everything is fine, Your Highness, but I appreciate the thought."

Marcellus cleared his throat, his eyes fixed on Selene. "If ... um, if you're free, I'd like to see if I can have some of your time," he asked.

Selene finally looked at him and sighed. "It's fifty glint an hour. Can you afford me?"

Marcellus nodded enthusiastically. "Yes!" he exclaimed as he pulled out a pouch filled with coins.

It was a silly question for her to ask. He was a prince, after all. He could afford anything. But I could tell she was annoyed by his presence.

Selene's eyes narrowed slightly and she pursed her lips in thought. It wasn't about the money, of course; it was the principle. She was asserting her control over the situation, reminding both of us—particularly him—of her agency in this establishment.

I nudged her. "Just play some music for him and maybe a dance or two ... nothing else," I whispered.

She sighed. "I'll give you one hour," she relented, her tone cool.

Marcellus, looking like a child who'd just been granted his favorite candy, nodded eagerly. "That would be great. Thank you!"

Selene cast me a brief, searching look, as if silently asking if everything was okay. I offered a reassuring nod, silently asking her to play along for now. She gracefully extended her arm and indicated that Marcellus should lead the way. He hesitated for a split second, likely not used to such forwardness, before taking her delicate hand in his and leading her towards a private chamber.

I was conflicted by a mixture of emotions as they disappeared down the corridor. On one hand, it was almost comical to see the Prince of Valoria so enamored and out of his depth with someone so far beneath his station. On the other hand, it was a painful realization of the complexity of the world we now inhabited.

I sat back in my chair and took another drink as I watched the girls dance on stage. When I heard Selene begin to play the lute in her private chambers, I smiled. I would love for her to have an opportunity with Marcellus, but I knew there was no chance in this lifetime.

I tossed back the rest of the wine and was about to leave when Madam Rose approached my table. With her hands tapping a rhythm on her skirt, her bright red nails appeared more like crimson-tipped claws. I sighed heavily as she strutted my way and paused in front of my table.

"Well, well, look who we have here! If it isn't the infamous healer of the Central Plains. I hope you're not here to cause trouble?" she simpered.

I snorted. "As long as everyone behaves, there shouldn't be any trouble," I countered, flicking my attention to one of the dancers and trying to dismiss the madam.

Madam Rose glanced between me and the dancer with a knowing smirk. "I can always find you a male escort to accompany you for the night," she offered. "I'm quite flexible in that aspect."

I rolled my eyes. "I don't need your flexibility."

Her grin widened. "Unless ... you'd prefer one of my girls ..."

My attention snapped to her and I glared, not deigning to respond.

She threw her head back and laughed loudly, catching the attention of those around us. "I'm not surprised. You *are* quite close to Selene," she hinted.

I slammed down my empty cup of wine. "If you're going to continue talking nonsense, it's best if I leave."

"Oh, please, don't leave on my account. Enjoy the show." With another unsettling smirk, the madam snapped her fingers to snag the attention of one of the girls and walked away, laughing hysterically.

I couldn't wait for the day I'd drive a sword through her chest.

Ignoring the advances of the girl she beckoned, I kicked back my chair and stood. It was high time I left, anyway. The Rose Petal, for all its heady allure, was also a den of vipers. And with the Crimson Clan lurking in the shadows, it wasn't safe for me any longer.

With one last glance towards the direction Selene and Marcellus had disappeared, I pushed open the heavy doors and stepped outside. Cool, crisp night air greeted me. The streets were quieter now, and as I walked, the noise of the pleasure house became a distant memory.

Tonight, it was time to rest. Perhaps tomorrow, I would seek more answers.

11

I was on my way to my clinic when a little body bumped into me head on. I took ahold of his shoulders to straighten him and the boy looked up at me anxiously. In the darkness I couldn't be sure, but it looked like my new little informant. "Henry?"

He nodded. "Yes, Miss Leila. I was coming to look for you. You have to come quick!"

I frowned and held still when he tried to pull me away. "What happened?"

"The Valorian army is fighting the Crimson Clan!" he shouted. "They're overpowering them!"

"The Crimson Clan is overpowering the Valorian army?" I clarified.

He shook his head. "No, the Valorian army is winning. The man who was in your clinic this morning is hurt!"

My brows shot up. "Which one?"

"The Crimson Clan member."

My first thought was that Caelan had been hurt, and I relaxed when I learned my fear was misplaced. Not that I wished ill on Ronan, but I wouldn't be hasty to rush in and help him, either. Whatever the Crimson Clan did to get themselves in the situation they were in was their problem.

Henry tugged on my arm again and tried to get me to follow him. "Come on, Miss. Leila, we need to hurry!"

I stopped him and squatted to be at eye level. "Henry, listen to me. We shouldn't get involved in their business. Whatever the Crimson Clan did—"

Henry shook his head adamantly. "But they're *killing* them!" he cried. "You have to save him!"

"Who, Ronan?"

He nodded. "This morning when I left your clinic, he gave me a pouch of coins and told me if I needed more to come to him. He was so *nice*, Miss Leila. We can't just let him die!"

Ronan did that? Why?

Henry pulled on my arm again and threw me off balance where I was still squatting. I placed my free hand on the ground to keep steady. With a long-suffering sigh, I asked, "Where are they?"

"Up in the mountains!" he exclaimed. "On the cliff overlooking the river."

"Henry, what were you doing all the way out there? You know the mountains aren't safe."

He slumped. "I know … but I was trying to get some information for you."

At his admission, I felt guilty for putting him in that situation. He was just a child, after all.

He turned his frightened, tear-streaked face toward mine. "When I escaped, most of the Crimson Clan had been killed and Ronan was barely hanging on. *Please* …"

If I got involved, I would make enemies of both Caelan and the Valorian army. And using my blood to fight would be a dead giveaway to my identity, which I wasn't quite ready to reveal.

But ... I owed Ronan from when he saved me and Orion from the bandits the other night. I hated owing others.

I sighed and relented. "Okay, Henry, I'll help. But I want you to go to my clinic and stay there for the night while I go and see if I can help them. If I'm not back by tomorrow morning, go to Selene at the Rose Petal. You know who she is?"

He nodded. "The pretty mermaid."

"Good." I smiled and patted his shoulder. "Now go. I'll take care of it."

Without another thought, Henry spun on his heels and ran in the direction of my clinic. With another sigh, I glanced toward the post where horses were tied and debated if their owner would let me borrow one. I didn't know who to ask and I didn't have time for all that anyway, so I jogged to the nearest horse, untied the reins, and quickly climbed on. I'd find out tomorrow whose horse I stole and pay them for it.

Now, I needed to save Ronan.

∼

THE RIDE through the forest that led to the mountains was enveloped in an eerie silence only occasionally interrupted by rustling leaves and the distant cries of nocturnal creatures. The moon, half-veiled by swirling clouds, cast an enigmatic glow that painted the woods in shadowy hues of silver and gray. My heart raced, each beat resonating with the hooves of my steadfast horse that courageously galloped through the dark, uncertain paths.

As we broke through the dense forest, the imposing sight of the mountains loomed before us, standing like ancient sentinels. Their peaks pierced the star-studded skies, holding within them secrets and memories of ages long past. The air grew colder, and the biting wind carried tremulous whispers of what was to come.

With every hoofbeat we ascended higher, punctuated by narrowing paths and fierce winds. The echoes of the ongoing battle resounded through the silent corridors of the mountains, a haunting concerto of death and valor.

I arrived at the cliffs and gazed down at the tumultuous river below that seemed to roar in unison with the clashing swords and war cries. The Valorian army, like a sea of armored watchmen, had surrounded the cliff, their steel armor gleaming ominously under the moon's haunting light.

Ronan, injured yet unyielding, stood like a wounded lion, soaked with the blood of both friend and foe. The Crimson Clan, outnumbered though undeterred, fought with the unbridled ferocity of desperate men.

I didn't know how to penetrate the army to get to Ronan or how to alert Caelan and stop him, which was another concern of mine. I also didn't understand why my former friend – a prince from another country – was the one leading the Valorian army while Marcellus was lounging at the pleasure house. Something was off.

It would take too long to figure out where there was an opening or a weak spot in the Valorian army's line, which meant my only option was to forcefully push my way through and hope for the best. Leaning forward, I gripped the reins tightly and kicked the sides of my horse. Snapping the reins, I yelled, "Yah!"

The horse hurtled forward at a speed that startled the soldiers up ahead. They tried to stop me but couldn't without being trampled. I ran past Caelan and placed myself between him and Ronan, who was using his sword to hold himself up. A gash on his arm bled profusely, but it was nothing compared to the wound in his abdomen. Even in the darkness, I could see Ronan was covered in blood.

The ground was littered with dead or injured soldiers from both sides, but the Crimson Clan members were outnumbered by the Valorian army ten-to-one. Only a handful were still standing with Ronan. Silas was by his side, his sword raised and at the ready.

"What in the bloody hell are *you* doing here?" Ronan yelled. He tried to step forward but could barely move.

"That's what *I* should be asking!" I peered over my shoulder at him before turning my attention to Caelan. "Prince Marcellus is at the Rose Petal, Your Highness. Why are *you* leading the Valorian army?"

Caelan was a fearsome sight atop his horse, gripping a bow with a quiver of arrows strapped to his back. He laughed and sized me up and down. "I thought you two weren't close?" he yelled out to me.

"We're not!" I called back. "And you didn't answer my question!"

Caelan glanced back at the waiting army and then back at me. "And why should I answer you? You're nothing but the town healer. Who are you to question me?"

I paused, unsure how to answer. To him I was a nobody, and he had every right to think so. Even so, I never imagined Caelan to behave so ... high and mighty to those beneath his station.

I nodded. "I know I'm a nobody in your eyes, but you can't just march your army into the Central Plains. This is neutral territory. No nation is allowed to start a war here."

Caelan snorted. "Is that so? You would lay down the law ... for *them*?"

I shook my head. "I'm not doing it for them; this is for the innocent people of the Central Plains. You have no right—"

"I have *every* right!" he seethed. The vein on his forehead pulsed an angry rhythm. "They are holding Princess Lyanna hostage—"

"I told you they're not!" I shouted back in frustration.

Caelan scoffed. "We have proof. We sent scouts to the Grasslands. We know she's there!"

I frowned and glanced back at Ronan, who held firm, not giving anything away. I turned back to the prince. "Can you ... please just trust me? She's not—"

"Trust you?" he exclaimed. "Why would I do that? Because you saved my life twice? For all I know, this is part of your plan and you're working with *them*!" He grabbed an arrow from his back and nocked it on his bow, aiming for Ronan.

I climbed off my horse and stood in front of the clan chieftain's son to block Caelan's arrow. "I'm not working with them, Your Highness, but I'm telling you—"

"I won't let Lyanna marry him!" He aimed his arrow at me. "And I don't care who stands in my way. I *will* get her back. Whether you're dead or alive, doesn't matter to me."

The arrow whistled through the air and embedded deeply into my left thigh. I dropped to one knee as white-hot pain ripped through my leg. I looked down and saw I was bleeding profusely. He may have even struck an artery, but I wouldn't know until I looked at it. And in this darkness, I could barely see a thing.

"Stop!" Ronan called out. "Don't hurt her!"

Caelan laughed. "Looks like you care more about this healer than you do Lyanna."

Ronan dropped to the ground behind me and held my shoulders to keep me steady. "Are you insane?" he growled. "He is not the child you used to know! He will kill you without a second thought," he whispered in my ear.

"I don't care," I muttered.

Ronan shook me. "Get ahold of yourself, Leila! You can't be this careless. You're important ... Not just to them, but to many. You ..."

"I what? What's so important about me?" I craned my neck to look back at him. "If you know something I don't, now is the time to tell me, Ronan."

His forehead creased with worry, but he remained stubbornly quiet.

I turned my attention back to Caelan, who already had another arrow nocked. I stood on wobbly legs. "You will regret this," I warned. "Please ... you don't want to do this."

Caelan smirked as he aimed the arrow at me again. "I regret nothing," he snarled.

A split second later, the arrow plunged into my chest, right above my heart. My eyes widened and blood dribbled from my lips. I stumbled back and Ronan vaulted to his feet to catch me.

"Leila!"

I smiled weakly at him and coughed up more blood. "Please, Ronan ... don't fight him. He doesn't know ... he doesn't mean to—"

"Stop defending him!" Ronan growled. "You're only going to make me angrier."

Caelan laughed wickedly. "Aw, look at you two lovebirds." He shook his head. "And you claimed you're not close." He nocked another arrow and pulled it back until the string creaked, this time aiming for Ronan.

With a sudden burst of energy, I pushed Ronan out of the way when Caelan released it and took the arrow in my right shoulder.

"*No!*" Ronan screamed and dropped to the ground.

I stumbled backward. When I glanced over my shoulder, I realized I was perilously close to the cliff's edge. Just a few more steps and I would plummet to the churning river far below.

I turned my attention back to Caelan and smiled weakly, whispering, "I'm sorry." He frowned and said something I couldn't hear through my pain-filled haze, but none of that mattered because with one last faltering step, I tumbled over the edge.

"No! *Leila!*"

I heard Ronan call my name, but then all I heard was the

wind. I spread my arms wide and waited for the sweet release of death. The drop felt slow, as if time stood still. Just before I hit the water, a force fell on top of me and spun me around so I fell face first. I opened my eyes to see Ronan holding me.

"I got you." Ronan's voice, a fortress against the cold, biting amalgam of the wind and river, wrapped around me as he held me tightly, pressing my face against his chest, his body ready to take the brunt of our fall.

The jarring impact of the river rattled my teeth, but my discomfort was nothing like what it must have been for Ronan, who took the full impact. We gasped for air before sinking like stones into the frigid waters. The water's cold embrace enveloped us, a stark contrast to the scorching intensity of the battle we'd just escaped. Each water droplet clung to our chilled skin with icy fingers, pulling us deeper into the silent, ethereal world below. The chaos above was muted, replaced by the tranquil, albeit ominous, silence of the undulating depths.

Ronan was limp in my arms; the fierce warrior was vulnerable and silent, entrapped in the unconscious realm. His features, though pallid from cold and shock, emanated a quiet grace—a visage of peace amidst the storm of violence and treachery. We continued to sink, succumbing to the oppressive force of the water that sought to claim us.

Every attempt to wake him proved futile. The vibrant, unyielding force of Ronan's spirit was imprisoned within the confines of unconsciousness. Desperation and dread mingled within me, and the icy waters amplified the cold grip of terror that clutched my heart. Even in his unconscious state, his arms still banded my waist in an ironclad grip that only emphasized the fact that he was nothing but dead weight, and I was already hurt. I couldn't save us both.

Gripping his face, I hesitated before pressing my lips to his and blowing air into his lungs. His lips were soft as they pressed against mine, an island of warmth amidst the cold. Each breath was a silent plea for him to wake. My breath flowed into him, a silent testament of connection amidst the encroaching abyss. In the silent, chilling embrace of the water, I felt him begin to move. Knowing our lives depended on it, I pushed through the pain and kicked my feet toward the surface, using every bit of strength I had left.

My lungs screamed for air as we finally broke the surface. I gasped and swam towards the bank with him in my arms, focused on pulling us from the river's clutches. With great effort I managed to drag him onto the muddy bank until only his calves remained in the water.

"Ronan!" I hovered over him, wincing from the pain in my chest. My vision blurred, and I knew I would pass out as soon as the adrenaline in my body was depleted. "Ronan!" I called out again. I started doing chest compressions and was about to blow more air into his lungs when he gasped and coughed up a bucket of brackish water. "Oh, thank the gods!" I sat back on my haunches and pulled the arrow from my thigh, quickly pressing a hand over the wound.

After coughing up more water, Ronan sat up with a start and met my eyes. He gently gripped my arms and looked me over. "Are you okay?"

I shook my head. The effects of shock were taking hold and I struggled to breathe. "What ... what were you thinking?"

I didn't get the chance to hear his response before my eyes rolled back into my head and I passed out.

12

When my eyes slowly fluttered open, I realized I was in a cave. Flames flickered on the stone walls and the smell of moist dirt tickled my nose. I attempted to sit up, earning a stab of pain in my chest. I pressed a hand over the wound but found it had been treated and wrapped. So had the wound on my shoulder and thigh. I looked over to see Ronan tending a fire. I cleared my throat.

His head darted in my direction and he exclaimed, "You're awake!" With a broad smile, he walked over to where I lay and helped me sit up and lean against the cave wall. "Easy," he murmured.

Once I was situated, I looked over at him and shook my head. "Did you do this?" I pointed to my bandaged wounds.

He nodded. "Yeah, I'm not completely useless. Living in the Grasslands, you learn a thing or two about medicine since we only have witch doctors."

I'd heard about the witch doctors of the Grasslands. They were ... unconventional, to say the least. I didn't believe in that sort of sorcery, but I suppose it had its place. I cleared my throat and looked over at him. "You're insane. Why would you jump in after me?"

He shrugged and returned to stoking the fire. "I don't know," he mumbled. "I guess I don't want you to die yet."

"So ... your bright idea was to get yourself killed in the process?" I questioned with a raised brow. "Did you take my shirt off?" Every movement caused pain and I tried not to move too much, but my hand went to my chest, suddenly feeling embarrassed that he had to remove my shirt to treat the wound.

"Why, feeling shy?" He smirked as he finished tending the fire and came to sit beside me.

I snorted and rolled my eyes. "Not at all."

He laughed. "It's okay, princess. I didn't peek."

I attempted to nudge him, but grimaced and pulled my elbow back. The pain was still too fresh.

"Easy," he repeated. "He aimed for your heart, but luckily the arrow didn't get that deep."

"It pierced my lung," I informed him.

Ronan whipped his head in my direction. "What?"

I waved him off. "I have regenerative properties as a blood mage, so I should be okay in twenty-four hours or so. But if I start coughing up blood after that, I'll need to go to Lomewood and see a healer."

"We can't wait twenty-four hours." He started to stand.

I gripped his arm and pulled him back down. "I promise I'm okay, Ronan. Besides, it's not safe to travel right now. The Valorian army might be looking for us."

"So what are we supposed to do? Wait until they find us, or until you die?" he exclaimed.

I chuckled and winced from the movement. "I'm assuming Silas will lead whoever survived the battle from the Crimson Clan into the forest to find you. I mean, you *are* the clan chieftain's son."

Ronan snorted, his face grim. "*If* any of them survived. You saw how outnumbered we were."

I nodded. "Yes, but you jumped into the river after me. Caelan doesn't care about the others. *You're* his target."

"Hopefully you're right," he murmured.

I didn't want to overinflate his confidence in my hypothesis. I was learning that Caelan was way more ruthless than I remembered from our youth. I wanted to think it was because of the circumstances in which we found ourselves, but I wasn't sure if it was true, or if I was trying to convince myself of it.

"I ..." I whispered. "I know everyone changes as they get older, and I know he's not interested in me romantically – at least not the *me* I am now – but I thought he and I were at least friends," I whispered. "Now, I mean."

Ronan peered at me and sighed. "Honestly, I don't blame him." He turned his gaze to the night sky visible outside the cave's entrance. "He's in love with you. He has been ever since you were young."

My eyes widened. "How do you know?"

He scoffed. "It's obvious. He wouldn't go through all this trouble if he wasn't. He's a prince of Eldwain. He has no business in Valoria, yet he was leading their army to find you."

Well, I guess it was obvious to everyone except me.

"He wasn't always like this," I countered. "He was very gentle as a child. I don't know what changed."

"Your disappearance, for starters." Ronan peered over at me. "Do you know what's been going on in Eldwain lately?"

I frowned. "*Is* something going on?"

Ronan laughed and threw his head back. "Caelan's brothers are fighting for the Eldwain throne. Their father is ill and isn't expected to survive the year, but he hasn't named his successor."

"I didn't know," I muttered sheepishly.

"Of course not," he said. "You're hidden away in the neutral territory of the Central Plains, where information on surrounding nations doesn't filter in."

I hesitated and tried to figure out how to frame my question. "Do you know if Caelan is trying to—"

"He's not," Ronan answered before I could finish. "He has no interest in the Eldwain throne. He's spent most of his life in Valoria, trying to hide from all the spectacle and politics of it. That's why his brothers don't think he's a threat."

I frowned. "Do you think otherwise?"

Ronan nodded. "Caelan has the support of Valoria, since he's spent many years there. Your parents are his primary backers, which guarantees their countries will have strong ties. As such, his father may choose him, after all."

I'd purposefully tried to insulate myself in Lomewood and not keep up with the world around me, though I hungrily listened for any scraps about what was going on in Valoria. But even that was hard to find in the Central Plains.

"But all Caelan cares about is … *you*." Ronan looked down at me and furrowed his brows. "Why did you come tonight? You could have stayed in Lomewood where it's safe and he never would have singled you out."

I sighed and pulled at the fraying hem of my shirt. "I owed you … for the other night with the bandits."

Ronan laughed. "Well, I think you paid me back with interest. You nearly got yourself killed."

I shook my head. "He wouldn't have killed me."

"You don't know that, Leila. Don't put so much faith in Caelan. He's known for being ruthless. He doesn't know you're a blood mage, so he probably thinks he killed you."

"I'm tired …" Overwhelmed and overstimulated, my desire to continue the discussion quickly evaporated. Mainly because deep down, the reality that Ronan was right danced mockingly in front of me; a truth I wasn't prepared to accept.

"Here, lay down." He helped me adjust and lay on a bed of leaves.

I tried to curl into a fetal position to conserve warmth, a grimace painting my features as pain sent tremors rocketing through me. I turned away from him, the dampness of my clothes a cold, clinging reminder of earlier events. The chill gnawed at my bones, and despite my best efforts to wrap my arms around my midsection, the icy air was unforgiving.

I felt Ronan's presence behind me on my bed of leaves an instant before his enveloping warmth met my back. His arm encircled my waist and drew me closer.

"What are you doing …?" I started. Even though my voice held a faint tinge of resistance, his hold tightened and anchored me to the sanctuary of his warmth.

"Stay still." His whisper, gentle yet insistent, graced my ear. "Our clothes are wet, and the night is unforgiving. Body heat is all we have." Uncomfortable yet secure, I stiffened against him, the memory of our lips meeting earlier conflicting with my sense of propriety. "Relax, Leila, I'm not going to do anything … unless you want me to." His teasing voice was a darkened whisper laced with playful intent.

"That'll never happen," I muttered.

He chuckled. "I mean … we could transfer our body heat better if we were naked and out of these wet clothes … for survival and all."

"Keep dreaming," I retorted weakly, my attempt to elbow him failing in the echo of his low laughter.

His fingers traced lazy patterns on my forearm, the touch feather-light and surprisingly soothing. The sensation was hypnotic, making it hard to maintain the walls I'd built. "Your heart's racing," he murmured, his mouth close enough that I could feel the vibrations of his voice against my skin.

"You have a knack for making it do that," I admitted, my voice barely above a whisper. The nearness of him, his scent—a mix of rain, earth, and something uniquely Ronan—was intoxicating.

His fingers stilled, his breath warm against the curve of my neck. "And what if I wanted to do more than just make your heart race?" he whispered, his lips brushing against the sensitive skin just below my earlobe.

A shiver ran down my spine, not from the cold, but from the heat of his touch. "What are you suggesting?" I challenged, but the tremble in my voice betrayed the thrill his words evoked.

He gently turned me to face him, and our eyes locked in a silent dance of challenge and vulnerability. Our wet clothes were pressed against each other, the coldness serving only to heighten our awareness. "Just this." He closed the distance between us to capture my lips in a soft, exploratory kiss.

I responded, no longer willing or able to hold back. The warmth of his mouth was a stark contrast to the crisp night that surrounded us. It was a slow burn, an intimate dance of lips and tongues as we learned the other's taste and rhythm.

With a sudden jolt of realization, I gasped and pulled away, wincing from the movement. "You—"

"I didn't—no, I *did* mean to," he said after some thought. "But I know you're not ready yet. When you are, I'll be here." His lips brushed against my ear, igniting a cascade of shivers.

Silence fell. Within the sanctuary of his embrace, warmth seeped into my bones and beckoned slumber, eliciting reluctant comfort. Amidst the aria of the night, sleep claimed me, pulling me deep into its silent, peaceful abyss.

∽

THE GOLDEN HUES of morning light weaved through the intricate patterns of leaves and branches at the cave's mouth, painting ethereal patterns on the cave walls as I awoke. The rhythmic cadence of Ronan's breathing was the melody to the dawn's awakening chorus. I was ensnared in the warm fortress of his arms, my cheek resting against the solid plane of his bare chest. Panic and confusion swarmed, and with a jolt, I pushed away.

Ronan's groan, deep and gravelly, echoed the grumbles of awakening nature. His crimson eyes, a vibrant contrast against the softer hues of dawn, blinked open, squinting as spears of sunlight sought entry.

"What ... are you okay?" he grumbled. His voice was a fusion of concern and lingering drowsiness. "What's going on?"

My gaze, wide and alert, was fixated on his bare chest. "When did you take off your clothes?" I questioned, my voice still rough with sleep.

His eyes followed my gaze and hearty laughter erupted, rich and full. "Apologies, princess. But in the dead of the night, your affinity for warmth turned me into a furnace."

I scoffed and tried to ignore the heat that rushed to my cheeks as I hastily rose to my feet.

He followed as he collected his leathers and put them on. "And where do you think you're going this early in the morning?"

I gestured ahead, where the forest deepened into a tapestry of green and gold. "I know a place we can stay. It's safe."

He looked dubious. "Is it far?"

"About sixteen kilometers from here," I admitted.

A shadow of concern danced in his eyes. "You're wounded, Leila. Can you endure the journey?"

With a sense of bravado I was unconvinced I could maintain, I walked to the cave opening and managed to only wince slightly from the pain. "I'm okay. If we stay here much longer, we'll be in danger."

With grim determination to evade those who pursued us, we extinguished the fire and began our trek through the woods. With each step I took, the pain of my injuries became a distant echo beneath the lullaby of awakening life around us. Each footfall into the lush expanse was both an escape and a journey deeper into the shadows.

Despite the lingering pain, an invigorating energy flowed through my veins, a gift from the verdant sanctuary that surrounded us. Ronan walked beside me, a silent guardian whose presence was both a reminder of the night's haunting intimacy and a fortress against the echoing threats that lurked beyond the forest's embrace. I was acutely aware of his gaze, the way it flitted towards me with every wince, his silent promise of strength and protection echoing louder than words.

We walked in silence, yet in the quietude, echoes of unspoken words and unuttered feelings resonated, painting emotions as vivid as the blossoming flora that adorned our path.

Several hours of traversing the rhythmic heartbeats of the forest led us to a small clearing, where my cabin sat ensconced in nature's embrace. Framed by sturdy oak trees and overshadowed by the majestic mountains beyond, the cabin was a quaint structure—a testament to the simplicity of the woods.

"Is this it?" Ronan glanced around warily. "How do you know about this place?"

"It's mine." I walked to the unlocked door and pushed it open. "I stay here whenever I come up to the mountains to pick herbs and plants."

The cabin door creaked to reveal its cozy interior. While not expansive, the space was thoughtfully utilized. Sunlight streamed through one window to illuminate the rustic wooden furniture and the single bed adorned with quilts, hinting at many nights spent beneath the stars. A pile of blankets, waiting to be fashioned into a makeshift bed, rested in one corner.

"And you're sure no one will be able to find us?"

"You mean can the Valorian army find us?" I corrected, then shook my head. "I know these mountains inside and out.

Unless you're from the Central Plains, you won't know how to get here."

Ronan dug through his pockets and pulled out a dripping wet flare. "Well, there's no way for me to inform Silas of our location."

I chuckled as I went over to a bureau and pulled out a dry flare. "Here. I always have them here to notify Selene."

He snatched it from my hand with a smile. "Perfect! Hopefully my clan will be able to find us."

"If not, they can always go to Selene. She knows how to get here," I said.

Ronan nodded, then slowly looked around the space. "Do you have anything to eat here?"

"No. We'll have to go hunting for some food, but I—"

"Don't worry about it," Ronan cut me off. "You managed to make the long journey here while being injured, so for now I need you to rest. I'll find us something to eat." He gripped my uninjured shoulder and gently nudged me toward the small bed in the corner of the room. "Rest. You must be exhausted. I'll be back soon." Without looking back, Ronan left the cabin with the flare in hand.

∽

An hour later, Ronan returned with two dead squirrels. After raising them in the air victoriously, earning a small smile from me, he stepped back outside to start a cooking fire. Once the squirrels were roasted and crispy, he brought them back inside just as my stomach growled.

I took my first bite and swallowed. Squirrel had never tasted so good. "Did you send out the flare?"

Ronan nodded and started to eat. "Silas will come looking for us soon."

"I told Henry to go tell Selene if I didn't return by this morning, so she'll be here soon as well."

"Good." Ronan took another bite and chewed thoughtfully. "Leila, have you thought about the aftermath?"

I raised a brow. "The aftermath? What do you mean?"

"Well, Caelan probably thinks you're dead, which means you won't be able to return to Lomewood easily."

I scoffed. "I'm not hiding, Ronan. I have a life in Lomewood ... a *good* life. He's not going to take that away from me."

Ronan watched me carefully before placing a bone down on the scarred dining table that I also used for sorting and grinding herbs. "I'm sure you know this already, but just to clarify, you *must* know that Caelan was only able to bring the Valorian army through neutral territory with the governor's permission ... which means the governor is in his pocket. Living in Lomewood after this won't be easy."

I couldn't argue with his logic. Unfortunately, he was right. There was no other way for Caelan to have done what he did unless the governor was a willing participant. And no matter how popular I was as a healer within the Central Plains, the governor would choose royalty with deep pockets over me.

Ronan cleared his throat. "Come with me to the Grasslands," he proposed. "I can keep you safe there."

My attention snapped to his face. "What?"

"Once Silas arrives, we can make plans for our return to the Grasslands. We might have to cut through Eldwain and Ellyndor, but we'll get there before—"

"No!" I cut him off and shot to my feet. "Was this your plan all along?"

Ronan stood and shook his head. "No, Leila, it wasn't. But the Central Plains are dangerous now. You can't *possibly* stay here! I can provide safety, and I promise not to tell anyone who you are. You can go with us as a healer and—"

I waved off his words. "I would just be placing myself into

my enemies' hands. If staying in the Central Plains is dangerous, then going to the Grasslands is even worse." I sighed and shook my head, wincing from the movement. "I won't let Caelan run me out of my home."

Ronan stared at me for a moment before he nodded and sat back down. Running a hand through his long dark hair still tangled from our hasty swim in the river, he finished eating his dinner. It seemed he didn't have the energy to argue with me.

∼

THAT NIGHT, Ronan slept on a pallet of blankets beside my bed. The tension between us was as tangible as the chilly air that seeped through the cabin's wooden frames. We didn't know how to behave around each other after the close quarters we'd employed the night before.

I handed him a pillow and pointed to the sleeping pallet I made. "Uh ... you can sleep here. I hope that's okay."

"Yeah, it's no problem." He laid down and made himself comfortable, then sent a mischievous smirk my way. "Unless you need a little warmth tonight as well?"

I rolled my eyes. "In your dreams."

Ronan's laughter filled the space, a jarring contrast to the tension that had silently built between us. "I don't have to dream. Last night, you quite literally got me out of my clothes, you were so cold! I thought you were going to squeeze me to death!" he joked.

Heat crawled up my neck and the crimson hues of embarrassment painted my features. Fortunately, he couldn't see me from where I lay on my bed. The flickering flame of a single candle cast an intimate glow from the bedside table, but it wasn't enough to dispel the lingering shadows of the small cabin. Our proximity, though not as close as last night, bred an awkwardness that made the confined space we shared feel even smaller.

I pulled my quilts up to my chin and peered down at him, surprised to catch him watching me with a serious expression.

"Leila," he said, his voice filled with tension, "you know I would never do anything you didn't want me to ... right?"

I frowned. "Yes," I answered confidently.

He nodded. "So rest easy. Nothing will happen tonight."

With those final words, he shot me a small smile before turning onto his side, presenting his back to me and silently telling me goodnight. I leaned over to the bedside table and blew out the candle.

∾

THE NEXT MORNING, Ronan rose early and went fishing. He returned with our breakfast—two fishes from the river—and roasted them over the fire outside the cabin. We had just sat down at the table to eat when we heard a knock on the door. We froze and locked eyes as we held our breaths.

"Ronan?" a male voice called out. "Ronan, it's me, Silas."

We both exhaled a sigh of relief and Ronan walked across the cabin to open the door. I followed on his heels and peered around him to see Silas standing there with a handful of Crimson Clan members. Unfortunately, their numbers had dwindled substantially after the skirmish with the Valorian army.

"Thank the gods!" Ronan motioned for his friend to enter. The rest of the clan members stayed outside to guard the perimeter.

Silas grabbed Ronan in a fierce hug and patted him on the back with relief. "I thought you were dead," he admitted.

Ronan smirked. "As if I'd die that easily."

Silas glanced over at me and nodded stiffly before returning his attention to his leader. "Unfortunately, I don't have the best of news."

I ushered them to the table. Once we sat, Silas sucked in a deep breath before speaking. "Prince Caelan has all but declared victory. He is announcing your death all over Asteria. It won't be long before the chief hears the news."

Ronan pressed his lips into a firm line. "I see someone is counting their eggs before they hatch."

"Did you see Selene on your way here?" I interrupted. When Silas only shook his head, I frowned. It was odd that the Crimson Clan arrived before Selene. Where the hell was she?

"This can't stand," Ronan started. "Head back to the Grasslands. You must inform my father that I'm still alive. If he learns of my death, he'll declare war."

Silas furrowed his brows. "Shouldn't we declare war anyway? They attacked on neutral territory—"

Ronan shook his head. "No. We can't afford a full-scale attack unless we team up with Keldara ..." Ronan peered over at me before looking back at Silas. "Which we can't do."

I wanted to ask why, but from Ronan's cagey expression, he didn't want to divulge any information. Deciding to ask him about it later, I kept quiet.

"However, I want to attack Caelan before he leaves the Central Plains," Ronan continued. "Once you inform my father of my survival, come back with reinforcements."

His friend's eyes widened.

Ronan smirked. "If they can break the rules, so can we."

Silas smiled back and nodded. "Will do. Would you like me to leave the others here with you?"

The chieftain's son shook his head, sounding every inch the leader in his own right. "No. Take them back with you to the Grasslands. It's not safe here anymore."

"We'll head back now."

They stood and gripped each other's forearms in a firm shake. "Be safe, brother," Ronan said, to which Silas repeated.

With a whistle, Silas and the remaining Crimson Clan members jogged through the forest, heading back to their Grasslands home.

13

Days turned into nights and back again, but there was still no sign of Selene. Each silent dawn intensified the worry gnawing at my insides. I sent out flares, hoped and waited, but silence was all that greeted me.

Ronan, seemingly attuned to my growing restlessness, walked into the cabin one afternoon carrying a dead rabbit for our supper. "Are you okay? How are your wounds?"

Though touched by his concern, I was consumed by the echoing silence from Selene. I slumped in the chair where I sat at the dining table and sighed. "They're mostly healed," I replied distractedly, the weight of Selene's absence heavy in my voice. "But I'm more worried about Selene. It's not like her to not show up when I send a flare."

Ronan took the rabbit outside and came to sit across the table from me, his gaze steady. "When Silas returns, do you want me to check on her?"

I shook my head. "When Silas returns, I assume you'll be attacking the Valorian army if they're still in the Central Plains, correct?"

He nodded.

"Then I'll head back to Lomewood."

He leaned forward. "Are you sure?"

"Yeah. I need to check on Selene myself." Rapping my knuckles on the table, I stood and grabbed a basket I'd filled with clean clothes and other toiletries.

"Where are you going?" Ronan stood and followed me to the door.

"I was just waiting on you to return so I could take a bath in the river," I answered. "I didn't want to leave without letting you know."

Ronan looked surprised. "You can't go out there alone, Leila. The Valorian army could be scouring the riverbanks as we speak!" He grabbed my arm to stop me.

"I have to bathe, Ronan. I haven't in days." I sniffed under my arm and scrunched up my nose. "I'm starting to smell ... and so are you."

He sighed. "Fine, but I'm coming with you." Grabbing the sword Silas left for him, he strapped it onto his waist and followed me out of the cabin.

Ronan's insistence on accompanying me was both a comfort and a reminder of the lingering danger. The woods, once a familiar sanctuary, now held shadows of uncertainty as we left the safety of my cabin.

Our steps crunched against the foliage underfoot, an anthem of sounds that pierced the heavy silence. The atmosphere was dense with unsaid words that echoed the worries and fears we carried. Every rustling leaf and distant animal sound accentuated the rawness of our solitude in these vast woods.

The forest was rich with the lush greenery of early spring, and each tree and shrub seemed to bask in the renewed fullness of life. But there was an eerie quietude that prevailed, a stillness that suggested the woods too, were holding their breath, waiting for events not yet known to unfold.

We journeyed to the river in tacit agreement marked by the silent companionship that had become a comfort in recent days. Ronan walked with a vigilant eye, his senses attuned to the environment, while I was lost in the tumultuous sea of my thoughts. Selene's silence echoed louder than the sounds of the forest.

The path to the river was a familiar one, yet each step felt heavy with the weight of the unknown. The towering trees, usually a source of solace, now cast long, ominous shadows that seemed to stretch out with grasping fingers.

The river's murmur grew pronounced as we ventured deeper into the woods. The rhythmic flow was a soothing balm to the clamorous thoughts that consumed my mind. When the woods finally opened to reveal the river, its water glistened under the tender touch of the sun, an oasis of calm amidst the unfolding chaos. The trees stood sentinel along the banks, their branches swaying gently in the breeze and casting dappled shadows that danced in harmony with the gentle lapping of the waters.

I placed the basket at the river's edge as Ronan stood nearby, his gaze lingering a beat too long before I motioned for him to turn around.

"What?" he asked, confused.

I scowled. "I need to undress. Turn around. You can't just stand there gawking at me."

He snorted but turned around, nonetheless. "Nothing I've never seen before," he grumbled as he turned his back to me.

I rolled my eyes and undressed. Once I was fully naked, I gingerly walked into the chilly water, watching for unsteady rocks that could send me careening onto my behind with one wrong move. Gritting my teeth against the frigid water, I plunged beneath the surface before I could change my mind. The river enveloped me in an intimate embrace. The sun's tender rays danced on the water's surface, casting reflections that shimmered like fleeting moments of reprieve. I stood back up and pushed my hair out of my face.

"So ..." I started, feeling odd with the silence stretching between us. "What do you plan to do when Silas gets back?"

Ronan shrugged, his back still turned to me. "Since it's okay for Caelan to attack on neutral territory, I don't see why we can't as well."

"Can you ... Will you do me a favor?" I asked hesitantly, then turned my attention to washing my body with the bar of soap so he didn't see how much I invested in his answer.

"What is it?"

"Can you ... not hurt Caelan?" I asked softly.

For a brief moment, the world paused. Silence, then a storm. Ronan whirled around with an enraged countenance, a startling contrast to the peaceful flow of the river. His crimson eyes grew darker as his jaw ticked with annoyance.

"Turn around!" I shouted as I covered my breasts, even though they were fully submerged.

"How can you ... *Why* do you still want to protect him after everything he did to you?" he exclaimed, barely able to control his mounting anger.

"Ronan, turn around!" I chastised again.

Instead, he stormed to the edge of the river and squatted to be at eye level. "How can you be so forgiving of Caelan, who has been nothing but cruel to you even after you saved his life?" He took a deep breath and released it. "You weren't even attacking him on the cliffs. You showed up to negotiate peace and he still shot you with his arrows ... and one was aimed to kill."

I felt the dull ache in my lung at the reminder of Caelan's attack. Realizing Ronan had no intention of granting the privacy I requested, I decided to answer him. "Because Caelan is like family to me. I can't hurt him," I whispered. "He doesn't know who I am, and—"

He narrowed his eyes. "That's no excuse, Leila, and you know it. Unless you tell him who you are, you will always be in danger from him."

I bit my lip nervously. "Do you want me to tell him ... who I am?"

Ronan stared at me for a moment before shaking his head. "You telling him who you are is not part of my plan ... at least not yet."

"And what exactly is your plan?" I demanded. He remained quiet, never taking his eyes from mine. I looked away, disappointed. "We need to learn to trust each other, Ronan."

"Do you trust me?" he asked.

I returned my gaze to him. His brow was raised, and the look on his face was open and curious. The truth of the matter was, I *couldn't* trust Ronan. He was still the enemy, no matter how much time we'd spent together. I glanced away without answering.

He snorted and stood. "I thought so."

Feeling my face turn hot from frustration and embarrassment, I yelled, "Turn around so I can get out and get dressed!"

Ronan smirked. "Of course, Your Highness. I wouldn't want to tarnish your reputation. Although ..." He paused, his grin widening. "Spending days with me in a cabin ... alone ... will make tongues wag. So what reputation do you really have to protect?"

"No one needs to know about our time here," I growled. "I would hate for others to learn I had to share space with a savage like you!"

His grin turned murderous. Instead of being offended and walking away, which is what I hoped to achieve, he stormed into the river fully clothed. Surprised into stillness, I watched as he waded toward me until we were a foot away.

"Are you insane?" I covered my breasts with folded arms and took a step backward.

"Obviously," he spat. "I'm obviously insane if I continue risking my life for someone who only sees me as a villain and doesn't appreciate a single thing I've done for her!"

I returned his heated glare. "How can I appreciate what you've done when I don't even know your motives?"

In the blink of an eye, he closed the space between us and grabbed my face, squeezing it tightly. I raised out of the water, exposing my breasts.

"Do you know Caelan's motives?" he growled, his crimson eyes staring me down.

I frowned and tried to rip my face out of his grasp, but he held on tightly. Bringing me up to his face, my breasts flattened against his rough, wet clothes.

"Of course I know his motives! His goal is to rescue me," I insisted stubbornly.

Ronan laughed and shoved me away from him. I nearly lost my balance and fell, but managed to find my footing at the last minute.

"Don't be so naïve, Leila."

He turned to leave the river, clearly exasperated with me. Without thinking, I latched onto his arm to stop him. "If you know so much, then why don't you tell me what Caelan's motives are?"

He ripped his arm from my grasp and I stumbled back. He leaned down to eye level and growled, "No. Since you trust him so much, you can continue doing so until he shows you his true colors."

Disgust rippled through me by his callous tone. Even so, I couldn't help but be distracted by the wet clothes that clung to his body and highlighted the firm contours of his muscles, though the heat of anger and irritation was clear in the way they tensed. I followed a water droplet as it traced the hard lines of his face, sliding down his neck and soaking into his chest. His crimson eyes drilled into mine with an intensity that momentarily made me forget the chill of the river and the vulnerability of my nakedness.

The closeness of our bodies and the dripping wetness only heightened the tension, shifting the atmosphere from anger to electric lust. Our frustrations and conflicting loyalties blended into an intoxicating cocktail neither of us could resist.

"I wish," I whispered, my voice thick with emotions I didn't understand, let alone know how to express, "that things were simpler." Bringing my hands up to his chest, I pushed him back slightly only to feel the strength of him beneath my fingertips.

He captured one wrist and brought it to his lips, where he placed a tender kiss. "And I wish," he murmured against my skin, "I could show you all that I am. All that I want to be for you." His lips trailed up my arm, his breath warm and inviting against my goosebumped skin.

Torn between pulling away and drawing him closer, my body betrayed my intentions and I leaned into him, our wet forms melding together in the cool embrace of the river. Sliding his hands to my waist, he tugged me against him, every inch of him hard and dominant, yet yielding to my every move.

"You infuriate me," he whispered, his voice husky with desire. He captured my lips in a searing kiss that left me breathless.

I finally pulled back and rested my forehead against his. "The feeling," I panted, my voice trembling, "is entirely mutual."

And just like that, amidst the tension and unspoken words, there was a fleeting moment where the world seemed to disappear and all that mattered was the electric connection thrumming between us.

The gurgling river became a muted whisper as the world condensed into this singular moment. Ronan's fingers traced patterns on the small of my back, each touch a promise and a plea. Our noses brushed, breaths mingling, as the distance between our lips became an unbearable chasm.

"You have no idea how much I want you to understand me, Leila," he murmured, his voice a soft growl filled with yearning.

"And you have no idea how much I fear that understanding," I whispered back, my fingers curling into his wet shirt, emboldened by the feel of his heartbeat racing against mine.

With a low groan, he claimed my mouth again and deepened the kiss as our bodies swayed with the river's gentle ebb. The water became a cloak around us, a world where past betrayals and looming threats ceased to exist. It was a stolen moment, a treasured respite from the storm of our lives.

Pulling back, Ronan brushed a thumb over my swollen lips. "But I can never forgive what Caelan did to you," he whispered. "Don't ever ask that of me." He studied my face, searching for acceptance I wasn't ready to give.

"If you hurt him ... I'll never forgive you," I said carefully.

His face fell. "You would really go that far for him?"

"I would."

Ronan clenched his jaw, a vein ticking at the side of his head, then stormed out of the river in drenched clothes, disappearing down the winding trail that led back to the cabin.

∽

I QUICKLY TRUDGED out of the river and got dressed in the clean clothes I brought in my basket. Grabbing the woven handle, I hurried back down the trail, intent on smoothing things over with him. I'd never seen him so angry. While I still didn't agree with him, we were forced to share the cabin until Silas returned, which meant we had to find common ground.

Wet hair clinging to my face, I ran through the forest heedless to danger with my heart and mind in turmoil. Was I blind to Caelan's true nature? Ronan's reaction suggested a deeper, darker narrative I had yet to comprehend. The tranquility of the forest was lost to me now; every rustling leaf, every whisper of the wind echoed my inner tumult.

Engulfed in my thoughts, I barely registered the change in scenery until I was in a clearing. Before I had a chance to realize the danger in which I'd found myself, they were there. Three Valorian soldiers, unmistakable in their armor, with crescent moons marking their foreheads. I stopped dead in my tracks and the basket in my hand almost slipped.

"Halt!" One of the guards held up a hand to stop me. Snatching two papers from the hand of one of his companions, he stared at it a moment before glancing back up at me. He did it several times before announcing, "It's her!"

In moments, they swarmed me on all sides. I was trapped.

"What's going on?" I looked between the three soldiers, unsure how to proceed.

The leader held the papers up so I could see them. One was a hastily drawn portrait of me, and the other was of Ronan. They were wanted posters. My eyes widened in surprise and shock. Caelan was going this far?

The posters said we were wanted by the crown dead or alive, but if dead, he wanted proof of our demise. This wasn't good.

"Listen, I don't want any trouble." I held up my hands. "I have no qualms with Valoria ..."

The leader scoffed. "You've sided with the Crimson Clan. You're nothing but a Crimson whore!" he spat.

I flinched, feeling more hurt than offended. These were my people, and now they viewed me as the enemy. There was no way to get out of this without fighting. I just had to do my best not to hurt them.

The leader unsheathed his sword. When the other two held out their arms and readied their stance, I realized they were mages. As one, they launched their attack. I brought up a magical shield to protect me and they bounced off with shock painted on their faces, surprised to learn I was a mage. A mage from the Central Plains was a rarity, an anomaly. In that fleeting moment, a bitter realization settled in me—there was no middle ground here, no room for peace.

I focused all my energy on maintaining the shield. My arms trembled under the relentless assault of the two mages. Each spell that collided with my protective barrier sent a shockwave of energy that reverberated through my bones. Every hit, every burst of magic, was a reminder of the daunting reality that I was outnumbered and the soldiers were relentlessly focused on killing me.

My muscles ached, strained by the sustained effort of maintaining the barrier. Each impact was a brutal dance of force and resistance. The mages' spells crashed against my shield with daunting ferocity. Each explosion lit the tranquil forest clearing, casting ominous shadows that danced menacingly amongst the trees.

I dropped to a knee and gasped for air, feeling my stamina wane. I couldn't hold the defensive shield much longer. My arms trembled and slowly drooped, and my eyes started to close. Before my shield winked out, the wind gusted and a figure swept through in a blur of motion and steel. In seconds, the three soldiers had sliced throats and lay on the ground, twitching.

My eyes widened. With a sudden burst of adrenaline, I raised my arms again and was about to attack when the stranger slowly turned around, covered in the soldier's blood.

Ronan.

"Why did you kill them?" I shouted.

He wiped his bloody sword on one of the soldiers' sleeves and glanced at me, unaffected by my outburst. "And what was I supposed to do? Try and negotiate peace?" he deadpanned.

That was obviously a jab at me for what I attempted to do

between him and Caelan. I knew I was asking for the impossible, but I didn't want the death of my people on my hands.

"They were innocent," I said coldly.

He snorted. "Innocent? There are no innocent soldiers in war."

I opened my mouth to retort, but nothing came out. I couldn't argue with his logic, which frustrated me to no end.

"Come on. Let's go before more come looking." Ronan sheathed his sword, grabbed my wrist, and hauled me out of the clearing.

"Wait!" I attempted to stop him, but he was undeterred. "We can't just leave them there!"

"Don't worry about them. You need to start worrying about yourself," he gritted out, his stride never wavering.

"We need to at least bury them!"

Ronan stopped and gave a heavy sigh before turning around to face me. "I'll come back later and bury them, Leila. But first we need to get you out of here before more Valorian soldiers show up!"

Knowing it was useless to argue, I took one last look at the dead Valorian soldiers and let Ronan drag me back to the cabin.

14

During the few days that had passed since the incident with the soldiers, Ronan and I had barely spoken beyond what was necessary to coexist. I'd be lying if I claimed I wasn't slightly uncomfortable. Not with him, per se, but with the situation in which we'd found ourselves. Every day spent with him enmeshed me further with the Crimson Clan chieftain's son. No matter how mad he was at me, Ronan was still protecting me. And that was something I couldn't deny, even if I didn't understand his motives.

We were finishing up breakfast when there was a knock at the door. We waited with bated breath until we heard, "It's me, Silas."

Ronan quickly went to open the door, but I stayed seated. I no longer felt comfortable knowing about Clan business. Even so, it was hard to feign ignorance since they weren't whispering and the cabin was so small.

"How was your journey here?" Ronan asked as he patted Silas on the shoulder.

"Not easy," Silas admitted. His crimson eyes flashed

between me and Ronan. "Eldwain closed their borders to all outsiders. Our reinforcements are waiting on the east side of the Central Plains while a small group of us cut through Lomewood to get here."

"Good work, Silas." Ronan smiled for the first time in days. "Where is the Valorian army now?"

"Gathered around the borders of Lomewood, close to the mountains," Silas answered. "There are wanted posters all around town looking for you and ... *her*." He motioned to me stiffly.

Ronan peered over his shoulder at me and then quickly looked away. "We're ... aware."

"What is our next move?" Silas asked.

"Let's meet up with our reinforcements, and then we'll talk about the plan."

An awkward silence followed and Silas looked over at me, which let me know they intended to keep their plans a secret from me. I rolled my eyes and stood, deciding it was time to start collecting my things to leave.

"Where are you going?" Ronan asked as I started to shuffle around the room.

"Packing up." I carefully packed the herbs I'd collected while we were marooned here and avoided his gaze.

"You should probably stay here for now," he said as he followed me around the room, leaving Silas standing by the door. "It's safer."

I shrugged. "Eventually someone will stumble upon this cabin. I'm not going to hide here forever, and I need to find out what's going on with Selene." Her stony silence worried me. Something was wrong.

"I can find out what happened to Selene and bring her to you," Ronan offered.

I paused my packing and looked over at him. "Why?"

"Why what?"

"Why are you putting so much effort into protecting me?" I raised a brow.

Ronan looked over at Silas cautiously and then back at me.

I raised my chin defiantly. "Say it."

"Leila," he said sternly.

"Is it because I'm—" I started to say, before Ronan hurriedly covered my mouth.

Our faces were inches away as he gripped the back of my head. He glared at me. "Are you insane?" he whispered. "Unless you have a death wish, I suggest you keep quiet!"

His crimson eyes darkened as he stared me down and kept his hand over my mouth. I unconsciously licked my lips, which made him furrow his brows. He slowly released me. I didn't realize how fast my heart was beating, but when his touch left me, I felt its absence and craved his touch again.

The thought made me frown. I shouldn't crave a single thing from him.

"I'm protecting you because you're *mine*, do you understand?" he said loud enough for Silas to hear.

"I'm not property," I growled. "I belong to no one!"

He smirked. "Think again, princess," he whispered before turning around to face Silas. He peered over his shoulder at me and said, "If you're returning to Lomewood, fine, I won't stop you. But don't get yourself captured or get hurt. Do you understand?"

I cleared my throat and looked away.

"Do you understand?" he repeated a bit louder.

"Yes!" I exclaimed, clearly exasperated.

With that, he and Silas left me alone in the cabin. After all the days we'd spent clustered in the small confines, the emptiness felt like a void. I'd gotten used to Ronan being there, and I didn't like that at all. Not one bit.

I waited until nightfall before making the trek back to Lomewood, hoping the darkness would shield me from anyone searching for me in the mountains. When I entered the capital of the Central Plains, I didn't bother going to my clinic. As foolish as it was, I went straight to the Rose Petal.

The light illuminating the pleasure house was a welcoming sight after so many nights spent by candlelight. It was packed with patrons, and lilting music filtered out into the street every time the door opened.

I opened one of the heavy doors and was stopped immediately by the male employee who handled the security of the place. I frowned. "Thomas, what's going on?"

His face was stony. "Sorry, Leila, but you're no longer allowed on the premises. You need to leave."

I frowned. "What? Why? Where's Selene?"

"She's safe," he replied cryptically.

"That's not an answer, Thomas. Where is she?" I demanded, taking a step closer and encroaching on his personal space.

"Please, Leila," he groaned. "I don't want to hurt you."

"And I don't want to hurt *you*. So answer me."

He was about to speak when Madam Rose sauntered up to the entrance, looking entirely too pleased with herself. Her lips were painted bright red and her hair was pulled back in its customary chignon. Her knowing smirk annoyed me to no end.

"Well, look who has finally decided to grace us with her presence!" Madam Rose announced.

"Where is Selene?" I demanded.

"She's safe. That's all you need to know," she smirked. "Although, I think you should be worrying about your own safety instead of the mermaid's. Due to our ... *friendship*, I won't report you, but that won't stop my patrons from reporting you and collecting the bounty in your name."

I glanced at some of those who were loitering near the door, eavesdropping on our conversation. "Did you ... did you sell Selene?" I asked hesitantly, wondering if Marcellus really bought her.

Madam Rose threw her head back and laughed. "You think I would really let go of such a rarity?"

I shook my head, frustrated. "Then what is going on?"

She sighed. "Prince Marcellus is ... concerned with your relationship with Selene and has paid for her protection. She is not to leave the Rose Petal until he says so."

My eyes widened at the news. I tried to look over their shoulders to see her, but Selene was nowhere in sight.

"I suggest you leave, Leila ... before I decide to turn you in, after all," Madam Rose threatened.

I glared, wanting nothing more than to unleash my blood magic to attack this establishment and finally free Selene, but I couldn't. It wasn't the right time. No one could know who I was.

"I'm leaving," I said, defeated. "Just ... tell her I came by. Please."

Madam Rose nodded and waved for her security guard to escort me out. Shrugging off Thomas' apologetic fingers, I stomped back down the steps and onto the street. If anything, I was even more worried about Selene than before.

As I walked the streets of Lomewood, I noticed the town folk behaved differently than they used to. They would glance up, notice who I was, and quickly look away. I found it odd, but brushed it off and hurried back to my clinic. It was probably stupid to return to the places I was known to frequent, but my clinic was the only place I had. It was my home.

I unlatched the wooden gate and crossed the lawn to my door. I opened it to find Henry lying down on the cot I used for my patients, illuminated by the scant light provided by the gas lamp outside.

"Henry?" I called out in the darkness. I quickly lit a candle and peered around the space.

Henry scrambled off the cot and to his feet, clearly startled. Then he ran to me and hugged my mid-section. "Oh, thank the gods you're back!" he exclaimed.

I brushed his hair and patted his back. "What are you still doing here?"

He pulled back and smiled sheepishly. "I've been staying here, waiting for you. I hope that was okay."

I smiled down at him. "Of course, Henry."

His smile brightened. "How is Ronan?"

"He's ... good," I replied. "You don't need to worry about him. Now, tell me: what's going on at the Rose Petal? Did you take my message to Selene?"

He nodded. "I did, and she was about to leave the pleasure house when a group of soldiers stopped her. Then Prince Marcellus appeared and made a deal with Madam Rose. The soldiers dragged Selene back to her room, and I haven't seen her since."

"I see ..." I went to sit down.

His version matched Madam Rose's, so at least I knew the infernal woman wasn't lying. Marcellus's motives were simple to decipher. He was infatuated with Selene, but it didn't excuse his actions. He couldn't keep her prisoner. I decided to pay my dear brother a little visit tomorrow.

"I won't be opening the clinic for a few days," I said. "You can stay here if you want."

Henry nodded quickly. "Thank you, Miss Leila!" His face was excited, but then he turned serious. "You might have noticed the wanted posters with your face on them, but you don't have to worry. The town folk have been ignoring the soldiers' inquiries about you and refusing to talk to them. No one has sold you out."

I chuckled. "Well I'm glad to hear it, but there's really

nothing to report." It was nice to know my neighbors supported me, even if the army of my homeland didn't. It comforted me to know I could roam Lomewood's streets with a small degree of safety without glancing over my shoulder. "Get some sleep, Henry. Tomorrow is going to be a busy day."

∼

I WOKE the next morning before the rooster crowed, though I tossed and turned all night. I'd grown used to having Ronan beside me on the floor, but now I was alone and his comforting presence was clearly missed. I shook away those thoughts and got dressed, fully intending to visit the governor's house to speak with Marcellus. When I shared my plan with Henry, he stopped me.

His eyes were wide and frightened. "You can't go there, Miss Leila! They'll arrest you!"

"They can do whatever they want, but I need to see Prince Marcellus." I bypassed him and strode to the door.

"Then why has everyone been protecting you if you're just going to turn yourself in?" Henry countered shrewdly.

"While it's very much appreciated, Henry, I never asked anyone to protect me. I have nothing to hide," I lied. "Besides, I refuse to sit idly by while Selene is kept prisoner." With a firm nod, I left the relative safety of my clinic and walked purposefully down the street toward the governor's house.

Many of the shop owners and neighbors I'd worked with and lived alongside waved hello and shouted words of encouragement as I walked by. I appreciated them more than they would ever know.

When I arrived at the governor's residence, Marcellus was walking out the front door with the governor following closely behind. The governor and I made eye contact and his eyes widened in disbelief. He pointed at me with terror in his gaze and yelled, "There she is! Leila! She's there! Someone catch her!"

Before the soldiers could descend, I strode to Marcellus and grabbed his arm. "What are you doing?" I exclaimed. "You can't keep Selene prisoner at the Rose Petal!"

He scoffed and flung my hand from his arm. "You're already in hot water, Leila. Don't push it," he warned, adjusting his clothes as if I'd soiled them with my touch. "I'm doing this for Selene's protection. Something *you* clearly wouldn't do."

I furrowed my brows. "She doesn't need your kind of protection. Controlling her movements won't make her love you."

His gaze whipped in my direction and he shot daggers my way with his glare. "Watch it, Leila. You are speaking to a prince."

I snorted. "And what kind of prince lets someone from another nation control his army?"

His expression turned furious. If he could strangle me at this moment he would, although he was probably afraid touching me would get his hands dirty. "Guards!" he yelled. "Arrest this woman!" He waved me away as if I was nothing but a pesky gnat.

Guards swarmed in from all sides, but I was ready. Calling on my magic, I blasted them away. My brother's eyes widened in shock, but it only lasted a moment. He slowly approached me and conjured his own magic—his blood magic.

I narrowed my eyes on his hand and stood still. I wouldn't attack my own brother. Unfortunately, he didn't have such scruples. Then again, he didn't know I was his long-lost sister.

He directed a bolt of magic toward me and knocked me square in the chest. My body lifted and flew across the governor's front yard. I fell to the ground with a crack I felt all the way to my bones and rolled to my side, where I coughed up blood. He'd blasted my vital points. This would take a while to heal.

Marcellus smirked and looked down at me disdainfully. "As if you're a match for a blood mage." He rolled his eyes and motioned for the guards to take me away.

15

They tossed me into Lomewood's filthiest dungeon where scurrying rats were my only companions. I peered around my new cage, which was barely large enough to hold one person. The pain in my chest was severe. My brother had inflicted severe damage. The guards secured the cell with locks that were guarded against magic, and my hope for escape dwindled.

Ronan's parting words to me were not to get captured or hurt, and that was exactly what I had done. I would laugh if the pain didn't make even breathing difficult. I couldn't think of a single way out of here unless I used my blood magic to free myself, but that was risky because in so doing, I would expose my true identity.

I dragged my body closer to the moldy stone wall and leaned my back against it for support, then focused all my efforts on controlling my breathing and redirecting the pain. However, Marcellus was an accomplished blood mage and the hit inflicted serious damage. I wouldn't be anyone's match for a while.

The day passed in a painful blur, each hour marked only by

the guards who patrolled the dank corridor. For dinner, one shoved a bowl of water and a piece of stale bread inside my cell, which I left untouched. The urine-soaked straw mounded in the corners of my cell was enough to put off my appetite, even if I wasn't concerned about being poisoned.

Then, the person I least expected dropped by.

Caelan strolled in without any guards, looking like the victorious captor as he preened and strutted in front of my cell. He leaned against the bars and looked at me curiously. "How did you survive that fall, pray tell?" he inquired. "I know you're a famed healer, but I can't imagine the state I left you in would allow you to recuperate so quickly." He grinned maliciously.

I scoffed and rolled my eyes. "I bet ..."

"I hope I didn't hurt your feelings," he said. "It wasn't personal, you know."

I shook my head slightly and gave a heavy sigh. "Listen, Your Highness, I don't care what kind of issues you have with Ronan. I've tried to help you and you don't want to believe me. So whatever is going on between you two, just leave me out of it." I leaned back and tilted my head to the side against the wall.

Caelan fixed me with a shrewd stare. "You see, I find that hard to believe, Leila. You seem to be *very* important to Ronan. I would even go as far to say he might be *in love* with you."

I laughed. "You are dead wrong. Dreadfully so."

"I mean," he blew out a breath and clasped his hands over his heart mockingly, "the way he jumped over the cliff after you was just ... *so* romantic. I'm touched, truly."

Irritated by the direction my former friend's line of questioning was veering, I decided to change topics. "So, what's your plan? Keep me hostage until Ronan returns the lost princess to you?"

He shrugged. "That's one option. But what I truly want to know is why you aren't with Ronan now. Were you two lovebirds separated in the river? I can't imagine him voluntarily leaving you alone."

I narrowed my eyes. "Like I said, we're not close," I reiterated.

Caelan chuckled and shook his head, unconvinced. "No, if there's one thing I know and admire about the Crimson Clan, is that those demons love once and it's unconditional. Ronan never would have left you alone, unless ..."

"Unless what? I told you, he's not in love with me."

He furrowed his brows. "No, I don't think so. I think maybe *you* don't love *him*, and you got away the first chance you could."

I wanted to laugh at Caelan's outrageous claim, but this situation was far from humorous. Instead, I stared back unflinchingly, hoping he would see his childhood friend beneath the layers of grime and praying he wouldn't at the same time.

A sinister gleam twinkled in the prince's eye, and he leaned forward as if he was about to divulge a juicy secret. By his sudden shift in demeanor, I was positive I didn't want to hear it. "I would love to send you back to him ... in pieces," he added with a cruel smirk. "Why don't we begin?"

I frowned at the monster who stood at the door of my cage. With wicked delight, he whistled for the guards to unlock my cell.

"Bring her out," he commanded.

Two guards entered my cell and pulled me up roughly. I grimaced and groaned as they dragged me out, my wounds screaming for relief. A shiny trail of blood marked my passage as I continued to cough, evidence of the internal damage that had been inflicted.

Caelan watched me, his brows raising to his hairline in surprise. "Who hurt you, little healer?"

My head lolled to the side and I fixed him with a pain-glazed stare. "Prince Marcellus."

The guards remained silent as they dragged me into a room that had been outfitted for torture. Torches placed every couple feet along the wall provided the only light in the dim, dank-smelling place. I wondered how many times they'd witnessed or even participated in the torture of prisoners, and if they did it eagerly or saw it as part of their job. In the end it didn't matter; the result was the same. Shoving me down onto a heavy wooden chair, the silent guards latched my wrists and ankles to the legs and arms of the chair with heavy iron manacles.

Caelan laughed. "Wow, you even got Marcellus mad enough to hurt you?" He perused a metal table nearby that was littered with a variety of torture implements and reached for a pair of pliers. He approached slowly and snapped the pliers in front of my face for added effect. "What do you think? Should I send your teeth back to him?"

I scoffed. "Do you even know where he is?"

His eyes gleamed in the firelight. "No. But you'll tell me."

I shook my head. "I don't know anything. You're wasting your time."

"I don't think so," Caelan mused. "I think you know *exactly* where he is and what his plans are. You think I don't know about the army he's amassed on the eastern side of the Central Plains?"

I fought to maintain an emotionless expression. "I don't know anything about that."

Caelan's mouth twisted into a cruel sneer. "If that's the game you want to play, so be it." He switched out the pliers for a poker that was being heated on a fire. Donning a thick leather glove, he grabbed the red-hot poker and aimed it at my face. "This is your last chance, Leila. I really don't want to hurt you."

I stared him down and lifted my chin defiantly. I wasn't

scared of his taunts. I'd been through worse. "Do what you have to do, *Prince*."

He paused for a moment as if disappointed that he didn't elicit the response for which he'd hoped. "Very well." He inched closer and slowly pressed the poker to my arm.

I gritted my teeth against the pain and my stomach roiled at the smell of sizzling, burning skin. If I clenched my teeth any harder, they would splinter and chip, but I refused to scream.

After several searing seconds, he removed the poker from my skin. "Come on, Leila, just give us a location," Caelan cajoled.

I gasped and sweat trickled down the sides of my face. "You already know his army is on the east side of the Central Plains. What else do you want to know?"

He leaned close to my face. "*Everything*."

I shook my head. "I don't know anything!"

The prince rubbed his chin and seemed to contemplate my response. "You see, I don't entirely believe that. Maybe you need a bit more incentive." Leaning in, Caelan pressed the poker to my arm again. I grimaced and pulled against the chains, but there was no escaping the skin sizzling assault. His eyes gleamed in triumph. "Have you had enough?"

I laughed and gritted out, "Not even close."

His brows rose in surprise, and he tossed the poker with a clatter and picked up the pliers again. He snapped them a few times in front of my face. "I heard that pulling out one's fingernails can be quite painful. Want to try it?"

I shrugged weakly. "This is your party ... I'm just here for the ride."

For the first time since Caelan arrived in Lomewood, I looked at him – truly *looked* – and came to a startling realization. Ronan was right. The man standing beside me so callously inflicting torture upon the town's healer wasn't the same gentle boy I once knew. Whether he'd morphed into this monster to survive his own harsh reality or for some other reason entirely, I wasn't sure, but the childhood friend I knew was long gone.

It was a good lesson.

"Why?" I mumbled as I looked up at him. He frowned in confusion. "Why are you like this, Caelan? What happened?"

The shock of me using his name so casually made him widen his eyes. And although he could have corrected or tortured me for disrespecting him, he only stared back as if lost in a trance.

"What did you say?" he asked softly. His demeanor and voice were a complete contrast to how he was just a minute earlier.

I cleared my dried, parched throat. "I asked what happened for you to become like this. I doubt this is the person your lost princess once knew."

"You don't know anything," he croaked.

I shrugged. "Maybe not. But I know one thing: she would be so disappointed in the way you are right now. Torturing an innocent person just to get back at your enemy. If you weren't a prince, I'd have pegged you for one of the bandits running around the Central Plains."

"I'm nothing like them!" he growled. In a flash, he leaned down, rested his hands on my shackled arms that rested on the torture chair, and shoved his sneering face in front of mine. "*I am a prince!*" he yelled, as if trying to convince me of the validity of his birthright.

I scoffed and met his eyes unflinchingly. "You could have fooled me. You seem more like a tyrant."

Caelan's glare was murderous. Staring me down far longer than I cared for, he finally pushed himself up and took a step back. "Guards!" he yelled, his eyes never leaving mine. The same two guards who strapped me to the chair marched to his side with a smart salute. "Take her back to her cell," he commanded. Spearing me with one last disgusted look, he spun on his heels and marched out of the room, his boots rapping sharply on the flagstone tiles.

∽

THE GUARDS DUMPED me back in my cell with new wounds to care for, but I didn't have the energy to heal myself. The damp dungeon made it hard to breathe, pushing my already strained lungs to the breaking point. When a rat scurried past my foot and brushed my toes with its long, pink tail, I didn't even have the energy to be disgusted.

I was weak and frail, the product of malnutrition and exhaustion, and desperately needed a healer or access to the medicine back at my clinic. Unfortunately, neither was an option.

Selene was under house arrest, Ronan was dealing with his army on the other side of the Central Plains, and poor little Henry was in my clinic without any way to help me. I was truly on my own.

Unable to hold my body up, I slumped to the side and hunched over in the fetal position. With my arms loosely wrapped around my stomach, I closed my eyes and prayed for a quick death.

16

My prayer for a quick death was not answered. The days passed in a blur until I had no idea how long I'd been there or if it was day or night. Each time Caelan came to visit he got more creative with his torturing methods, and he seemed to take great delight in pushing me to the edge. Unfortunately, his patience wore thin because I didn't give him what he needed—which was either Ronan's exact location or his plans. It was all for naught, as I truly didn't know anything. This was why Ronan and Silas were so careful not to discuss anything in front of me, although the prince obviously didn't buy that.

I had just been returned to my cell after a particularly brutal interrogation. Crawling across the mildewed straw that littered the floor to a bowl of filthy water, I grimaced and poured it out, then clinked the bowl against the steel and croaked out, "More ... water ... please." My voice was rusty and hoarse. Lately, the only sounds I'd made were my screams.

After several minutes, a guard marched to the cell bars and kicked the bowl out of my hands with a hearty laugh. "Don't be so greedy!" he smirked. "You've had more than enough water to—"

But the man never finished his sentence, because someone crept up behind him and snapped his neck in one smooth movement. I was in too much pain to fear the newcomer. Instead, I prayed my end would be as swift. When the guard's body slid to the floor in a lifeless heap, I looked up and met Silas's crimson gaze.

He gave a lopsided grin. "We can't leave you alone for two seconds before you find trouble, Leila."

I chuckled. "Nice seeing you, too."

With a shake of his head, Silas leaned down and patted the guard's body for the keys to my cell. Once he found them, he shoved the body to the side and opened the door. With a gentleness that surprised me, Silas reached down and lifted my body into his arms. "Come on, Leila. Let's get you somewhere safe."

Like Ronan, Silas had long, dark hair that was braided at the sides of his head. His arms and body were covered in crimson tattoos that told his story, and he shared the same deep-set crimson eyes. Whereas Ronan had a more rugged look, boyish charm resonated from Silas. I could tell he was younger than Ronan, but I didn't know by how much.

My chest lightened with each step Silas took with me out of the dungeon. I lacked the strength to hold my head up, but I saw the ground littered with dead guards. When we left the stagnant cells behind and stepped outside, a small group of Crimson Clan members were waiting.

I inhaled the fresh air deeply into my lungs, feeling better than I had since this nightmare began. "Where's Ronan?"

"He's with the army ... preparing," Silas answered cryptically. Even though he was saving me, it was undoubtedly under Ronan's orders. Silas didn't trust me much.

We soon left the horrors of the prison dungeon behind and

stepped onto Lomewood's eerily quiet streets. It was dusk and the sun sank into the horizon, painting the sky with vivid streaks of orange and pink. Shopkeepers along the route took one look at our ragtag group and closed their doors immediately to hide from the dangerous Crimson Clan.

Henry was waiting outside the prison gates. The moment he saw me, his eyes widened in shock. "Miss Leila!" he exclaimed. "Are you okay?"

I attempted to nod. "I'm fine, Henry. Why … why are you here?" Without slowing so Henry's little legs could keep up, Silas continued walking down the street flanked by his clan members.

"I heard you were arrested!" he said quickly as he followed slightly behind Silas. "I searched for Ronan and found him in —" Silas cleared his throat and sent the young boy a glare, a not-so subtle hint to keep his mouth shut. "Sorry," Henry mumbled.

"Ronan was very upset to learn that you'd not only been captured, but also injured," Silas chastised. "He's waiting for you with a healer back at camp."

With those reassuring words, I rested my weary head on Silas's shoulder and closed my eyes. Sleep came quickly.

∼

WHEN MY EYES FLUTTERED OPEN, I was lying in an unfamiliar tent. The gentle glow of candles cast warm light to chase away the shadows, and a furnace hummed softly, assuring the night would be wrapped in warmth. Confusion, followed by the recollection of preceding events, slowly crawled into my awakening consciousness.

I wasn't alone. Henry's silent form was huddled on the floor, his head resting on the corner of my cot. An unsettling mix of gratitude and concern filled me and I wondered how long he'd maintained this silent vigil. Reaching out, I gently brushed his hair away from his face. He stirred and his eyes snapped open. After a fleeting moment of disorientation, he straightened.

"Miss Leila?" His voice was groggy but laced with relief. "Are you finally awake?"

I nodded. "Yeah. Why don't you get some rest?"

He shook his head. "No. I have to inform Ronan that you're awake." He rose, each movement echoing the weariness that clung to his bones, and left the tent in search of Ronan.

The pain in my body had receded and I felt some of my strength return, but I still wasn't in top shape. What should have been a slow recovery had been hastened by the healer who had obviously treated me. I attempted to sit up, but my bones and joints were stiff. I lay there with a blend of impatience and relief coursing through me until the tent flaps rustled and Ronan's towering form entered.

"You never listen, do you?" Though stern, his voice held a level of concern that was touching. The chieftain's son stopped by my bedside. "How are you feeling?"

"Better," I muttered. "Where are we?" I glanced around warily, but I didn't see a distinguishing characteristic to announce where we were.

"Don't worry about that for now. Just get better." Ronan pulled the blankets up and tucked them under my chin. "Are you hungry?"

His tenderness was disconcerting, a deviation from the Ronan I thought I knew. My brows knitted together, suspicion and curiosity intertwining. "What's wrong?"

A laugh, rich and deep, escaped him. "Nothing is wrong! Does something need to be wrong for me to be nice to you?" The warmth in his eyes belied the stern tone that followed. "When what I *really* want to do is wring your neck for disobeying me."

"Now that's more like it," I chuckled.

Ronan's eyes held a mix of frustration and relief. The silent interplay of emotions was a dance we were both learning. "Why do you always have to be so stubborn?" he asked, the firmness in his voice softened by the unmistakable concern in his crimson eyes.

"You should know by now that it's part of my charm," I replied, my attempt at lightness barely masking the undercurrent of vulnerability that lay beneath.

Silence enveloped the inside of the tent. While fraught with unspoken words and tensions, in this quietude, a strange comfort persisted.

He pulled up a chair and settled beside the cot. "You should rest, Leila." Ronan's voice was imbued with tenderness that seemed as foreign as it was familiar.

"I've been doing nothing *but* resting," I protested. The restlessness within sought an outlet, a breach from the confines of the cot and tent.

Ronan's gaze held mine and our silent exchange seemed to echo the unsaid, the known, and the unknown. "You were hurt badly, Leila. You need time to recover." He paused and looked me over. "You'll have permanent scars," he said hesitantly as he fisted his hands. "I'll kill him," he growled, growing angrier by the second. "I promise you."

I reached out and placed a hand over his. "Ronan—"

"Don't!" He stopped my words and pulled his hand from my grasp. "Don't you *dare* defend that coward to me. Caelan doesn't deserve your consideration."

I shook my head. "I'm not trying to defend him, but I also don't want you to be consumed with hatred because of what happened to me. I'm not worth it."

A flicker of surprise. "You're more than worth it, Leila, and you know it."

I snorted. "Why? Because I'm the lost princess?"

He frowned. "That has nothing to do with it."

I nodded in understanding. "I know you're angry and I know you consider me a ... *friend*, but—"

"A friend?" he repeated with a raised brow. "Interesting choice of words."

I sighed. "Come on, Ronan. Don't make things difficult."

He scoffed. "*Me*? Make things difficult for *you*?"

"You know that's not what I meant—" I rushed to backpedal, but he wasn't having it. The temperature in the tent rose several degrees.

Ronan was livid. "I had to orchestrate your rescue from someplace I couldn't go because of the bounty on my head. Do you have any idea how much I have sacrificed for—"

"For me," I finished with a barely restrained eye roll. "I know."

"Aren't you angry?" he asked with furrowed brows. Confusion laced his expression.

"Yeah ... I am," I answered honestly. "But being angry and seeking revenge won't make me feel better. It won't change what's already happened."

His gaze was penetrating, and he seethed with an anger that boiled not from a place of personal vendetta, but from a deeply rooted protective instinct. Every word that escaped his lips echoed the furious storm that brewed within him.

"Inaction is not an option, Leila," Ronan responded, his tone resonating the finality of a judgement pronounced, along with his uncompromising resolve. "Not while the enemy still draws breath."

Veins pulsed along his temples as a silent testament to the rage of his inward battle. Amid the night's stillness, punctuated by the tranquil hum of the woods, every uttered word was a clash of swords and every silence was a field of unmarked graves.

"I'm not seeking revenge for the sake of revenge, Leila," he continued, his voice laced with painful restraint. "But every scar on your skin, every mark—is a testament to an unspeakable violation, an unforgiving reminder of a man unbridled by honor or humanity."

I felt the welling up of my own storm, a tumultuous tide of emotions that sought a release from the ones who wronged me. But where Ronan's storm was fiery, mine was icy, a chilling tempest born of painful betrayals and haunting truths.

"I refuse to be defined by scars, Ronan." My voice, though steady, barely masked the icy fury that raged beneath the calm exterior. "Every mark is a battle won, not lost. A testament to survival, not defeat."

His gaze held mine, a silent battlefield where storms raged and tempests clashed.

"I won't stand idle, Leila." Ronan's voice, though restrained, echoed the unyielding resolve of a warrior marked by countless battles.

"And I won't be a prisoner of my scars, Ronan," my retort, though whispered, bore the chilling echo of icy storms, unyielding and untethered.

He stared me down, his crimson gaze never leaving mine. "Then it seems we're at an impasse."

∼

RONAN HAD LEFT my tent hours earlier. It seemed he and I couldn't agree on a single thing. We were both frustrated, but we had different ways of dealing with our annoyance. Where he wanted to skin Caelan alive, I wanted to let things go. Caelan would get what he deserved once he realized who I was. To me, that was punishment enough.

My stomach grumbled. Fully intending to get up and seek food, I sat up on the cot and prepared to swing my legs over the edge. But it seemed Ronan and I were thinking the same thing.

The tent flaps opened and Ronan stepped inside carrying a

tray of food. Even though we argued the last time we saw each other, he smiled at the sight of me. "I figured you'd be hungry," he muttered as he approached. The tantalizing aroma of spiced meats filtered into the tent and my stomach grumbled again. "Oh, yeah, I came just in time."

He walked to my cot and set the tray down beside me, then pulled up a chair alongside. There was more than enough food for two people. I raised a brow as I looked between the tray and him.

He laughed. "I figured I'd eat dinner with you ... *if* you don't mind."

My brows shot up to my hairline. "Aren't you upset with me?"

He blew out a breath. "Honestly? Yes, I am. But I also understand your point of view. So I can't hold a grudge, now can I?"

"I guess not." I picked at the meat and licked my finger, savoring the taste.

I was struck by the contradiction of the man before me. Ronan—a warrior, forged in the fires of conflict, who extended grace amidst the unyielding stances we each held. A complexity of emotion and thought was woven through every fiber of his being, marking him as both an enigma and an open book.

As I indulged in the food's rich flavors, the silence that descended was reflective and calm. It was neither charged with the vibrant clash of our conflicting stances nor haunted by the shadow of unspoken grievances.

"I haven't thanked you yet," I said between bites, the rich tapestry of flavors melting in my mouth.

"For?" Ronan's eyebrow arched, the inquiry shadowed with a depth of meaning.

"For saving my life, yet again." The weight of gratitude coursed through every word.

Silence fell, charged yet contemplative. Ronan's gaze lingered, a silent dance of reflections and revelations. "We're allies, Leila. Perhaps more." His assertion was neither a confirmation nor a denial, but a space where possibilities thrived.

"Allies ..." I repeated. "I'm not too sure about that."

"Oh?"

I chuckled awkwardly. "Just because you've saved my life twice doesn't mean I'm suddenly allied with my enemy."

He leaned in, placing his elbows on his knees. "What if I told you a secret of our people that could possibly change your mind?"

"A secret? Now you've got my attention," I smirked.

His grin widened as he reached for the tray and snagged a piece of meat, popping it into his mouth with great relish. I followed the motion, hyper-aware of the grease that stained his bottom lip, and then as he slowly licked it clean. I was so entranced by his mouth that I had to shake my head and look away.

I cleared my throat and frowned. "What kind of secret?"

"What if I told you we were no longer allied with Keldara?" he whispered as he leaned in closer. "What if I told you it's been ten years since we were allies?"

My frown deepened. "Ten years ..." I gasped. "You mean since the invasion of Valoria?"

He nodded.

"How? Why?"

He tsked and wagged his finger at me. "Now, now, Leila. I can't tell you *all* our secrets." He grinned and reached for another sliver of meat. "But I hope this little secret will warm you up to the Crimson Clan ... even if only a little."

A million theories coursed through my mind as I tried to piece everything together. "Didn't the Crimson Clan *want* to invade Valoria?"

He tilted his head and smirked. "Now, I didn't say anything about that."

"Then what happened?" I pressed.

Ronan looked behind him to make sure no one had entered the tent or was strolling nearby, and leaned forward again to whisper. "Let's just say Keldara and the Crimson Clan had a deal in which Keldara didn't deliver."

My brows shot up. "You wanted something from Valoria," I murmured.

Ronan slowly nodded.

"What was it?"

Ronan laughed. "I think you've had enough secrets for now. Finish up before I eat it all." He nodded toward the tray of food.

I rolled my eyes and reached for the bowl of soup, then proceeded to drink it in a few gulps. The warmth of the soup coursed through my veins, lending a semblance of calm to the storm of questions swirling in my mind. Every revelation, each unveiled secret, painted intricate patterns of complexities and entwined narratives to create a world where alliances and enmities were as fluid as the shifting sands.

Once we finished our dinner, Ronan lifted the tray and called out for Silas, who must have been standing guard outside the tent. The Crimson Clan warrior hurried inside to retrieve the empty food tray. Without another word, he exited, leaving Ronan behind.

"You're not leaving?" I asked with a raised brow.

He shook his head slowly. "No, unless you want me to?"

I bit my lip and contemplated his question. Did I? Did I want Ronan to leave me here alone? Or did I want his company like when we were hiding in the mountains?

"Stay," I whispered as I peered into his darkening crimson eyes.

"As you wish."

The tension in my tent climbed to levels even I couldn't

handle. I fumbled with the edges of my blankets, the intricate weave coarse against my nervous fingers. The quietness around us felt tangible, a thick, charged silence that threatened to consume the tent's confines.

The candle flames danced precariously, casting an enigmatic dance of shadows that echoed the array of emotions churning within me. Ronan's presence, both a solace and a storm, rendered the night's silence as articulate as the unspoken words that hung heavily in the air.

Ronan reached toward me and swept my hair behind my ear, slowly caressing me as he withdrew his hand. Had this been weeks ago when I first met him, I would have slapped his hand away. But now ... I didn't understand where my thoughts and feelings were. My brain told me this was all wrong. Once an enemy, always an enemy. But my heart ... my heart fluttered at his touch, his soft, intense gaze, and his warmth that I'd grown to crave.

"Leila," he whispered. He retracted his hand, but I quickly grabbed his wrist and stopped him. He looked at my hand and his gaze fell on me again. "What I want ... I'm not sure you're willing to give ... yet."

"What do you want, Ronan?" I asked, my voice heavy with need. I tugged at his wrist, bringing him closer.

His brows furrowed in confusion and then understanding. "I want you," he murmured. "All of you."

My heart stuttered as I stared into his darkening eyes. "I can't give you all of me."

"I know," he said confidently. "But one day you will." He caressed the side of my face with his free hand and intertwined his fingers through my hair as he pulled me closer. "But for now, I'm willing to accept just a taste," he whispered.

My heart raced like the hooves of a thousand horses. I held my breath for fear of breaking the moment. Just a taste was what he wanted ... the question was, was I willing to stop there?

The gap between us was gradually diminishing. Not just the physical, but the emotional chasms that kept us at arm's length had started to unravel. The piney scent of the surrounding woods and the cool night air mingled with his scent. It was wild yet comforting, alien yet hauntingly familiar.

As the distance between our lips shortened, a torrent of memories rushed through my consciousness—my journey so far, unveiled truths, the battles we'd fought together, and the impending war that lurked in the shadows. Each memory, revelation, and prediction laid bare the undeniable—the enemy was not the man before me, but rather the circumstances that brandished us as adversaries.

Our lips met, and the dam of restrained emotions burst forth. It was not a mere physical union but an amalgamation of complex sentiments—the subtle union of resentment, attraction, resistance, and surrender. It was passionate and restrained, exploratory and familiar. A conflict and a resolution, a question and an answer, all rolled into a coalesced moment that seemed suspended in eternity.

"I …" The words trailed away and I slumped toward him.

"I know," he responded. We were in uncharted territories; lands where crimson flags and crescent moons didn't dictate loyalties and hatred. "If a taste is all you can give me, then a taste is what I'll accept."

I couldn't pinpoint the moment when things shifted between us. All I recognized was the pull that grew stronger as each day passed. It was harder and harder to say no.

He pulled me toward him again and his lips crashed against mine. The raw intensity that lingered between us was drawn taut like the bowstrings before a war.

The conflicting realms of our existence, of crescent moons and crimson flags, warriors and princesses, captors and allies, dissolved in the intimate space where touch was the language, silent yet eloquent, expressive yet restrained. In the sanctuary of that moment, titles were irrelevant and roles were inconsequential. We were but two souls, warring though yearning, separate though inseparable.

I couldn't get enough.

I reached for his leathers, fumbling as I tried to undo them. His hand settled over mine and he stopped me before pulling away.

"Now ... is not the time," he said.

I stared deep into his eyes, confused by his reaction. Then again, we were in the middle of the woods, surrounded by the Crimson Clan right outside my tent. It wasn't exactly the most romantic of places.

As if he could read my thoughts, he chuckled. "Trust me, Leila ... I want to. But there are things you don't know." He murmured the last part and glanced down at our intertwined hands with a pained expression.

"Like?" I questioned.

He looked away. "I ... I can't say."

I nodded and tried not to get upset. Of course there were secrets still being kept from me. Why wouldn't there be? It seemed everyone knew something to which I wasn't privy. The question was, did it revolve around me?

"I won't force you to tell me everything," I whispered. "But just tell me one thing ... Does this secret affect me?"

His gaze found mine and he slowly nodded.

My mind raced as I tried to connect the dots, but without more details, I was at a loss. Details that Ronan wouldn't share. It was a stark reminder that even though he didn't consider himself to be my enemy, Ronan and the Crimson Clan were not to be trusted.

I pulled my hand out of his and put some distance between us. The rush of coldness that swept between us made me shiver.

"Leila—"

"You don't have to explain further," I stopped him. "I don't want you to have to lie to me."

He remained quiet, a silent admittance, then nodded again and slowly stood to leave.

I grabbed his arm to stop him. "I didn't say I wanted you to go."

He looked over at me in shock. "You still want me to stay?"

"At least until I fall asleep," I said. "Will you stay with me?"

"Always."

17

The next day when I woke, Ronan was gone and a food tray with a steaming bowl of porridge had been placed on the table. He must have recently left.

Groaning as I sat up and stood, I gingerly made my way to the table to eat. I sat down carefully and rolled up my sleeves to see the burn marks on my arms. They were healing, but Ronan was right: I was scarred for life. I smoothed my sleeves back down and tried to forget about the time I spent in the dungeons with Caelan.

I'd just taken a spoonful of porridge when Henry called from outside my tent.

"Miss Leila?" he yelled. "Are you awake? Can I come in?"

I smiled. "Come in, Henry!"

The tent flaps opened and the young boy walked inside with a bounce in his step, looking cleaner than I'd ever seen him. His face was clear of dirt and grime, and his clothes looked new. It could only be Ronan's doing.

He sat in the empty chair across from me. "Miss Leila, how are you feeling?"

I smiled brightly and ignored the pains in my body. "Much

better, Henry. All thanks to you, of course." I winked and ruffled his hair.

He attempted to duck, but I was too fast. His cheeks brightened in embarrassment.

"I didn't get to properly thank you for letting Ronan know of my ... circumstances." I offered him some of my porridge, but he waved me off.

"Of course, Miss Leila," he said. "I couldn't let you get hurt. I should be the one thanking you for all you've done for me."

"Aren't you hungry?" I asked when he declined my offer.

He shook his head. "I already ate with the men. Ronan made sure I had plenty! Please, eat your breakfast."

"Okay." I smiled and continued eating. "What are you doing now?"

He sighed and leaned back, resting his hands behind his head. With a bright smile, he admitted, "I have the easiest job in the world!" He paused. "Watching over *you*."

I laughed. "I'm guessing Ronan told you to keep watch?"

His eyes sparkled when he nodded. "He's paying me a glint a day."

My brows shot up in surprise. "Well, that's very generous of him."

He furrowed his brows. "So no funny business, Miss Leila. You need to rest and get better."

"Of course. I won't make things difficult for you, Henry," I said. "But ..."

He threw his head back and groaned. "I knew there would be a *but* coming ..."

I finished my breakfast and set the bowl aside before leaning forward and whispering, "Want to be a double agent?"

He straightened and his wide eyes gave me the answer I wanted. My proposition had certainly snared his attention.

"Ronan is keeping some ... information from me," I started. "I'm wondering if you can find out what secrets he and the

Crimson Clan might have regarding the lost princess. Can you do that?"

Henry tilted his head in confusion. "But that has nothing to do with you, Miss Leila. Why ...?"

"Um ... no, not necessarily. But I need to know their secret."

"Do you plan to use it against him?" Henry frowned. It seemed he was conflicted on who he should remain loyal to.

I shook my head. "No. I don't have any ill intentions," I clarified.

He blew out a breath and slumped back in his seat, looking as if a huge weight had been lifted. Henry loved a good adventure. "Oh, thank the gods. Then sure, Miss Leila. I'll find out for you." With a wink over his shoulder, Henry crept out of my tent, intent on learning what the Crimson Clan was hiding.

∽

A FEW HOURS passed and true to my word, I remained in my tent to recuperate and not make any trouble. At noon, Henry returned with a tray of tea and pastries but left again. Night had fallen and I expected him to return soon, so when my tent flaps opened, I was surprised to see Silas instead.

Silas was formidable on the battlefield, but still cut a domineering figure with his six feet frame, all bulk and muscle covered in the crimson tattoos of his clan. His long, brown hair fell below his waist. My stomach dropped when he closed the tent flap and tied it from the inside so no one would easily enter.

I watched Silas grab a chair and bring it next to my cot. "What are you doing?"

"Nothing. I just thought we should talk."

I sat up and faced him, feeling uncomfortable and vulnerable lying down. "I don't think we have much to discuss."

He smirked. "On the contrary, Healer, we do. You see,

Ronan has been preoccupied with you since we arrived in the Central Plains, which goes against why we came here. He almost got himself killed just to save you."

I ticked my head to the side. "And what did he come here for?"

"The lost princess," Silas answered without hesitation. "It's obvious he confided in you and admitted we don't have her. What I don't understand is *why*. Which brings me to question whether you practiced some sort of witchcraft to make him—"

I burst into laughter, which cut him off mid-tirade. "I'm no witch, Silas. And I haven't done anything to Ronan."

He shook his head. "You must have. All his life, he's known the lost princess was promised to him. She's the only female he's ever cared about. Then *you* came along."

I frowned. "He ... he was promised to the lost princess?"

Silas nodded and straightened. "There are things you don't know of our people, Leila. Things we can't share. But as a member of the Crimson Clan and Ronan's closest friend, I must intervene for the sake of our clan."

My frown deepened. His words confused me. "I don't understand."

"You may have heard that members of the Crimson Clan only mate once for life, unlike the men from surrounding nations who like to marry multiple women—"

"Yes, but what does that have to do with the lost princess?" I blurted out.

He scoffed and looked away, then he smoothly veered the conversation away from the lost princess. "The survival of our clan depends on Ronan, and you're a distraction. So I suggest you end things before they begin. Once you've recuperated, I'll provide you with an opportunity to slip out of camp without his notice. That's the best I can offer."

It didn't bother me that Silas wanted me gone, or that Ronan was supposedly promised to someone else—ironically, me. What I cared about was what the lost princess—*I*—had to do with this. His claim didn't make sense. Was this the secret Ronan was keeping from me?

I cleared my throat and met the warrior's steely gaze. "I'll leave ..." I started, "but first, I want you to tell me how the Crimson Clan is involved with Valoria's lost princess."

Silas snorted. "That is confidential, and it has nothing to do with you. You're just a random female from the Central Plains who has no business being involved with us. If our chief ever found out about you ... you would need to pray to your gods in hopes of survival."

The irony wasn't lost on me. As much as I wanted to keep my identity a secret, I had the nagging feeling my secret would be revealed to the world fairly soon. Too many threats were being lobbed at me and my only chance of survival was to reveal the truth.

But I wasn't ready. Not until I learned why I'd been forced to hide all this time. Suddenly, I had an idea. One I wasn't sure I believed in, but it was worth a try.

"Silas, I'll leave ... if you do me a favor."

He furrowed his brows, wary about the bargain I wanted to strike. "Depends on the favor," he replied diplomatically.

I smirked. "I've heard tales about the witch doctors of your people ... how they commune with the dead."

His frown deepened. "Yes, that is true."

"If you bring me a witch doctor, I'll leave as soon as possible. Deal?"

He watched me carefully before nodding. "Deal."

∽

HENRY AND RONAN arrived an hour later, carrying a dinner tray heaped with soup and different meats. I hadn't seen Ronan all day, but I knew he was busy preparing his army. Being here made me feel like a traitor to my own people.

"How are you feeling?" Ronan asked. "The healer said you were on the mend."

I nodded. "I'm much better, thank you. Though I'm surprised you got a healer from the Central Plains instead of using one of the clan's witch doctors."

He chuckled. "I figured you'd be more comfortable with a healer than a witch doctor from the Grasslands. Most outsiders don't believe in them."

"Hm ... that's true." When he placed the tray on my bed, I started picking at the food. "You were gone this morning when I woke up."

"Yes, I had some things to do, but I left Henry in my stead." He ruffled Henry's hair affectionately. My little informant stood at the foot of my bed and shyly lowered his head with a small smile on his face. "Go on, Henry. There's a whole feast going on outside. Go join them."

Henry lifted his head and his eyes widened, then a wide smile stretched from ear to ear. "Yes sir!" Without a backward glance, he rushed out of the tent as fast as his short legs could take him.

I chuckled at the boy's exuberance, then puzzled over what Ronan said. "There's a feast going on out there?"

Ronan nodded.

"Why aren't you with them, then?" I asked hesitantly.

"Because I wanted to be with you."

His honest answer and the seriousness of his gaze made me squirm and I bit my lower lip. "You don't have to be so straight-forward all the time, you know," I mumbled before turning my attention to the tray of food as if it was the most interesting thing I'd seen all day.

Ronan laughed. "Oh, don't tell me you're suddenly shy. That's not in your nature."

I snapped my attention back to him and fought the smile that threatened. "And what is *that* supposed to mean?"

He snorted and gave me a knowing look. "You're the one who took down three Crimson Clan warriors the first time we met. In a drunken stupor, you were able to fight bandits in the street, and you had the gall to show up in the mountains and place yourself between me and Caelan's army. You're definitely not shy, Leila."

I rolled my eyes. "That makes me brave, but I'm still a woman."

He sized me up and down. "Yes. I'm well aware."

I laughed and threw a chicken bone at him, but with his quick reflexes, he easily caught it before it hit his chest.

"I must say, your aim is impressive even with non-lethal weapons," Ronan teased, holding the bone between his fingers.

"You better be glad it's just a bone," I retorted. This playful banter, light and free of the heavy burdens of a looming war and complex allegiances, was a refreshing escape.

Ronan's smile mirrored my own as we stared at one another. His crimson gaze dropped down to my lips for a split second before meeting my eyes again. The temptation was there. We both wanted it. But he held back for reasons he still hadn't divulged.

He cleared his throat. "Are you … are you feeling better? You look better." He asked for the second time since he arrived.

I grinned. "Yes, I do feel better. I'd say I'm at roughly seventy percent. Just a few more days and I'll be good to go."

His smile faltered. "Go? Do you plan on going somewhere?"

I tensed. It was merely a turn of words, but they held so much meaning. Meaning he wasn't aware of yet. "Oh, I didn't mean it like that," I blustered. "I just meant I'll be back to my normal self."

He frowned for a moment before he nodded in understanding. "I don't want you going anywhere, Leila. You're safest here in camp. Do you understand?"

"Yes, I do." I wanted to promise I wouldn't go anywhere, but that was a lie. I'd already struck a deal with Silas.

"Good. If you need anything, just let me know and I'll get it for you."

I smiled. His expression wasn't one of joy. If anything, he looked suspicious. But I'd been hiding my identity for ten years already, which meant I was an excellent pretender.

"You know what I want?" I looked into his eyes. "Wine."

His suspicion cleared and he laughed. "Of course you want wine. Unfortunately, I can't get your favorite 'A Thousand Roses' from the Rose Petal, but could I offer you some Drunken Mead from the Grasslands?"

I sighed. "I guess …"

He rolled his eyes. "I'll get you some wine tomorrow. How about that?"

I perked up. "Thank you!" I hated tricking him, but I needed him out of the camp tomorrow so I could meet with the witch doctor Silas promised. So far, everything was going according to plan.

18

While we waited for Ronan to leave camp on his way to Lomewood to acquire my wine, Henry was in my tent sharing the latest information.

"I haven't been able to learn anything from Ronan or Silas, but I've heard whispers around the camp about something else," Henry whispered as he sat beside me on the edge of the cot. I nodded for him to continue. "Supposedly, there's a prophecy from the Grasslands that has to do with ..." He twisted his mouth to the side and scratched his head.

"With what?" I pushed.

"I've never heard of this before, so I don't know if I heard correctly, Miss Leila, but they mentioned something about a blood weaver ... The first *female* blood weaver."

I froze.

A blood weaver? What was that? Was it the same as a blood mage? If it was, the prophecy could refer to me, as I was the first female blood mage in the only family of blood mages. My family line had only produced males, which was great for continuing the blood line, but then I came along. Besides being a girl, something else that set me apart from my male counterparts was the healing properties of my blood.

"Are you sure that's what you heard?" I asked, just to make sure.

Henry nodded. "Yes ... I think so," he mumbled.

I didn't doubt him. If anything, my persistent questioning was making him doubt himself. I wrapped an arm around him. "Thank you, Henry."

"Of course, Miss Leila. I wish I'd learned something more."

I smiled down at him. "You've done more than enough, Henry. Way more than I should be asking of you."

Someone cleared their throat outside the tent before they spoke. "It's Silas."

"Come in!" I called out.

Silas entered the tent and his crimson eyes landed on Henry immediately.

"He won't tell Ronan," I said quickly. "Not unless it brings him harm."

Silas nodded. "Very well. The witch doctor is outside, so whenever you're ready."

I squeezed the young boy's arm. "Henry? Would you mind waiting outside with Silas?"

He frowned. "Miss Leila, are you sure? I've heard those witch doctors from the Grasslands are quacks."

I snorted and tried to hold in my laugh and ignore Silas's glare. "I've heard that too, Henry, but don't worry. I know how to take care of myself. And if anything goes wrong, find Ronan." I looked up at Silas, a silent warning in case he had any malicious thoughts toward me.

Henry twiddled his fingers and looked down at his sandaled feet before nodding. "Okay ..." But he sounded far from convinced.

"Go on, now." I slightly pushed him toward Silas.

The two exited the tent. Less than a minute later, the enigmatic presence of the witch doctor entered. She was garbed in clothes that seemed woven from the fabrics of various realms, an intricate interplay of colors and patterns that danced in harmony with every movement. Her skin, a canvas of artistry, was adorned with intricate tattoos. Every line and curve bore testament to ancient incantations, each etching a silent hymn of power that echoed the chants of her ancestors. They crawled gracefully up her arms, encased her neck, and sprawled across her chest, emanating an aura of sacred potency.

Her eyes were crimson, deep as blood, bestowing upon her a gaze that seemed to peer into the soul. A necklace of bones, beads, and amulets graced her neck, each piece a repository of energies and a guardian of sacred powers.

"I am Amina," she introduced herself. Her voice was eerie and uncanny, and held the sound of much wisdom.

I regarded her with a mix of apprehension and fascination. "Hello, Amina, I am—"

"I know who you are, Leila of the Central Plains."

"Then I'll get to the point." I stood and approached. "I need your help. I need to contact someone who is deceased."

She furrowed her brows. "Not many from the Central Plains, or any of the surrounding nations, believe in our abilities. Why do you?"

I sighed. "Honestly? I don't. But I'm sort of desperate and willing to try anything."

"I appreciate your candor," Amina said. "Who are you trying to reach?"

"My former guardian ... Sir Edric of ... Valoria," I said hesitantly.

Amina didn't react. There was no shock or knowing look. She was poised and calm as she waited for me to continue.

"So how does this work?" I asked.

Amina inched closer, each stride appearing as if she floated on water. "First, we must establish a connection. You need to think of this Sir Edric and not get distracted. Your mind must remain steady. If he is near, he will appear ... through me."

"You mean he will possess you?" I raised a brow and she nodded. "Will you be ... aware of what's said?"

She shook her head. "No, I won't. You will have complete privacy."

"Why should I trust you?" I asked.

She smirked. "You shouldn't."

"Of course not," I muttered. "Fine. Let's get started."

Amina moved the table and chairs to the edges of the tent, making a clearing in the center of the spacious area. She sat on the ground, criss-crossed her legs, and motioned for me to do the same. After I was situated, I waited for her instructions.

"I need you to close your eyes and think solely about Sir Edric. Think of a pleasant memory you shared. If he is here, he will make himself known." The witch doctor closed her eyes and sat motionless in front of me.

I closed mine, then took a deep breath and exhaled. Amina began to chant in a language I didn't recognize, but I tried to focus and push aside the distractions that threatened to pervade my thoughts. My eyelids felt heavy, bearing the weight of uncertainty and hope. In the darkness behind my closed eyes, images of Sir Edric slowly began to materialize. Every scene, every shared laughter and stern reprimand echoed the complex tapestry of our relationship.

Amina's chant was hypnotic, a melody that resonated with the silent hum of the universe. It was a symphony that reached into the untethered spaces of existence, seeking connection beyond the physical realm.

I was transported to a time of innocence when I was eleven years old, holding on to Sir Edric's big, warm hand as he guided me through Asteria. Sir Edric, with his stern yet loving gaze, his voice a blend of authority and affection. Each memory was a portal, drawing me closer to a space where dimensions intertwined.

Amina's voice grew louder, her tone imbued with a mystic power that seemed to defy the earthly realm. The energy within the tent shifted. It was as if the air was charged with an inexplicable force that bridged the gap between here and the beyond.

As her chanting reached its zenith, profound silence engulfed the space. In this silence, a presence manifested. The air was thick with an energy that seemed both foreign and familiar.

"Leila," a deep voice called out.

My eyes flew open. "S-Sir Edric?" I stuttered. When I looked at Amina, I didn't see anything different until she opened her eyes, which were milky white. The disembodied voice sounded exactly like the guardian I once knew. The sound gave me chills and brought on memories that had long since been forgotten.

"I'm here, Leila … You've done well for yourself," he said. "Although I know why you seek me."

"Have you been watching over me?"

He chuckled. "Of course I have. Even in death, my duty is to protect you."

A lump in my throat kept me from saying all that I wanted to say. Sir Edric had been a father figure to me during our time together. When I was sixteen, he died in an accident and no amount of blood I fed him would bring him back.

"I need to know, Sir Edric. Why did I have to leave Valoria?"

After a pause, he said, "When Keldara invaded Valoria for their land, there was another objective, a darker one … To kidnap you."

My eyes widened and I gasped. "Why?"

"That was the deal Keldara made with the Crimson Clan," he answered. "Your parents knew since the day you were born that the Crimson Clan would come for you one day."

I shook my head, confused. "I don't understand, Sir Edric. What is so special about me that they'd go to all that trouble?"

Amina looked around the room to make sure no one was around before divulging, "Because you're the Blood Weaver, Your Highness."

The Blood Weaver ... That was the same thing Henry overheard. So it *was* me. But if so, then...

"What does that mean, Sir Edric?" I asked. "I don't know what it is."

Amina nodded. "Your blood is special, Your Highness. Not only do you carry blood magic and can heal with your blood, but your blood can be woven to create things."

I frowned. "Such as?"

"Such as weapons," he answered matter-of-factly. "With a slit of your wrist, your blood could pour out of you and form shapes as solid as metal."

My stomach rolled and my eyes grew impossibly wider. "How-How is that possible?"

"I don't know, Your Highness." The witch doctor shook her head, though the mannerism was all Sir Edric. "This is all ... legend. I never attempted it with you because I was afraid you'd get hurt."

"So if I really am this *Blood Weaver*, why isn't it safe for me to return to Valoria? I've stayed away because that's what you said before you died, but it's been ten years. When can I go back home?"

The witch doctor waved off my question. "There are too many spies in Valoria, even now. You will never be safe there, no matter how much the King and Queen love you. Not many people know what you are, but one day, for the safety of Valoria, your parents will—"

"Trade me," I finished in a horrified whisper.

Amina nodded. "You were never safe there, Princess. I

disobeyed orders because I couldn't bear to see you betrayed in that manner. It was best if you disappeared."

"Okay ... so the Crimson Clan wants to use me as a weapon?" I asked.

Amina shook her head and her eyes narrowed. "No, Your Highness. The Crimson Clan wants you for something far more sinister than that."

My blood ran cold at his words. I wondered what exactly Ronan had planned.

"Whatever you do, Lyanna, you must NEVER trust the Crimson Clan, and you must NEVER trust—"

Suddenly he stopped speaking and Amina's body began to convulse. The witch doctor fell to the side, her body making a loud thud as it hit the ground. Her eyes slid shut and I hurried to her side, trying to shake her awake.

"Sir Edric!" I shouted. "Sir Edric!"

Silas rushed inside the tent when he heard me yelling and looked between me and the witch doctor. He helped me lift Amina and she slowly opened her eyes. They were back to normal.

"Bring him back!" I demanded.

Amina stared me down. "I can't."

"Wh-What? Why?"

"The connection was lost and I'm completely drained. It will be a few weeks before I've recuperated enough to try again."

"A few weeks?" I gasped at the absurdity.

Silas helped Amina stand and I followed suit. "Witch doctors can only contact the dead once a month," he explained.

I didn't trust them one bit. Just as Sir Edric was going to confide something in me, the connection was extinguished? It was a little too tidy.

"No! I need to reconnect with him. You have to try again!" I said desperately.

Silas whispered something in Amina's ear, and she left the tent without another word.

"Where is she going? Tell her to come back!" I shouted.

Silas shook his head. "I gave you what you wanted. Our deal has been met. Now it's time for you to complete yours."

She wasn't coming back. That was what he was telling me.

"I need three more days before I'm fully healed," I said, stiffening my spine and raising my chin defiantly. "Then I'll leave."

"Good," Silas said. "Three days from the stroke of midnight, be prepared to leave." He turned and swiftly left my tent.

Henry rushed inside with worry etched on his face. "Is everything okay, Miss Leila?"

"Yes, Henry," I murmured as I stared at the tent flaps where Silas had exited. "Everything is fine."

19

I spent the rest of the day alone in my tent, contemplating my conversation with Sir Edric. For starters, it was surreal to speak to him. Because his death was so sudden, I'd never gotten closure and spent years ruminating on what I could have or should have done. Beyond the sense of closure, I was decidedly uncomfortable in the Crimson Clan's camp. I still didn't know where we were, and based on Sir Edric's warning, they were not to be trusted.

I was sitting at the table, stirring the bowl of medicine the healer left for me when the flaps of my tent opened and Ronan strode in with a bright smile and two massive jugs of wine. "Your wish is my command," he declared as he approached and placed the two jugs on the table. "I hope these will be enough. It wasn't easy stealing them from the Rose Petal."

My brows shot up. "You *stole* them?"

He smirked. "It's not like I can walk through the front door, Leila. I'm a wanted man."

I chuckled. "Right. Of course."

He frowned. "Are you okay? You don't seem like ... yourself."

"Oh, it's nothing. I'm just trying to work up the nerve to take this bitter medicine the healer concocted for me. If only I had something sweet to eat it with." Though not the truth, it wasn't solely a lie, either. The medicine smelled disgusting.

Ronan sat down across from me and his grin spread. "Well, you're in luck, then." He pulled a wrapped bundle from inside his vest, then unfolded the cloth to reveal two moon cakes. "Selene told me these were your favorites."

My eyes widened. "You saw Selene?"

He nodded. "I thought you might want to know how she's doing."

I leaned toward him and gripped his hand. "Is she okay?"

He nodded again. "She's doing well. Luckily, Marcellus paid Madam Rose enough so she no longer has to entertain. She spends much of her time in her room or in the back garden, but she's surrounded by Valorian guards at every turn."

"At least she's not working," I muttered.

Ronan offered me the moon cakes. "Go on; take some so you can drink your medicine."

I gave a tight smile before grabbing one and taking a bite, then quickly drinking the medicine. Thankfully, the bitterness was absolved by the sweetness of the moon cake.

Ronan uncorked one of the wine jugs with a pop and slid it toward me. "A Thousand Roses, just what you've been craving."

I watched Ronan for a moment. He was behaving much ... sweeter than he normally did. Was there a sinister purpose behind it all, as Sir Edric suggested? Or was Ronan simply being kind? My heart was torn by what I wanted—*Ronan*—and what I knew was wrong – *also Ronan*.

Ronan knew I couldn't give him all of me. That eventually I would have to return to Valoria and when I did, we would have to permanently part ways. Even though Sir Edric told me it wasn't safe in Valoria, the end of my hidden identity would come soon. I could only continue being Leila and stay hidden for so long before the truth came out.

"Leila?" Ronan snapped his fingers in front of my face. "You're zoning out. Are you sure everything is okay?"

I shook my head and smiled. "Yeah. Everything is fine."

Just then, I was struck by a thought. If I wanted to get the truth out of Ronan, these jugs of wine might do the trick.

"Drink with me," I begged, clasping his hand in mine. "It's lonely drinking by myself."

Ronan laughed. "I got these for you! Don't worry about me—"

I pouted, "But there's more than enough for both of us. Come on!"

"I was hoping these jugs would last you a couple of days, at least. I didn't think you wanted to drink them all in one night!" he laughed.

I shrugged. "Let's have some fun."

He eyed me for a moment before agreeing. "All right, fine. Let's get drunk." He uncorked the other jug for himself and took a big swig. I did the same.

The atmosphere in the tent shifted with each sip. The heaviness of our reality, the unsaid words, and the complex dance of emotions flickering between us were temporarily muffled by the intoxicating effect of the wine. The air was infused with a rare lightness.

We laughed harder and spoke more freely. In those fleeting moments, we weren't Crimson Clan's most feared warrior and Valoria's lost princess. We were simply Ronan and Leila, two souls unburdened and unfettered, reveling in the magical euphoria that A Thousand Roses lent us.

His laughter boomed throughout the tent, rich and unrestrained. Amidst this uncharted territory I dared to probe, hoping to unravel his hidden secrets.

"So, Ronan," I started. "Do you plan to attack Valoria soon?"

He chuckled. "No ... I have no plans to attack Valoria ... but Caelan's army? That's another story."

"But Caelan's army *is* Valoria's army. Aren't they one and the same?"

He shrugged and took another gulp of the wine. "I guess," he murmured.

The conversation wove through a dance of playful jests and silent revelations. Each swig of wine ushered in the courage to delve deeper and venture where we hadn't dared. As the night drew on, the two jugs of wine became silent witnesses to confessions and surprises, to laughter and unutterable words. Every gulp was an unmasking, and as the intoxicating liquid coursed through our veins, the walls we'd meticulously built crumbled.

I pushed back my chair and stood. Walking over to him, I sat down on his lap and wrapped my arms around his neck. "Do you love me, Ronan?" I whispered, my eyes narrowing as I stared at him.

His cloudy gaze widened and he placed his long, tapered fingers around my waist. "And if I do?"

I leaned against him and lightly brushed my lips against his. "I might consider giving myself to you," I purred.

He blinked a few times, trying to clear his head and probably wondering if he heard me correctly.

A Thousand Roses was strong wine, known to reduce a man into doing just about anything, hence why it was mostly sold in the Rose Petal. I'd drank so much of it over the years that it hardly had any effect on me, but even I wasn't completely immune to its potency.

"You're drunk, Leila." He picked up the nearest jug and shook it to reveal it was almost empty. "We *both* are."

I crossed my arms over my chest defiantly. "And? What does that matter?"

"It matters, Leila," he whispered, his tone serious. "You're a princess. Even though you've been in hiding for the last ten years, I'm almost positive no man has ever had you."

While that was true, I was willing to do anything at this point to get to the truth. Even if it meant giving something away I shouldn't.

I caressed his face and he leaned into my hand. His eyes fluttered closed. "I wish I could take you right now," he murmured. "But there are things you don't know, Leila."

"Like?" I probed.

He shook his head, trying to clear the cobwebs. "Like ..." he started, but then left the thought hanging.

"Ronan?" I whispered, trying to snare his attention again.

"Hmm?" He opened his eyes and stared at me. "You're beautiful, do you know that?"

"Then why don't you want me?" I asked. "You said you wanted all of me, and that's what I'm offering."

He shook his head again. "No. You'll just give me one night. I want forever."

I froze in his lap and replayed his words in my mind. Those were dangerous words. Forever was a long time. I remembered what Caelan said in the dungeons about how the Crimson Clan members mated once for life. Maybe his words weren't complete nonsense, after all.

"Why do you want more of me? You hardly know me," I muttered. Not quite two months had passed since the night we met, which was hardly long enough for him to have such lingering thoughts. Was it my true identity he loved? Silas claimed Ronan was promised to marry the Princess of Valoria, which would explain his fascination with me.

He brushed strands of my hair away from my face and swept it behind my ear, caressing my face as his cloudy gaze stared into mine. "I've known you my whole life."

I frowned. "What?"

He chuckled and dropped his head onto the back of the chair. "You don't remember, do you?"

"Remember what?" I asked, my drunkenness dissipating in a blink.

He shook his head. "Nothing," he murmured with another laugh. "You'll remember one day." Dropping his head onto my shoulder, Ronan nuzzled the crook of my neck. "You smell like roses."

"That's the wine," I reminded him. "You're smelling the wine."

"I don't care," he said as he snuggled deeper. "Promise me Leila, that no matter what happens, you'll forgive me."

I ticked my head to the side. "What will I have to forgive?"

"Just promise me. Promise me you won't believe everything you hear until you've spoken to me first," he murmured in the crook of my neck. "I'll never hurt you. I promise you that."

I sighed and ran a hand through his long, dark hair. "Oddly enough, I believe you, Ronan," I whispered.

He lifted his head, reached for the remnants of the wine, and tossed it back in one hearty swallow. "I should get out of here before we do something we'll *both* regret."

I tightened my hold around his neck to prevent him from sliding me off his lap. "Stay with me tonight."

He peered at me with eyes glazed with lust. "I'm still a man, Leila."

"You've stayed with me before," I countered.

"That's not what you're asking of me," he said. "And there's only so many times I can say no before I break."

I gulped at the meaning. He was patient, but not overly so. If I kept pushing him, we would end up in bed.

Before I could utter another word, Ronan stood and cradled me in his arms. He smirked as he walked over to my bed and gently laid me down.

I gripped his arms. "Stay," I repeated.

"Leila," he growled.

Before he could pull away, I grabbed the front of his shirt

and pulled him down toward me, our lips crashing in a mess of sloppy kisses. His weight fell on top of me, and he quickly turned us over so he was on his back and I was on top of him. His fingers combed through my hair, tugging slightly at the roots and pressing me closer to him.

He moaned into my mouth and I felt his hardness between my legs. I tensed, but without giving me a chance to change my mind, I sat up and straddled him, then ripped off my shirt and bra. His crimson eyes darkened as they took in my naked torso, and he slid his rough hands around my waist and up my abdomen until he was cupping my breasts. He looked mesmerized, as if he'd finally gotten what he craved for so long.

He sat up slightly and his mouth went to my right breast, sucking and biting my nipple until I moaned in ecstasy. I rocked my hips at the sensation and rubbed against his hardness to soothe the building ache.

When he swirled his tongue around my nipple, I gripped his hair and pressed him closer. His free hand latched onto my left breast, kneading and pinching in all the right places.

"Oh, gods," I moaned. Wanting to feel his warmth against my cool skin, I tore open his shirt by ripping the fabric straight down the middle, then tore it off his body to expose his tattooed skin. I tugged his hair, pulling him away from my breasts until he was staring up at me. We watched each other for several silent seconds before I crashed my lips to his and pressed my bare skin against his.

"Leila," he panted in my mouth. "Tell me to stop."

"No."

He flipped us over until I was on my back and he was on top of me. Hovering over me, his gaze scanned my body as if trying to memorize every inch. "There's no going back after this," he whispered. "Once we cross this threshold, you're *mine*. No matter what anyone says. Do you understand?"

"Yes!" I reached for the buttons of his trousers impatiently, quickly undoing them and lowering the fabric until his engorged cock popped free.

He reached for the buttons of my trousers, but where I was feverish and bold, he unbuttoned them slowly as if giving me time to come to my senses. He slid them down my legs along with my underwear until I was completely bare for him. I attempted to cover my nakedness with my hands, but he grabbed my wrists and pinned them to the bed.

"Don't ever hide from me," he whispered. "You're ... you're more beautiful than words can express." He pressed a gentle kiss on my lips.

My muscles gradually relaxed and I wrapped my legs around his waist. The tip of his cock was slowly penetrating my folds when ...

"Ronan!" Silas called out and stormed into my tent. With a surprised grunt, Silas spun around with his back to us when he saw what we were doing.

Ronan quickly grabbed the blanket and covered every inch of me, his expression darkening with anger. "You better have a gods damn good reason for coming in here unannounced!" Ronan growled.

"Uh ... I do," Silas stuttered and started to peer over his shoulder.

"Look away!" Ronan commanded.

Silas looked straight at the entrance of the tent. "Ronan, the spies we sent to the Valorian camp were found floating in the river ... dead," Silas said nervously.

"Damnit!" Ronan climbed off me to stand, then stepped into his trousers and buttoned them in a flash. "Meet me in my tent in ten minutes," he commanded.

"Yes sir!" Silas peered over at us as Ronan looked away, but I didn't miss the heated glare he sent my way before he disappeared from my tent.

Ronan dropped to his knees beside the bed and brushed

my tangled hair away from my face. "I'm sorry," he murmured. "I—"

"I know," I cut him off. "Go do what you have to do. I understand."

He nodded and grabbed his torn shirt from the floor before rushing out of my tent.

I released a deep breath, my body trembling from the sudden coldness as I laid under the covers, completely bare.

If Silas hadn't interrupted us ... I would have given my virginity to Ronan. I didn't know if the idea made me happy or not. A whirlpool of emotions swirled in my gut until I no longer knew what was right or wrong.

But what I *did* know was that tomorrow, Silas would demand I leave. My three-day grace period had just been voided.

20

The next morning, Ronan didn't come to see me. Henry told me he left camp in the middle of the night with a small group of warriors and appointed Silas to look over the camp. I knew Silas would come to see me soon.

Someone cleared their throat outside my tent. *Speak of the devil.* "It's me."

I looked over at Henry and whispered, "When Ronan returns tonight, give him this letter." I handed him an envelope and clenched his hand around it. "Promise me."

Henry nodded. "Yes, Miss Leila."

I tried to convey my earnestness as quietly as I could so Silas wouldn't know Henry had my letter. "Make sure no one knows you have it," I said, glancing at the outside of my tent where Silas lingered.

"Yes, ma'am." He stuffed the envelope into his vest where no one could see.

"Thank you," I whispered. Then I straightened and called out for Silas to come in.

Silas entered my tent with a scowl and shooed Henry away.

After sending one last look at me over his shoulder, the young boy ducked outside my tent.

Now, it was just me and the hulking Crimson Clan warrior. I stood and met him with straightened shoulders. "I'm ready whenever you are."

Silas grunted. "I'm glad I didn't need to force you out."

I chuckled. "After last night, I figured your patience had run out."

His eyes flashed dangerously. "I warned you, Healer, and you didn't listen."

I smirked. "Yeah, I have a hard time listening sometimes. But you have nothing to worry about. Ronan only loves the lost princess." I grinned knowingly. "He won't settle for anyone less."

Silas frowned, confused. He walked in on us last night, so in his mind, Ronan was about to settle for someone far less than the princess. But I wasn't going to explain. He would find out soon enough.

"Come on," he said, ignoring me. "Patrol shifts are changing in ten minutes. This is your only chance to escape."

"After you."

∼

Leaving the camp was far easier with Silas by my side than if I would've had to do it alone. His presence lent legitimacy to our errand. With a cloak wrapped around me and the hood pulled low over my face, no one knew or questioned who I was. Even when we were stopped by Crimson Clan guards, Silas easily explained away our errand. In a matter of minutes, we were leaving camp and stepping onto a nearby road where a carriage was already waiting.

I'd be lying if I said Silas' desire to be rid of me didn't sting a little. "I guess you had it all planned out," I noted wryly.

"Like I said, Ronan holds the fate of our clan in his hands. He can't ruin it all for some Central Plains woman," Silas said, uttering the words *Central Plains woman* like a curse.

I chuckled. "Right. Well, thank you for escorting me safely out of camp. You might not believe me, but I appreciate it."

He nodded curtly. "I hope we don't see each other again."

My smile tightened. "Hopefully."

With those parting words, I climbed up into the carriage and closed the curtain, shutting off my view of the world outside the seating area. After a few moments, the carriage jostled down the road toward Lomewood.

My ride back home was introspective, a journey both physical and emotional. The landscape unfurled before my eyes as I stared out the window, a procession of natural beauty that seemed to mirror the myriad of emotions surging within me. Each tree that whispered secrets with the winds and each brook that babbled stories of times long past drew me into deeper reflections.

Every now and then, the driver cast his glance backward, as if ensuring my safety or perhaps curious of the mysterious passenger he ferried. We exchanged no words and the journey was marked by respectful quietude, each absorbed in our worlds.

The transition of the landscape outside my window told of the passing time. Lush forests adorned with the glistening dew of dawn gradually transitioned into stretches of meadows basking under the golden embrace of the afternoon sun. Shadows lengthened and silhouettes of distant homesteads emerged, whispering the nearing proximity of Lomewood.

As the outlines of the town became distinct, anxiety and relief coursed through me. The familiar terrains beckoned with the comforting allure of home, yet they were also reminders of an identity and a destiny that was as uncertain as the paths that stretched before me.

I was still a wanted person, and it was no longer safe to walk along the streets of my home, but I had nowhere else to go. With no other option, I told the driver to take me to my clinic. When we arrived, I tipped him with a glint, even though I knew Silas had already paid him. He scrambled off the carriage driver's seat to help me climb down, then watched quietly as I swiftly stepped inside and shut the door.

My clinic looked the same as always, if a bit dusty from disuse. I unwrapped the cloak from my shoulders and hung it on the peg by the door, then headed upstairs to freshen up and change clothes. As I did, I considered my next steps. I couldn't leave Selene at the Rose Petal. Sneaking her out was my priority, but I needed a safe place to hide afterwards. If we came back to my clinic, we would be sitting ducks. This was the first place Madam Rose and Marcellus would look.

There was an inn located right outside Lomewood's borders on the way to the Silent Mountains. That might be the safest place for us to lay low and figure out what to do next. With a new plan in mind, I hurried and dressed in dark colors and wrapped the black cloak around me once again. Lowering the hood over my head, I quietly stepped outside my clinic and headed down the street.

I briskly walked toward the eastern exit of Lomewood, intent on reaching the inn before nightfall to make a reservation. The walk was lengthy, but it was my only option. I couldn't hire a driver for fear they would turn me in for the bounty.

With my head down, I was hurrying down the street with my attention fixed on my boots when someone slammed into me. "Sorry," I muttered and sidestepped around them.

"Is that all you're going to say to me?" a man said.

I recognized his voice instantly. I lifted my head to see Orion, who wore his customary smirk. "I've been waiting for you, dear Leila."

I sighed and fought the eye roll that threatened to escape. "What do you want, Orion? I don't have time to play games."

"I want to help you," he offered. "Are you really heading into the mountains to escape?" he asked, glancing down the road and back again. On this stretch of road, it was clearly my only destination. "Not many know about your cabin, little one, but if they decide to torture Selene for the information, she will eventually divulge your secret hideaway."

I narrowed my eyes at the overly curious fae. "And how do *you* know about my cabin?"

He chuckled and looked far too smug for his own good. "I know many things, dear. Some might even consider me all-knowing."

"You're no god," I deadpanned.

He snorted. "No, I'm not. But I *am* a full-blooded fae, which makes me much stronger than many."

"Why should I trust you to help me?" I asked.

He shrugged and gave me a knowing look. "Because Sir Edric would have wanted me to help you." With a sigh, he added, "I made a promise to your guardian—"

"What?" I gasped.

Orion glanced around and took my elbow. "Out on the open road isn't an ideal place to talk about such delicate matters. Follow me."

As a blood mage, I was more powerful than Orion, whether he was a full-blooded fae or not. Confident I could protect myself from whatever he threw my way, I didn't protest when he prodded me down the street and into a nearby tavern that was relatively empty.

The establishment was a stark contrast to the normally bustling streets of Lomewood. It was quiet and somber inside with a few patrons scattered about, lost in their ale. Creaky wooden boards flexed under our feet, echoing the weariness and stories of countless travelers and locals who had sought refuge and solace in this hidden gem.

A haphazard assembly of chairs and tables, each bearing the marks of time and heavy use, gave the tavern a rustic charm. The lighting was dim, with the occasional flicker of candles to cast enigmatic shadows that danced in a hypnotic rhythm, concealing as much as they revealed.

Orion's grip on my elbow was firm yet reassuring as he guided me through the hushed space. A sense of unnerving tranquility loomed, as though the tavern was insulated from the tumultuous upheavals that seemed imminent outside its sheltering walls.

We found an isolated corner, veiled from overt gazes by the interplay of shadows and the strategic placement of furniture. The air was thick with unspoken tension, the silence echoing the gravity of impending disclosures.

As soon as we sat, the tavern keeper ambled towards us. His silent gaze bore the testament of years of silent observations. A nod from Orion and the man disappeared, only to return with two chalices of wine. The dark red liquid reflected the flickering lights and brought an even more somber mood.

Orion leaned in. "I'm sure you have many questions," he began.

"Yes, but mostly I want to know if you know. Who I am, I mean," I added haltingly.

Orion slowly nodded. "Your guardian tasked me with looking after you if he passed while you were still in Ellyndor."

I grunted. "Great job protecting me. I've been shot, jailed, tortured—"

"I heard," he cut me off. "I was away in Ellyndor and didn't find out what happened until Ronan had already staged a rescue."

I eyed him carefully. "I hope you don't mind me saying this, but you don't seem like a normal fae. What are you?"

His intense gaze never wavered. "Don't worry about who *I* am, Leila. That's not important. What's important is getting you out of Lomewood. I've already scheduled transportation to take you to Ellyndor. I can keep you safe there."

I frowned and stiffened. "Ellyndor? I don't want to go back there."

Orion sighed. "Don't make things difficult, Leila. You don't know everything that's happening—"

"Then tell me!" I shouted as I kicked back the chair and stood. "I'm tired of being kept in the dark about my own life!"

Orion slowly stood. "Everything will be shared in due time, but first you need to go somewhere safe. Lomewood isn't—"

"I'm not going anywhere with you," I seethed. When I turned toward the door, he grabbed my arm.

"Lyanna," he growled.

"Don't call me that," I murmured, shocked that he spoke my real name in public. "That girl died a long time ago."

"You will always be Princess Lyanna," he whispered.

The next thirty seconds seemed to unfold in slow motion. I saw his hand curl and dart toward one of my pressure points and realized he would knock me unconscious to whisk me toward what he deemed as 'safety'. But I was faster.

I swerved under his arm and forced him to release his hold, then took a measured step back. "You might be a full-blooded fae, Orion, but *I'm* a blood mage. You'll never be stronger than me."

I held my hand aloft with my palm facing him and focused on the blood coursing through his veins. In the next second, I started to make it boil. Orion dropped to his knees in agony, his face contorted as he scratched his skin.

"Lyanna, please!" he begged.

The use of my royal name caught the attention of several tavern workers. "Oh my gods, it's the lost princess!" one of them exclaimed.

With my free hand, I lowered my hood further and flung Orion against the wall with enough force that he crashed through it and into the building next door.

Orion's revelations sent shivers down my spine; a cascade of emotions flooded every fiber of my being. The secrets, veiled alliances, and untold narratives were almost too much to process. The walls of the tavern that echoed the silent whispers of countless hidden stories suddenly felt too confining. I needed air, space, and the liberty to breathe and confront the upheaval that inwardly raged.

I darted out of the tavern, the door swinging shut with an echoing thud that marked my abrupt departure. The streets of Lomewood were veiled in the serene embrace of the night and stars glittered like silent sentinels overseeing the unfolding drama below. Each step towards the inn was fueled by the tempest of emotions that warred inside my head.

I reached the inn with a sigh. It seemed a tranquil haven amidst the surrounding turmoil. Pale moonlight cast a serene allure on the establishment, marking a stark contrast to my racing heart.

The innkeeper, a silent observer of transient visitors, handed me the keys with an unintrusive nod when I placed my reservation under a fake name. I made my way up the winding staircase to my reserved room and closed the door.

The room was a harmonious blend of modest comfort and serene solitude. The bed was adorned with simple, cozy linens that extended a silent invitation for rest, a haven amidst the storm. A solitary window opened to the moonlight and shadows, a world where I was no longer free to walk around, especially after the scene I'd just made in the tavern. Everyone would know who I was by morning.

I couldn't waltz into the Rose Petal and whisk Selene away in plain sight. No, my plan required stealth, which meant I needed to pretend to be a man to enter the pleasure house. Only then could I reach Selene's room and plan our escape.

After pulling my long hair into a bun at the top of my head, I removed my memorable cloak and wrapped a cloth around the bottom of my face to obscure my features. I left my room and had just stepped onto the staircase to head back downstairs when the inn's front door burst open and a group of men stormed in with another man nestled between them.

"Help! We need help!" one of them called out.

Startled, the innkeeper jogged from around the front desk and met them in the foyer. "What's going on? Is he okay?"

"We were up in the mountains and he fell from one of the lower cliffs!" one of his companions panted. "He injured his leg, but it could have been a lot worse."

The innkeeper ushered them to a sitting area and told the men to lay their injured friend down on one of the tables. As perplexed guests started to filter out of their rooms due to the commotion, the innkeeper looked around and called out, "Is anyone a healer?"

With a groan, I realized my plan would have to wait. When no one else responded, I yelled out, "I am!" and jogged down the stairs toward the injured man.

"Who are you?" one of his companions asked.

I made sure the cloth still obscured my face and pitched my voice deeper. "I'm a healer ... that's all you need to know." I stood beside the man and tried to clear my mind.

The man tossed and grimaced in pain. Sweat beaded on his temples and upper lip. "Help me ... please," he begged.

"I will. Just tell me where it hurts." I pressed my hands over his arms, chest, and abdomen, searching for broken bones.

"No," he exclaimed. "My leg! It's my leg!"

"Okay." I lifted his pant leg and exposed the skin of his left shin. "I don't see anything," I muttered.

"No, *here!*" he pointed to his thigh.

"Does someone have a knife?" I called out. One of his companions swiftly produced a knife and handed it to me. After carefully slicing his pant leg to expose his thigh, the injury became evident when I saw his femur sticking out of his skin.

Everyone in the vicinity grimaced and gagged at the sight, but I'd dealt with far worse injuries and was able to maintain my composure.

I ignored the squeamish spectators and focused on the injured man. "Okay, I need to push your femur back in. It's going to hurt like hell, and I don't have any sedatives with me to ease the pain. Do you understand?"

"Yes," the man grunted. "I don't care. Just do it."

"Very well." I glanced around the room. "Does anyone have alcohol?" A server from the dining area called out that he did and rushed over with a jug of wine. After washing my hands with it, I splashed a bit of alcohol on the man's wound. He screamed so loud, you would have thought someone was murdering him. When no one was looking, I made a slight cut on the tip of my finger. "I need two logs of wood and some rope," I called out. In minutes, the items were placed in front of me. After sanitizing them with alcohol, I went to work.

Using a sizable amount of force, I pushed the man's femur back in place, ignoring his bloodcurdling screams. Once it was properly fitted, and without others seeing, I sliced my finger and rubbed my bloody finger over the wound so it would heal faster. A few drops of my blood wouldn't completely heal him, but it would speed up the process. Placing the rope beneath his leg, I nestled the logs on his left thigh to use as a splint.

After asking one of his companions to hold the logs still, I slowly bent the man's knee, then lifted his thigh slightly and gingerly wrapped the rope around his leg with the splints in place. Once it was secure, I lowered his leg.

The innkeeper handed me a cloth to wipe my hands, and I

peered into the man's feverish face. "You need to see a healer as soon as you're able. They'll do a more thorough job than I did with better supplies. But don't delay, or you'll be left with a limp for the rest of your life."

"Thank you! Thank you so much!" one of his companions exclaimed. "Please, tell us who you are."

"Are you ... are you the renowned healer of the Central Plains named Leila?" someone else asked.

Murmurs filtered all around the inn. To some, the name was unfamiliar. But a knowing spark came into others' eyes as recognition hit. The collective focus was unyielding, and in that moment, the clandestine serenity of my disguise was shattered. I was a spectacle, and with each murmur and speculative whisper, the cloak of anonymity was ripped away stitch by stitch.

"No," I retorted quickly, my voice steady, a lie woven with the finesse of necessity. "I'm just a healer passing through. My name is of no significance."

But doubt lingered in the air, thick and palpable. Each gaze seemed to pierce the cloth that veiled my identity. My hands, stained with the evidence of healing, betrayed a narrative far more complex than the simplicity of a transient healer. There was recognition in their eyes, a silent acknowledgment that transcended the barrier of the cloth that concealed my face.

"We won't tell anyone, Miss Leila," one of the men murmured as the crowd continued to stare at me.

I smiled beneath my face covering. "Thank you." I stood. "I must go." Though my voice was resolute, an underlying tremor betrayed my rising anxiety. The room had become a stifling confinement.

With unspoken urgency driving each stride, I left the inn and turned toward the pleasure house. The night's chilly air was a liberating embrace, the silent whispers of the moonlight a soothing balm to the intrusive scrutiny of watchful eyes. The cobbled streets were largely empty, and many of the shops and storefronts were closed for the day. By the time I reached the other side of town, it was late.

Admittedly, my disguise was severely lacking. Even I was hard pressed to believe I looked like a man. My hair and the lower part of my face was covered, but not showing my face would only arouse suspicion, not dampen it.

With no other plan in place, I crept toward the bright lights and open doors of the Rose Petal and blended into a group of men as they entered, keeping my attention fixed on the sumptuously carpeted floor beneath my steps. Music and laughter filled the air, a stark contrast to the clawing anxiety I felt. The interior was as opulent as always, the rich colors and extravagant décor showcasing the house's wealth and the kind of clientele it attracted.

I needed to move quickly to avoid detection, but staying invisible in a place like this would be challenging since the girls were incentivized to mingle amongst the guests. I kept my head down, relying on the ambient noise and crowd to cover my movements.

The group of men I'd sheltered with were absorbed in their own world, and their raucous laughter and crude jokes created a diversion that allowed me to slip away unnoticed to the grand staircase that led to the upper chambers. Each step was a mixture of caution and speed; the less time I spent in the open, the better.

The upstairs corridor was quieter, providing a soft backdrop against the muffled sounds of ongoing revelry downstairs. The way to Selene's room was ingrained from previous visits. I walked briskly, my ears tuned to any sound that wasn't meant to be there, any indication that I'd been spotted. But fortune was on my side, and I reached Selene's door undetected. My hands, steady despite the adrenaline coursing through my veins, turned the knob.

The door opened silently, a testament to the well-maintained luxury of the Rose Petal. I slipped inside and closed the door gently behind me. The noise from downstairs became a distant echo as I stepped into the silent sanctuary of Selene's chambers and let out a silent breath of relief. My hands trembled as my adrenaline waned and the reality of the risk I'd just taken started to set in. I tugged down the cloth that covered my face and took my first deep breath.

The room was dimly lit by a single lantern casting a soft, golden glow that highlighted Selene's elegant furniture and lavish decorations. The serene space was a stark contrast to the chaos and opulence of the tavern below. I scanned the room as my eyes gradually adjusted to the muted light and saw her lying on her bed with her back to me. I slowly crept toward her and tapped her shoulder. She jerked and whirled around with a dagger clenched in her hand, ready to attack. I caught her wrist just in time.

"Selene!" I whispered. "It's me."

Her hand relaxed and she sat upright to get a better look. "Leila?" she gasped.

I nodded and released her wrist. "Are you okay?"

She scrambled out of bed and dropped the dagger. "By the gods, Leila, where have you been?"

"It's a long story." I sighed and pulled her into a hug. She squeezed me tightly, her small frame trembling in my arms. "I'm sorry I didn't come sooner," I murmured.

She shook her head and pulled back. "As long as you're safe, that's all that matters. I ... heard things ..."

I was almost positive I knew what she heard. Stories of Caelan torturing me. Tales of my alliance with the Crimson Clan. Truths mixed with lies.

"I'm okay," I repeated. "How are you?"

"I'm fine," she answered. "Prince Marcellus paid Madam Rose a hefty amount of coin to keep me locked in my room."

I frowned. "Your door wasn't locked."

She nodded. "It can only be opened from the outside. I can't open it from inside."

Realization dawned and I looked back at the door I'd unwittingly locked. Glancing at the open window, I thought I could jump from Selene's room to the next roof. I filed my escape route away and turned my attention back to Selene.

"I need to talk to you, but we don't have a lot of time."

Sensing the urgency of my request, she pulled me toward her seating area and we sat down. "What is it?"

"First, I need to know what happened between you and Marcellus." Ever since hearing my brother had locked her away, I struggled to understand why he would go to such lengths. Unless ...

Selene bit her lip and shrugged. "Nothing."

If she didn't want to tell me, I wouldn't push. But I still needed to know ... "Do you like him, Selene?"

Her eyes remained locked on her clasped hands in her lap. "Yeah, he seems nice."

"No." I shook my head. "That's not what I mean. Do you *like* him?"

Her eyes widened and she finally met my eyes. "I—"

I squeezed her shoulder. "It's okay if you do. That's nothing to be ashamed about."

She returned her attention to the clasped hands in her lap. "He seems so ... genuine, Leila. But realistically, I know nothing can happen. We're too ... different. Our worlds are not the same."

I wanted to agree but didn't know how without hurting her feelings. "If you feel safe here, that's fine and completely understandable. But if you want to leave, let me know now so we can come up with a plan to free you."

Her brows shot up. "Free me?"

I nodded. "I don't like the idea of you being locked in your room against your will. We already know Madam Rose is not to be trusted. You better believe that old bat has something up her sleeve. There's no way she would allow her most popular girl to sit out for so long, no matter how much Marcellus paid her. It's bad for business if others get the idea they can pay to have their favorite girl be all theirs."

"Madam Rose has been unusually quiet lately," Selene admitted.

I leaned closer, the urgency of our situation prompting a fervency in my voice. "Then you understand why I'm worried. If you want to leave, we need to act fast."

Selene's eyes drilled into mine and a storm of emotions swirled within them—fear, uncertainty, and the shadow of longing for freedom she hadn't allowed herself to fully embrace.

"But don't feel pressured, Selene. If you truly want to stay, I'll understand. I just want to give you a choice."

Selene shook her head. "No, you're right. I need to leave. If I don't now, I never will."

"Alright, then. What's our plan?"

21

After climbing out of Selene's window and hopping to the next roof with no issue, I returned to the inn to rest for the few scant hours left of the night. Unfortunately, sleep never came. I tossed and turned and anxiously thought about my plan the next night for breaking Selene out of the Rose Petal. The plan was dangerous and risky. Madam Rose would dispatch slave hunters the instant she discovered Selene was missing. Unless ...

I considered Orion's offer to go to Ellyndor. Slave hunters couldn't step foot in that place.

I was adamantly opposed to returning to fae lands, but for Selene's sake, I would. Ellyndor was a lovely place, but it was the last place I'd resided with Sir Edric before he died, and it held sad memories. And although his death was an accident, you never knew with the fae. They were a tricky lot.

Once the sun slowly inched over the horizon, I finally admitted I wouldn't find rest. Sitting up with a groan, I bathed and got dressed, then carefully wound the cloth around my face and hoped no one would recognize me.

When I went downstairs for breakfast, Orion was waiting

for me in the dining room. I almost laughed ... Almost. Knowing it was futile to try to slip away before he saw me, I took a seat across from him. "I guess I can't hide anywhere in Lomewood."

He smirked. "Good morning to you, too. I told you, Leila, I'll always find you."

"Because *that's* not creepy," I mumbled. "You're like, a million years old and—"

"Trust me, Leila," he cut me off. "I'm not interested in you romantically. Not even a little. Compared to me, you're a child. Now Selene, on the other hand ..." He grinned.

Merfolk lived long lives, similar to the fae. Selene would outlive me by centuries. That was probably why Orion was interested in her. "Don't even think about it. Selene deserves someone better," I growled.

Orion snorted. "Like who? Prince Marcellus?" he scoffed. "He'll make her his what? Fifth wife? You and I both know your brother wouldn't look at her twice if she weren't one of the merfolk."

Marcellus wasn't married, to my knowledge, but I did remember him saying he would make Selene his second wife. The thought made me furious. "That doesn't mean *you're* worthy of her!" I snapped.

"Oh?" He raised a brow. "You seem quite protective of the mermaid. You should be careful of showcasing your attachment so openly. Someone might get the idea to use her against you to get what they want."

I snorted. "They could try it, but they'll feel my wrath. And I won't hold back."

"You would expose your blood magic for her?" he asked quietly.

I nodded. "In a heartbeat."

"Are you sure you two are just friends?" he asked with a sly smirk.

"What we are is none of your business!" I glared at him. "What do you want, Orion?"

He shrugged. "You already know what I want, but I'm a patient person. I can wait."

I frowned and considered his offer. "If I follow you to Ellyndor ... could I bring Selene with me?"

His brows shot up. "She wants to run away? Wouldn't that bring you even more difficulties than you have today?"

"Slave hunters can't cross the borders of Ellyndor," I replied confidently. "Besides, I can't leave her behind."

He nodded. "I could always buy her freedom," he offered. I was about to interject when he cut me off. "*And* I would provide her with her slave release documents immediately. She would be free."

My eyes widened. "Really?"

"Really," he confirmed.

If Orion bought Selene's freedom, then I wouldn't need to sneak her out of the Rose Petal tonight. But I still needed to let her know about the change of plan. Otherwise, she would be waiting for me all night and worry when I didn't show up.

I held Orion's piercing stare and attempted to discern the sincerity behind his words. Every ounce of instinct warned me of the peril in trusting the fae, yet the allure of Selene's freedom was an undeniable force.

"Why?" I finally asked, my voice a low murmur amidst the growing hum of the inn's waking life. The question hung heavily in the air. Why would a powerful fae extend such an offer? What did he want in exchange?

"Consider it a gesture of goodwill," Orion replied smoothly, his eyes glittering with an unreadable expression. "A demonstration of my commitment to protecting you as promised."

I leaned back, my mind a storm of emotions and thoughts. The complications of accepting help from Orion were evident, yet Selene's safety, her freedom, was paramount.

"Alright," I finally conceded. "But secure Selene's freedom first. *Then* we can talk about my journey to Ellyndor."

Orion's lips curled into a victorious smile. "Deal," he said, extending his hand towards me.

I eyed it warily, the gravity of an unbreakable pact with a fae not lost upon me. With a reluctant yet determined grip, our hands met, sealing an alliance forged in the fires of mutual need and expedience.

The day unfolded with a looming sense of the impending journey ahead. As the sun began its descent, painting the skies with hues of fuchsia and purple, I began my preparations.

Evening arrived with an eerie silence, a haunting prelude to the journey ahead. I walked to the Rose Petal for hopefully the last time, the heavy burden of the deal I'd made with Orion weighing down my shoulders.

Bright lights illuminated the Rose Petal's front steps. Bypassing the front door, I strode out of the darkness toward the back of the pleasure house when someone slipped out of the shadows and stood in front of me. At first, I thought it was Orion and rolled my eyes. "What do you want now? Our conversation is over. I already agreed to—" I started, but didn't finish.

The man before me snorted and slid into the moonlight. With a start, I realized it *definitely* wasn't Orion.

I furrowed my brows. "Who are you?"

"I can be whoever you want me to be," he stated and took a step toward me.

He was tall and muscular, with broad shoulders and arms that dwarfed many others. He wore black from head to toe like me, and his grin widened when he saw me checking him out. I couldn't see the full details of his face from the darkness, only the angled contours of his body, but the man was obviously a warrior.

"I think you have me confused with someone else." I tried to sidestep him, but he moved with me.

"No. I think I got the right person. Leila, isn't it?" he questioned.

"The healer?"

I frowned. How did he know who I was? My face was covered. It may not be a good enough disguise for those who knew me, but it was certainly sufficient to pass amongst strangers. "Who are you?" I demanded.

His grin widened. "I'm your worst nightmare." Reaching over his shoulder to the scabbard on his back, he unsheathed his sword and charged toward me with murderous intent.

Adrenaline surging through my veins, I quickly jumped out of the way and ducked under his swing. Every sense was amplified. The night's eerie silence was punctuated by the harsh rasp of our labored breaths and the cold ring of steel. His sword cut through the air where I stood seconds earlier. Moonlight glinted menacingly off the blade, a reminder of the razor-thin margin between life and death.

I was unarmed, aided only by my mage magic which I wasn't ready to reveal. The locals thought I was human, which allowed me to blend amongst the populace. The instant they learned of my magic, those days were over. That left only my instincts against an armed assailant whose intentions, though unclear, were undeniably lethal.

I darted away, my nimble agility proving advantageous against his lumbering brute strength. He was fast, but I was faster. Every swing of his sword met only air as I dodged, though my breath came in ragged gasps.

Despite the terror and adrenaline, my mind raced. Who was this man? Why did he want me dead? The questions swirled in my head, each one amplifying the palpable danger of the moment.

I scanned my surroundings as I moved, searching for anything that could be used as a weapon. My assailant was relentless. The cold determination in his eyes was a haunting mirror of the lethal precision of his attacks.

I felt exposed and vulnerable in my dark attire, a target against the moonlit night. Each slash of his sword, each near miss, amplified the chilling realization of the peril in which I found myself.

In the adrenaline-fueled dance of attack and evasion, a plan began to form. I needed to disarm him or, at the very least, create enough distance to escape. The streets were deserted and the usual nightlife of the Rose Petal was absorbed within its walls, oblivious to the deadly attacks unfolding in its shadows.

A near miss and the harsh rasp of steel cutting the air beside my ear brought my focus back. In that moment of lucid clarity, I saw my opportunity. When he lunged, I sidestepped and grabbed his extended arm, then used his momentum to send him crashing into the wall.

Temporary relief was found when the sword clattered to the ground, but I knew I didn't have much time. He was bigger, stronger, and would recover quickly.

I spun on my heels, ready to make a mad dash out of there when I slammed into someone else's chest. Startled, I looked up to meet Caelan's hazel eyes.

He gripped my upper arms to steady me and keep me from falling. "Leila?" he asked with a raised brow. Reaching for the face covering, he pulled it down to expose my face.

I guess I wasn't as hidden as I thought I was.

I stumbled away from Caelan, knowing he was just as bad as my mystery attacker. When I turned to run, the prince grabbed me and swung me to the side. Only when I heard the swish of a sword did I realize he'd just saved my life.

I furrowed my brows, confused. In Caelan's eyes, I was the enemy because of my complicated relationship with Ronan. Why would he help me?

Caelan's sword clashed against that of my mystery attacker, the metallic resonance echoing in the otherwise still night. I stood there frozen, caught between the urge to flee and the bewildering sight before me. Caelan, a man who had every reason to despise me, stood between me and an assailant whose intentions were clear—to kill me.

My heart pounded loudly in my ears, a miasma of confusion and adrenaline. Every stroke of their swords, every parry and attack revealed a dance of deadly intent unfolding before my eyes.

In the midst of the chaos, my eyes locked with Caelan's. Cold fury lit his gaze with a darkness that had nothing to do with the night's shadows. Yet, in that moment, the enmity between us was eclipsed by a graver threat.

The mystery attacker was skilled, his movements precise and lethal. Caelan matched him stroke for stroke.

"I never thought the great Prince Caelan from Eldwain would protect Ronan's woman," the mystery assailant sneered.

His words caught me off guard. It was obvious the men knew each other.

Caelan smirked. "And *I* never thought the infamous Commander Mykal Kaiser of Keldara would dare show his face in the Central Plains. But what are the odds?"

Keldara?

My gaze whipped to the commander and I fisted my hands at my sides. Anger surged through me at the sight of my sworn enemy.

Caelan stood in front of me, using his body as a shield. "What are you doing?" I murmured so only he could hear me.

"You know who he is, Leila," Caelan muttered back. "I might not like you, but even *I* wouldn't wish him upon my enemy. Keldara will show you no mercy."

The clash of steel rang through the air as Caelan and Mykal locked in combat again. I knew the reputation of the Keldaran forces—brutal, merciless, and unyielding. My family and people suffered under their cruel hands when they invaded Valoria. Every stroke of Caelan's sword against Mykal's was imbued with the memory of their atrocities.

The menace in Mykal's gaze was as chilling as the winds that swept through the silent night. "You're making a big mistake, Prince," Mykal taunted as their swords clashed again. "We have a common enemy. We should be working together. Sending her head to the Crimson Clan would be a wonderful sight."

"Not if I kill you first!" I growled. I scanned the area for a weapon but found nothing. That left me with only one option. I was a mage; I had magic within me. Now that I knew who he was, I wasn't afraid to show what I could do. Besides, Caelan already knew I was a mage ... just not what kind. I still had to keep that part hidden.

I closed my eyes for a moment and summoned the energy within me. The power of my magic simmered beneath my skin, a fierce, wild force ready to be unleashed. Mykal's grating laughter echoed in the night, fueling the fire within me.

I stretched out my hand, my eyes blazing with untapped power. The air around us crackled with electricity, an ominous precursor to the storm of power about to be unleashed. Mykal's laughter ceased and his eyes widened when he comprehended his imminent danger. The cold, harsh light of realization dawned in his eyes.

"You have no idea what you're dealing with, do you?" I spat. The energy pulsing through my veins lent a fierce tremor to my voice. A sudden blast of power shot from my hand, swift and lethal. Mykal deftly dodged the flare, his agility a testament to battle-hardened skills. But I was unrelenting as I unleashed my power in a torrential downpour of wrath and vengeance.

The night was shattered by the fearsome clash of magic and steel. With Caelan fighting alongside me, our combined forces

—magic and sword—were formidable adversaries against the menacing threat of the Commander of Keldara.

Mykal, outnumbered but undaunted, fought with the vicious tenacity of a man with nothing to lose. Each swing of his sword was a stark reminder of the unyielding cruelty of Keldara—a cruelty that left scars etched deep within my soul.

Caelan and I fought side by side, the enmity between us momentarily suspended in the face of a graver threat. It was a reluctant alliance; each stroke of his sword and my magic was an acknowledgment of a mutual enemy.

Mykal careened over the asphalt when my magic blasted him several feet away from us. Battered but not broken, he used his sword to hold himself up. "This isn't over!" he growled.

As Mykal retreated into the night, defeated but not vanquished, Caelan and I were left in the haunting stillness of the aftermath. Our breathing was heavy. For many minutes, we didn't speak.

"Why are you here?" I asked once I'd caught my breath. "Don't you want to kill me, too?" I frowned.

He laughed and fought to catch his breath. "Yeah ... I thought I did. Guess not as much as I thought."

"I'm not your enemy, Caelan. I never was," I said.

"Excuse me?" He furrowed his brows and looked me up and down. "Aren't you getting a little too comfortable?"

Confused, I tilted my head and tried to remember what I said that must have offended him. Then I realized I forgot to address him as *Your Highness*. I smacked a hand over my mouth at my mistake. "I'm sorry," I muttered. "I didn't—"

He laughed and waved me off. "It's okay. I'm not as strict with honorifics as Marcellus is."

I winced at my blunder. "So what are you going to do now? Arrest me?"

He narrowed his eyes and then shook his head. "No. I'm not."

"Why?"

He raised a brow. "Do you *want* me to arrest you?"

"No! Of course not!"

He chuckled. "Then don't ask why. Just accept my favor."

"I know ... but you really didn't have to get involved."

"No, I didn't. But like I told you, the Keldaran might be human, but their force is in their military. They are trained to fight people like you and me, and Commander Mykal has a fearsome reputation for cruelty. I wouldn't want even my worst enemy to fall into his hands."

Having witnessed Caelan's cruelty first-hand, I shuddered to think how much worse Mykal would be. "He looks awfully young to be a commander of an army," I mused.

"He is. He rose up the ranks from a very young age and is the king's most trusted advisor. I suggest you be careful. Next to the King of Keldara, Commander Mykal Kaiser is the most powerful."

Understanding the situation before me, I nodded. I should have taken advantage of the situation and killed Mykal when I had the chance, but I didn't know how important he was to his people. Even if I had to expose myself, it would have been worth it to rid the world of such a menace.

"Are you okay?" Caelan asked. "You're gritting your teeth so hard, I'm afraid you're going to chip a tooth."

I snapped my gaze in his direction and relaxed a bit. "Sorry," I mumbled. "Just lost in thought. Why are you here, anyway, Your Highness? Shouldn't you be preparing to attack the Crimson Clan?" I asked cheekily.

"Marcellus is leading the army. It's *his*, anyway, as someone reminded me earlier." He narrowed his eyes on me. "Don't think I'll share any secrets with you, because I won't. I still don't trust you."

I laughed. "I know. I just found it odd that you're here and not out in the wilderness with the rest of the army."

He nodded. "I got wind of Commander Mykal roaming Lomewood's streets and decided to take advantage and get him off the chess board."

I winced. "Oh. I guess I messed that up for you, huh?"

He shook his head. "No, he's crafty. I knew there was a good chance I wouldn't catch him." He sighed and straightened. "Well, this is where we part, Leila. Stay safe."

I smiled up at him. "Thanks." When he turned to leave, I murmured, "Now *that's* the Caelan I know and love."

He stopped mid-stride and peered over his shoulder with a frown. "What did you say?"

My eyes widened in shock. "Nothing! I didn't say anything."

He paused for a moment before he turned back around and walked down the dark, lonely streets of Lomewood.

⁓

I SNUCK into the Rose Petal again and stealthily made my way to Selene's room on the second floor. I entered without knocking and shut the door behind me. Tiptoeing into the room, I found Selene sitting in front of her dresser mirror, combing her long, raven black hair.

"Selene?" I whispered.

She nearly jumped out of her skin, then spun around in her chair with a sigh of relief. "Oh, thank the gods! I thought you were never going to show up." She stood quickly and gave me a fierce hug. "All my personal belongings are packed and I'm ready to go."

I pulled away. "There's been a change of plans, Selene."

She frowned. "We're not leaving?"

"Yes, we are, just not tonight and not this way." I ushered her back to her seat and gently set her down. "I don't want you to be chased by slave hunters for the rest of your life. It's not fair to you, especially when the trouble is because of *me*. So I ... I made a deal with Orion." I bit my lower lip.

"A deal? With Orion? The fae?" she asked in succession.

I nodded. "Yes. He's offered to pay for your freedom before, but I always shot him down because I assumed there would be strings attached. But he promised me he would give you your slave release document right away, which would permanently free you. You wouldn't have to worry about it ever again."

Her eyes widened and she gasped. "Really?"

"Really." I smiled at her.

"Can ... can you trust him?" she asked worriedly.

That was a loaded question. Could I? I wasn't sure. But I knew what he was offering me, and I couldn't think of any possible loopholes that could possibly trip me up. Also ... he claimed he was here to protect me, and I had to believe Sir Edric sent him to me for a reason. I trusted Sir Edric with my life.

"Yes. I think we can," I answered with as much confidence as I could muster.

She nibbled her thumbnail, a nervous tick of hers.

"Don't worry, Selene. Everything will work out the way it's supposed to. I promise. I'll protect you."

She sighed. "I know you'll do anything to protect me, but that's what I'm afraid of. I don't want to put you in harm's way. I'm not worth it and—"

"Don't say that, Selene. You're more than worth it. Don't ever put yourself down like that. You're only in this situation because your shitty father sold you. Not because you *wanted* to be a courtesan. You're one of the merfolk, for God's sake! You shouldn't be here."

She lowered her head in shame. "I stopped being one of the merfolk long ago," she muttered.

I tipped her chin to look up at me. "Do you want to go back to the Luminar Sea?" I asked. The bioluminescent ocean was off the coast of Keldara and home to the merfolk. "Be honest with me, Selene. I will do everything in my power to send you home, even if I have to take you there myself."

Selene reached for my hand where it held her chin. "I would never ask you to cross the borders into Keldara," she whispered and squeezed my hand. "But if I ever want to go home, I'll tell you. I promise."

"Good." I smiled down at her. "Now be prepared, because Orion will be coming here in the coming days to buy you from Madam Rose. Wait for him, no matter what happens."

She nodded. "I will ... Thank you, Leila."

22

I escaped the Rose Petal through Selene's window and hopped from rooftop to rooftop until I could scale down a storefront and drop onto the street. Covering my face again, I was about to dart into the shadows when a familiar figure appeared in the quiet street. I narrowed my eyes and my stomach dropped when I realized it was Mykal.

He prowled toward me at a leisurely pace. Once he stood under the moonlight, I saw he wasn't alone. A group of six other Keldaran soldiers was with him.

"I underestimated you, Healer," he said. "I didn't realize you were a mage ... but it's all starting to make sense now." He laughed and ran a hand through his short brown hair. His companions shifted on their feet but remained quiet.

My earlier fear that I would expose myself if I used my blood mage magic reared its ugly head. I slowly edged back the way I came.

"You see, usually mages are from Valoria." Mykal pointed to his forehead. "But you're lacking the one element that would distinguish you as Valorian."

The crescent moon birthmark every Valorian has, he didn't add.

"I don't know what you think you know, but I don't have any ties to the Crimson Clan. Killing me will do nothing for your cause," I said with more bravado than I felt.

He tilted his head and grinned. "Is that so? On the contrary, darling. I think you'll be the match that lights this fire."

I frowned. I wasn't sure what he meant by that, and in all honesty, I didn't care to find out. I stopped inching back and stood my ground. "You don't want to fight me," I gritted through my teeth.

He smirked. "I like a challenge." Slicing his hand upward, he dropped it in a chopping motion, signaling his soldiers to attack.

Without hesitation, all six charged toward me at full speed. I could turn and run, but I couldn't outrun all of them. And even if I did, where would I run to? Back to the pleasure house? Madam Rose would gladly have me arrested to collect the bounty on my head.

When the first three soldiers reached me, I blasted them back with a burst of my power and then ran toward them, scooping a fallen sword to fight the other three who were closing in fast. Steel clashed against steel as I ducked and wove through the cadre of Keldaran soldiers. One swiped his sword in a killing arc toward my head, which I narrowly avoided by leaning back. As the blade sliced through the air where I'd stood, I ducked another sword thrust and slashed my borrowed sword through the man's back.

One down.

One of the soldiers grabbed my throat and squeezed my wrist hard enough to crack bone, then twisted it. My sword dropped from my useless wrist, but I caught it lightning fast with my other hand and stabbed him in the gut.

Two down.

The men didn't offer me a moment's respite. Chains snaked out from the shadows to wrap around my wrists and ankles.

One soldier tugged on the chains and my wrist slackened. My sword clattered to the street.

Slowly, Mykal strolled up to me wearing a smug grin. "You're a good fighter ... just not as good as we are," he said, gloating. "Also, we came prepared. You see, once I knew you were a mage, I realized you need the use of your hands to wield your magic. Which, as you can see, we've taken care of. But that's not all. Do you feel it?"

With a frown, I slowed my galloping heartbeat and felt the chains around me. With a start, I felt my power leaching from my skin. "What is this?" I tugged against the chains even more frantically.

Mykal laughed. "To fight Valoria, we discovered ways to conquer their mages. We learned that harsh lesson ten years ago, which was why we failed. But now ... we've found Aetherite. This material weakens mages as effectively as iron diminishes the fae."

My eyes widened. "Where did you get this?"

He chuckled. "Don't worry about that. Aren't you concerned with your life? It's completely in my hands."

I scoffed. "Kill me and do it quickly. I'm losing patience."

He stepped closer and tightly gripped my chin, pushing my face to look up at him. "Kill you?" He tilted his head and shook it. "No. Now that I can see you clearly, I realize you're too pretty to kill," he said with a knowing smirk.

Before I had a chance to muster a snarky remark, someone clubbed the back of my head and knocked me out cold.

∽

My eyes were heavy and gritty, but that discomfort was nothing compared to the throbbing pain in my skull that beat a rhythm with my heart. I slowly regained consciousness and my eyes fluttered open. I quickly noticed my hands were tied behind me, though thankfully with rope instead of the chains those goons had used earlier. My feet were unbound. Another stroke of good fortune.

I was in a tent, probably somewhere in the mountains or vast wilderness of the Central Plains wherever the Keldaran army was hiding. I sat up and leaned against the tree that acted as the tent's center pole, then glanced around for anything I could use to slice the ropes that bound my wrists.

I slowly rubbed the ropes back and forth against the rough tree bark with enough friction to hopefully shear the woven threads. This would take a while, which meant I had to employ patience that wore thin with each passing moment. Unfortunately, this wasn't the first time I'd been captured, but it meant I had experience in a situation such as this. Time was my greatest weapon.

The repetitive, sawing motion of my arms and shoulders was tiring, and I had to take several breaks. I was half-convinced I would pop my shoulder out of its socket before the ropes would fray, but eventually, I felt the rope tearing. Soon, I would be free. Then, I heard movement outside. I stopped and strained my ears.

"Is the Crimson whore inside?" someone with a gruff voice asked.

There was a grunt before someone else answered, "She's inside."

Heavy footfalls sounded before the tent flaps opened and two Keldaran soldiers walked inside. They were big, like *scary* big. I shrank inward as they took up most of the space within the tent.

One of the men scratched his bald head. "Well, look what we have here! The Crimson whore."

His companion laughed. "I'm sure after she made the rounds in their camp, they threw her out once they were done with her."

I narrowed my gaze. Their words didn't bother me. They could think whatever they wanted. What worried me was their intent.

The two soldiers circled me and slowly began to untuck their shirts and unbutton their trousers.

"She might as well be of use to us while she's here. Isn't that right?" the bald headed one asked me.

I kept quiet and steeled myself for the impending attack.

He knelt in front of me, grabbed my legs, and attempted to spread them wide. I tightened my knees together and tried to kick at him.

"Don't touch me!" I yelled. "I swear I'll kill you!"

He laughed. "You? Kill me? Well, isn't that funny. Right, Sam?"

His friend dipped his hand into his pants and groaned. "Come on, James," Sam rushed the bald soldier. "Quit your yapping and get on with it. I don't have all day!"

James reached for my trouser button and tore the fabric. Panic rose like bile, and I kicked and screamed for all I was worth. The force was enough to unravel the loosened rope threads and they broke loose with a pop. Grabbing the man's bald head with both hands, I dug my thumbs into his eye sockets.

His agonized scream alerted his friend to the fact I was no longer bound. Sam pulled his hand out of his pants and backhanded me hard enough to split my lip and draw blood. I released his filthy companion and cowered against the tent's edge.

"Stupid bitch!" The soldier grabbed a hunk of my hair and dragged me across the ground into an open space. Flinging me away forcefully, I fell onto my side with a wince. Then he dropped to the ground and grabbed my legs in a punishing grip I knew would leave bruises.

I kicked like my life depended on it, because it did.

"Come on, girl, play nice like you did for those Crimson barbarians," Sam grunted as he tried to restrain my flailing legs and arms.

"Get off me!" I screamed. In my panic-fueled state, I couldn't keep my powers at bay any longer. I began to boil his blood, focusing on the vessels in his head.

He wiped sweat off his forehead and breathed heavily. "James!" he called out to his bald friend. "Is it just me or is it incredibly hot right now?"

James, who was temporarily blinded and still kneeling on the ground answered, "It's just you, mate."

My hate was a living, breathing entity as I glared at my would-be rapist. "I said I'd kill you if you touched me!" I whirled my legs out and locked them around his neck before pinning him to the ground. Startled, he released my wrists.

"Fuckin' bitch!" Sam growled as I choked him.

James crawled around the tent with squinted eyes, trying to locate his friend. "What's going on, Sam?"

I tightened my legs and heard the satisfying crunch of broken cartilage. Sam tried to drag slips of air through his crushed windpipe and wheezed, "Help!"

When James crawled within arm's reach, I punched him in the throat and sent him careening to the ground with another howl of pain.

In the midst of all this, the tent flaps opened and Mykal strode into the chaos. He frowned and demanded, "What in the bloody hell is going on?"

Two soldiers ran inside the tent, their eyes wide and startled. They dipped their heads and saluted. "Where were you two?" he asked the guards.

"We uh ... were taking a quick break," one of them muttered. "We left her with Sam and James," he quickly added.

Mykal flicked his eyes over Sam and James, who gasped and

choked for air, then he turned his attention to me. "And you're free because?" he questioned with a frown.

"These two just tried to assault me!" I growled and tightened my legs around Sam's windpipe.

Mykal's expression darkened with a ferocity I'd never encountered on someone's face before. For a second, I thought it was directed at me. Then he lunged and grabbed James by the scruff of his neck.

"Is this true?" he demanded of the burly man who was still trying to catch his breath.

"We ... we weren't ... doing ... anything wrong, Commander!" the man gasped. "She's just a Crimson whore—"

"Watch your mouth!" Mykal yelled. "I don't care *who* she is! No one gave you permission to touch her!"

The bald man's eyes bulged. "But we thought—"

"You thought wrong." Mykal tossed him aside with a disgusted sneer. "You two!" He pointed to the hapless guards. "Forty lashings for leaving your post. As for these two ..." he motioned to James and Sam, "behead them and toss their corpses into the mountains for the wolves."

"Commander, please!" James begged. "We're sorry!" He crawled and grabbed Mykal's pant leg, but Mykal kicked him away.

"I didn't train you to be mindless savages," he spat. "You know my rules: no second chances." He pointed to Sam, but directed his command to me. "Release him. He'll get what he deserves. Follow me."

Without checking to see if I would obey, Mykal stormed out of the tent. I contemplated whether to stay or follow, and reluctantly chose the latter. I unlocked my legs from around Sam's throat and rushed past the stunned guards, jogging to catch up to Mykal's long strides.

The sprawling Keldaran camp was far larger than I imagined. Rows upon rows of meticulously arranged tents were separated with ample space for quick mobilization. Campfires glowed in the distance, the light reflecting off the Keldaran soldiers' polished armor. The murmurs of men, distant clangs of swords against shields, and soft horse wickers combined to create a symphony of organized chaos.

Giant banners bearing the emblem of Keldara—a fierce, rearing black stallion set against a backdrop of blood-red – billowed majestically in the stout breeze to mark the heart of the army's territory. Sentries stationed at regular intervals glanced suspiciously at Mykal and me as we crossed the camp, their eyes scrutinizing every movement, the grip on their spears unwavering.

After a few minutes, we arrived at a tent that was much larger than the ones surrounding it. I paused just outside before Mykal backtracked to the opening, grabbed my arm, and hauled me into the tent.

The opulence was evident inside the Commander's tent. Thick canvas walls were lined with ornate tapestries depicting glorious Keldaran battles. Torches were placed in bronze holders, casting a warm, golden hue across the spacious interior. The sleeping area was cordoned off with a lavish curtain of deep blue velvet, embroidered with gold thread. The plush bed, complete with intricately designed posts and drapery, looked inviting, the thick furs and soft pillows indicating a taste for luxury.

Adjacent to the sleeping quarters, the office area was dominated by a massive wooden desk with maps of different territories, inkpots, quills, and official-looking parchments cluttering its surface. The mahogany chair behind the desk had intricate carvings of Keldaran victories and a cushioned seat, emphasizing the importance of the person who sat there.

To the right, a dining area boasted a long wooden table, polished to a mirror shine, surrounded by chairs draped in furs.

Goblets and plates with remnants of food suggested a recently concluded meal.

But it was the throne in the center that snagged my attention. Majestic in design, it was made of dark oak with a high back that soared almost to the tent's lofty ceiling. The arms of the chair were adorned with carvings of rearing stallions, while the seat and back were cushioned with furs from beasts that must have been quite exotic. From the very aura of it, the throne screamed authority.

Mykal dragged me inside and tossed me onto the bed. But instead of attacking me, he walked over to his desk and sat down, shuffling through papers and ignoring me completely.

"Why am I here?" I asked, afraid to move an inch. "Are you really going to kill them? Are you trying to get to Ronan? What do you want with me?"

"What I *want* is for you to be quiet." Obviously irritated, his eyes flicked up from his documents to me.

"But—"

When he placed a finger over his lips to quiet me, I shut up immediately. His eyes were dark with fury, and I wasn't embarrassed to admit I was a bit terrified. With the imposing frame and large, muscular build that was known of all Keldarans, he could easily overpower me.

I made myself comfortable on his bed and waited. It didn't seem like he planned to ravage me, but I couldn't relax. I had to be alert in case he changed his mind.

Roughly a half hour went by before someone outside called into the tent. "Commander, I have a report!"

"Enter," Mykal answered. A soldier walked in with a rolled parchment in hand. "What do you have, General?"

With a sharp salute, the general unrolled the parchment and placed it on Mykal's desk. "We have movement in the east, with Valoria's army camped just north of us. They've sent spies, of course, but we've caught each and every one of them."

Mykal nodded and I stretched to see what they were looking at on the map. I could tell it was marked in different locations, but I wasn't close enough to see what the areas were.

"Send word that we'll attack the Valorian camp tonight," Mykal instructed as he gazed at the map.

The general nodded. "Do you think the Crimson Clan will show?"

Mykal nodded. "Yes. Ronan is reckless in that manner and will want to reap the spoils. Once he sees we're not there, he'll have no other option than to attack."

"Then *you'll* reap the spoils," I finished for him.

Both men looked my way. Mykal smirked, but the general glared. "Mind your business, little girl!" the man snapped.

I rolled my eyes. "I can't help it if you're discussing your plans so loud I can hear," I scoffed. "Also, you're wrong. Ronan won't be that stupid."

Mykal leaned back in his chair and rubbed his jaw, watching me with a calculating gleam.

I continued, "Ronan can be reckless at times, but he cares about his men. He won't send them to their deaths."

"Is that so?" Mykal mused.

"You won't benefit from it," I said with a shrug. "But go on, follow your plan and see how well it goes." I leaned back and reclined on his bed as if unbothered by the men staring at me.

"Don't listen to that Crimson whore, Commander. She doesn't know anything except how to spread her legs to any savage who comes her way!" the general spat.

I snorted. "For your information, I'm the town healer, not some prostitute like you're probably used to."

"You!" The general started to charge toward me, but Mykal stopped him with a raised hand.

"She's off limits."

"But Commander—"

"I don't like to repeat myself." Mykal sent the general a glare that stopped anything else he was about to say. "Continue with the plan. Let's see how accurate our dear Leila's information is."

"Yes, Commander." The general bowed and exited the tent, but not without sending me a final glare. I waved goodbye and sent him a cheeky smile.

"You sure like to stir the pot everywhere you go," Mykal chuckled as he watched me.

I shrugged. "I only speak facts."

"We'll see. Leila, I am curious about your relationship with Ronan." He leaned back and crossed his arms over his barrel chest. "I mean, he's been waiting for the lost princess for most of his life. It's ... odd to see him taken by another woman."

I looked away. "He's not taken by me."

"The fact that you think he's not is what makes you interesting." He gave me a knowing look. "Good thing *you're* not the lost princess." He sighed as he rolled up his sleeves and went back to his documents. "Now *that* would be rotten luck."

I frowned. "Why?"

He peered up at me and raised a brow. "You don't know?"

"If I did, I wouldn't be asking." I rolled my eyes.

Mykal laughed. "I just figured since you're such good friends with Ronan, he would have told you."

I shrugged and glanced away as if I wasn't hanging on his every word. "That just goes to show you we're not that good of friends," I muttered.

He smirked. "All right, I believe you. But why are you so curious about the lost princess? Do you know her?"

I shook my head. "Not at all."

"Good." He chuckled. "Death is all her future holds."

I whipped my gaze in his direction and gasped. "What?"

His grin widened. "Why so shocked? It's almost as if ..."

"I'm just curious!" I cut him off.

He looked at me and nodded. "Fine, fine, I'll stop messing with you. If you truly want to know what fate awaits the lost princess, I'll tell you." He raised one eyebrow. "But I'll warn you ... once you know, you can't unknow it."

I groaned. "Just tell me."

"Very well." He stood from his desk and strode toward where I sat on his bed. "There's a prophecy that the Crimson Clan is trying to realize. One that will bring back the Demon Fox, from whom they originate."

I sighed. "What does that have to do with the lost princess?"

He waved me off. "Slow down. I'm getting to it," he smirked. "The prophecy states that the only way to revive the Demon Fox, who was sealed away by the Moon Goddess, is with the return of the next female Blood Weaver."

"The Moon Goddess?" I murmured. The Moon Goddess was the deity in whom my people believed. Who we, the royal family, got our blood magic from. Until I came along, she was the one and only female blood mage in history.

Warming up to his story, Mykal continued. "You may or may not know that the Moon Goddess used to be the only female blood mage, which was for a reason. The Moon Goddess sealed the Demon Fox away using blood magic. The prophecy claims that only a female descendent can wake him, which was why she cursed her bloodline from ever producing a female heir ... until Princess Lyanna."

This history belonged to my people, yet I never learned it. Why? That was a question for my parents. Unfortunately, I had no way of asking them.

"So ... the Crimson Clan wants to use the lost princess to wake up the Demon Fox?" I guessed.

He shook his head and wagged a finger. "No, no. They don't just want to *use* her; they want to *sacrifice* her to the Demon Fox. Only her blood can wake him."

I frowned. "You're lying." I thought back to all my encounters with Ronan. He would never hurt me! At least, I didn't think he would. I couldn't see him agreeing to this. He—

Seeing the wheels spinning in my head, Mykal said, "If I'm lying, then you can ask Ronan yourself. Although," he sighed heavily, "you don't need to worry about any of this since ... you're not the lost princess," he smirked.

My mouth snapped shut. I was getting angry and reacting in a way that the simple healer Leila from the Central Plains wouldn't.

"I don't believe you," I scoffed. "You made all of that up to make them look like—"

"Like bad people? Because they *are*, Leila." His eyes hardened. "Ten years ago, they dispatched an envoy to Valoria to discuss a trade for the princess, but the King and Queen of Valoria refused to give up their only daughter. Hence, the Crimson Clan's alliance with us to attack Valoria and kidnap her."

"They ... they went to Valoria to ask for the princess?" I asked, my mouth hanging open in shock.

Mykal nodded. "This isn't common knowledge," he whispered. "So keep it between us." He winked and leaned against his desk. "Too bad we couldn't find Princess Lyanna when we invaded Valoria. Had I been the Commander back then, I would not have failed."

I snorted and mumbled, "Right," then stood from the bed and began to pace. "Let's say I believe you," I started. "Why does the Crimson Clan rely so heavily on Ronan to complete this prophecy?" I remembered Silas's words—*The fate of the Crimson Clan depends on Ronan.*

Mykal chuckled. "Ah, I'd rather keep *that* little tidbit to myself," he said, offering a secret smile. "Let's just say that Princess Lyanna's maidenhood is vital for the resurrection of the Demon Fox."

"You mean she has to be a virgin?" I asked with furrowed brows.

He grinned. "Yes, but it must be taken by Ronan."

My eyes widened until I was sure they would pop out of their sockets. My virginity needed to be taken ... by Ronan? Did he know about this the other day when we almost ...

I felt sick. Beyond sick. Lightheaded, I held on to the headboard to stabilize myself.

Mykal frowned. "Are you okay, Leila?" he asked sincerely.

I gasped for air as panic ensued. "I—I need—air," I choked out.

Mykal came toward me, gripping my face with both hands and tilting my head back to look up at him. "Breathe, Leila," he whispered to me. "Calm your racing heart and breathe. Don't make me use other methods ..."

I shook my head and my eyes welled with unshed tears. "I—I can't!"

"Damnit," he murmured before smashing his lips onto mine.

I sucked in one lungful of air before it was cut off. As his soft lips melded with mine and his tongue snaked into my mouth, I was lost, my panic momentarily distracted by the intensity of his kiss.

It was both desperate and commanding, as if he was trying to pull the panic from me through our joined lips. My mind spun until I couldn't comprehend the warmth, sensation, and sheer audacity of Mykal's actions. The juxtaposition of fear, anger, and confusion tangled my thoughts in a storm of emotions.

When he finally pulled away, I was in a daze. The world seemed to regain its focus slowly and I stumbled backward, touching my lips with trembling fingers. "Why ...?" My voice trailed off and the weight of the situation pressed down upon me.

Mykal's expression was inscrutable. Vulnerability lingered behind his eyes, which seemed at odds with his earlier aggression. "When the mind can't be controlled, distract it," he answered lightly, trying to maintain a nonchalant tone.

I tried to find my voice, my anger, my defenses, but all that came out was a feeble, "That wasn't a distraction. That was an invasion."

He sighed and ran a hand through his dark hair. "You were panicking, and I couldn't think of a faster way to snap you out of it."

"We're *enemies*, Mykal. You can't just … kiss me when you feel like it!" I retorted. As my wits returned, my indignant fire nipped on its heels.

He stepped closer and locked his intense gaze onto mine. "Maybe that's the problem. Maybe we shouldn't be enemies."

An eerie silence enveloped the tent and the weight of his words seemed to press down on both of us. The atmosphere was thick with unsaid words and unfinished business. In that moment, the world outside ceased to exist.

He didn't know it, but he would always be my enemy. Whether I was the healer Leila from the Central Plains or Princess Lyanna from Valoria. As long as he was Keldaran, I would always hate him.

I raised my chin defiantly. "Don't ever do that again." Spinning around, I primly sat back down on the edge of his bed.

I was ashamed that I'd lost control in enemy territory. And whether I wanted to admit it or not, Mykal was right: distraction was key. My panic attack was long forgotten.

I slumped and tried to remember the last night I spent with Ronan. He hesitated … He told me not to push him and I did anyway. Even so, he should have been upfront with me. He should have told me about this prophecy, if what Mykal said was true. The only way I would know for sure was if I managed to escape and confront him.

Mykal observed me keenly, likely trying to piece together my scattered emotions. His previously imposing figure was more subdued now, perhaps sensing the complexity of my internal turmoil. "You're thinking about him, aren't you?" His voice was barely above a whisper, carrying a mix of bitterness and resignation.

I glanced at him, taken aback by his unexpected perceptiveness. "That's none of your concern."

"You wear your emotions like an open book, Leila. Or should I say, *Lyanna*?" His gaze sharpened, revealing the depth of his resentment.

I narrowed my gaze. "You *knew* ...!"

He shrugged. "I put the pieces together. It was fairly obvious, given your rather visceral reaction to learning about the prophecy. I'm just surprised no one else has uncovered your true identity. So ... is the Princess Lyanna thinking about Ronan?"

"Again, none of your concern!" I snapped. "Ronan and I ... It's complicated."

He scoffed. "Isn't it always? Love, loyalties, responsibilities. They're all a web of entanglements. But remember, Princess, while you're tangled in your personal affairs, there's a war looming."

My eyes met his with a steely glare. "I'm well aware of that. And you? What are *you* doing here? Keldara has no business in the Central Plains."

He leaned in closer, his breath warming my face. "Perhaps we have interests that align."

A cold shiver ran down my spine. "Or maybe you're just here to further your own goals, and Keldara intends to use me as a pawn."

He smirked. "Ah, the sharp-witted princess emerges. Good. It's far more entertaining this way."

I took a deep breath. "Whatever games you're playing, Mykal, remember this: I'm not someone to be trifled with."

His gaze roamed my face, searching for any hint of vulnerability. "Oh, I don't doubt that for a moment," he replied, his voice dripping with dangerous intrigue. "But like I said, maybe we don't have to be enemies."

As much as I wanted to deny any possibility of an alliance with Mykal, deep down, a small part of me wondered if there was a sliver of truth in his words. The lines between enemies and allies constantly shifted in the game of war and politics. And in this treacherous dance, one could never truly know where they stood.

"We'll always be enemies," I growled before standing. "Am I a prisoner here, or can I leave?"

Mykal laughed. "So quick to go? Of course you're a prisoner. But don't fret, Princess, I'll let you leave soon."

I frowned. "What are you planning?"

He smirked. "Oh, you'll see." With those parting words, he stepped back and gave me a quick once-over, then laughed and strode out of his tent.

I wrapped my arms around my middle, not quite feeling uncomfortable, but feeling bare. Exposed. It seemed that my secret was no longer a secret. I was out of options.

It was time to return home.

23

I laid on Mykal's bed and picked at a bowl of grapes that had been delivered earlier. After Mykal left, I attempted to step out of his tent but was met with half a dozen guards outside watching over me. I should've known the commander wouldn't leave me with an escape route. Especially after what happened earlier with his soldiers.

Nightfall finally arrived. By my calculations, I'd been sequestered in the tent by myself more than five hours. A guard brought a tray with my dinner and two jugs of wine. Mykal was probably hoping to get me drunk, but he had the wrong prey. I knew when and when *not* to drink. And right now, I needed to keep my wits.

Laughter and shouts rang out from the camp as the Keldaran soldiers drank to their hearts' content and feasted on meat. I could hear them all the way across the camp, along with grumblings from my guards who were upset they were missing out on all the fun.

It was the ideal time to escape with the Keldaran army distracted by food and wine, but fighting the half dozen guards who stood outside the tent would cause a commotion I didn't want or need.

I was pacing the tent when I heard a rip behind me. I whirled around and watched as a knife cut through the back of the tent. With widened eyes, I watched a man in a black cloak slip inside. The hood of his cloak concealed his face. When he reached up to pull it back, Orion stood there with a mischievous grin.

"Ah, there you are," he whispered. "This camp is so large, I thought I'd never find you!"

I sighed in relief. "Thank the gods you're here!" For the first time, I was actually happy to see Orion. "What took you so long? I thought you were supposed to protect me!"

Orion chuckled. "Correct, but it's not easy getting through the Keldaran wards. They're set up to keep the fae and half-fae out. Luckily, I found an unprotected area."

"Don't you find that odd?" I questioned. Keldarans, particularly Mykal, were very careful and deliberate, from what I'd observed so far. He wouldn't leave the camp with any weaknesses.

"I find it extremely odd, but I'm not going to dwell on that now. It's best we leave while they're all drinking their fill." Orion extended his hand to me.

I frowned. "First, answer me this. Did you know what the Crimson Clan plans to do with me?"

He furrowed his brows. "You know, right now is not the best time to discuss this, Leila ..."

I stood my ground, stubbornly refusing his hand. "Answer me! Did you know they were planning to sacrifice me to the Demon Fox?"

Orion sighed and dropped his hand. "Yes. I knew."

My eyes widened and my mouth fell open. "So it's true?"

Orion nodded. "They want to resurrect the Demon Fox, and they need you to do that."

"So ... Ronan ... has been lying to me this whole time?"

"Yes. He has."

Anguish twisted my heart. My chest tightened and anger bubbled within me. The very man who ... I couldn't even put a name to it now. He was only lying, using me for whatever grand scheme the Crimson Clan had planned.

"Why didn't you tell me, Orion? Why let me discover it this way?" I whispered, pain evident in my voice.

He looked down, remorse clouding his eyes. "I wanted to tell you, truly I did. But the situation is more complex than you know. Sir Edric also told me to keep it secret for as long as possible. Ignorance is bliss, Leila."

My thoughts swirled in a maelstrom of betrayal. "And you were okay with them using me as some sacrificial lamb? As a means to an end?"

Orion's gaze met mine. "No, I wasn't. I've been trying to find a way to thwart their plans. That's why I'm here, Leila. I'm not just here to save you from Keldara, but also from the Crimson Clan."

His sincerity rang clear, but trust, once shattered, wasn't easy to mend. Still, I couldn't deny the reality of my situation. Mykal was not my ally, and Ronan ... Ronan had been playing me all along. Right now, Orion was the lesser of the many evils surrounding me.

"Have you freed Selene?" I asked.

"I will. Remember our deal?" He pulled the cloak's hood back over his silver hair and pointed ears, then reached out his hand again for me to take.

Reluctantly I took it. "Yes, we have a deal." With a sigh, I let him lead me out of the tent through the slit.

The cold night air hit my face, offering a brief moment of clarity amid the whirlwind of events. The Keldaran camp was vast and chaotic, with fires flickering in the distance and the raucous laughter of drunken soldiers piercing the stillness. But

Orion moved with purpose, guiding me expertly through the shadows, avoiding patrols and staying clear of the lit areas.

As we crept toward the edge of the sprawling camp, my thoughts turned to Selene. Would Orion keep his word and free her as he promised? And even if he did, where would she go? Once my secret was out to the world, I wasn't sure she could return to Valoria with me. Would she be safe with Orion?

"We need to be quick," Orion whispered, snapping me back to the present. "There's a forested area to the west where we can take cover until dawn."

I nodded and focused on putting one foot in front of the other, letting the rhythm of our escape momentarily drown out the overwhelming emotions that threatened to consume me. After what felt like hours but was probably only minutes, we reached the edge of the forest. The canopy of trees offered cover and a temporary sense of safety. We slowed our pace and took a moment to catch our breath.

"Wait!" I stopped as realization dawned on me. "There's going to be an attack tonight."

Orion frowned. "What are you talking about? What attack?"

"Keldara sent word that they plan to attack the Valorian camp tonight in the hopes it would lure the Crimson Clan into the open."

My fae rescuer furrowed his brows. "So?"

"*So*, Keldara is trying to start a war between Valoria and the Crimson Clan."

Orion shrugged. "That's *their* business, Leila. *Our* business is to get somewhere safe. Not only you, but Selene as well."

I ripped my hand out of his grip. "No! I need to warn Caelan." I started to double back.

"Leila!" Orion whisper-yelled. "If you do this, there's no going back from it."

I knew he was right. I also remembered how I defended Ronan to Mykal by saying he wouldn't be stupid enough to fall for his trick, but deep down I wasn't sure. Now that my eyes had been opened, it forced me to consider that everything I thought I knew wasn't real.

"Free Selene," I said, walking backward. "Get her to safety and I'll meet you at the inn near the Silent Mountains."

"Leila ..." he muttered.

But my mind was made. I spun on my heels and ran north toward the Valorian camp.

∼

THE FOREST FLOOR WAS UNEVEN, and roots and stones threatened to trip me with every hurried step. But determination fueled my pace. My heart raced and pumped enough adrenaline through my veins to speed my journey. Each labored breath reminded me of the looming danger and the weight of the responsibility I now bore.

I heard the Keldaran camp in the distance, the shouts and clinking armor growing fainter. But the sound was deceptive. A well-coordinated attack would move swiftly and stealthily. I had to reach the Valorian camp before they did.

Moonlight filtered through the trees, casting an eerie glow over the forest. Shadows shifted and danced, playing tricks on my mind, but I couldn't afford to be distracted now. My sole focus was reaching the Valorian camp in time.

I finally broke free from the trees into a clearing that signaled the proximity of the Valorian camp. Lofty watchtowers lorded over camp as wary guards patrolled the perimeters. I slowed and approached carefully, not wanting to be mistaken for the enemy.

"Halt! Who goes there?" a guard shouted as he caught sight of me.

"I have urgent news for Prince Caelan!" I called out, my hands raised in surrender. He eyed me hesitantly and several other soldiers approached, looking at me cautiously. "Tell him Princess Lyanna wishes to see him!" I yelled, launching a chorus of startled gasps from everyone in the area.

"Send a message to His Highness!" the first soldier yelled to another one who stood nearby. With a sharp salute, the other soldier rushed off to inform Caelan of my arrival.

The soldiers, after a moment's hesitation, surrounded me in a protective circle, spears and swords at the ready. While their formation was intended to protect, it also served as a cage to prevent me from moving. Murmurs spread among them, whispers of disbelief and surprise echoing through the clearing.

"Princess Lyanna? Is it truly her?"

"I thought she was dead."

"I've heard tales of her bravery and beauty."

"This woman doesn't have our crescent moon mark."

"Surely this can't be her!"

After a tense few minutes that felt like hours, the young soldier returned and whispered something to the one who seemed to be their leader. The guard hesitated for a moment before motioning for the others to make an opening for me. "Quickly, follow me." Without another word, he led me towards the center of a cluster of tents.

The Valorian camp was abuzz with activity. Soldiers were preparing for night watches, checking their equipment, and chatting by the fires. But the air was tense, with an undercurrent of anticipation that signaled they were already aware of the impending threat.

I was ushered into a grand tent where Caelan sat at a table studying maps and a bundle of documents.

He looked up as I entered, surprise evident in his eyes. "Leila? What are you doing here?" he asked as he stood. "I thought—"

"I know what you thought ..." Suddenly, I wasn't ready to reveal my true self. "Sorry for fooling you, but I came to warn you," I said urgently. "Keldara lied about their plans to attack tonight. They want to pit you against the Crimson Clan."

Caelan's face hardened. "So *that's* what they're hoping for."

"After we ... parted ways," I raised a brow, "Mykal returned with soldiers and captured me. I've been in their camp all day, and I heard their plan," I said, slightly out of breath. "They're hoping that if they draw out the Valorian army, the Crimson Clan will make an appearance in hopes of collecting the spoils."

"Making them attack *us* once they realize Keldara didn't show up," Caelan finished.

I nodded. "Correct."

Caelan grunted. "Commander Mykal Kaiser sure lives up to his wily reputation," he murmured. "Regardless, we must prepare for an attack. The Crimson Clan doesn't play games. If they believe there's a chance they can get what they want, they'll strike hard," Caelan said, his eyes scanning the maps on the table.

"You need to change your tactics," I suggested. "Instead of waiting for them, lure them into a trap. Let them think they've caught you off guard."

Caelan raised an eyebrow. "I thought Ronan was your friend," he asked cautiously.

I snorted. "Yeah, I thought so, too. Unfortunately, he's not who I thought he was."

Caelan nodded, but he didn't inquire further. "Your proposed strategy is risky, but it might just work. Do you have something specific in mind?"

"I've been thinking about it." I pointed to a narrow pass marked on the map. "This is the most direct route they could take if they decide to attack. You could use the terrain to your advantage. Set up a diversion here," I pointed to a thickly wooded area, "and when they're drawn to it, your forces can flank them from both sides."

A slow smile spread across Caelan's face. "It's bold, but it'll only work if they believe the diversion is our main defense. We need something to catch their attention and hold it long enough for our forces to get into position."

"What about fire?" I suggested. "A large bonfire, or maybe some makeshift fireworks. It'll draw their attention and give the illusion that you're celebrating, blissfully unaware of their approach."

"That's good." Caelan nodded. "It will require precise timing. Our soldiers must be in position before they light the fires, and we need scouts on the lookout, ensuring we know the exact moment the Crimson Clan approaches."

I raised one shoulder. "I can help with that. Once they reach this point," I pointed to a passage on the map, "I can send up a flare."

Caelan's brows furrowed and he narrowed his eyes at me. "How do I know this isn't a trick and you're not actually working for the Crimson Clan?"

"I wish I could say something that would ease your worry, but I can't ... at least not yet," I offered. "Just know that the Crimson Clan is my enemy and I want them defeated as much as you do ... possibly even more."

I wanted to tell Caelan I was Lyanna, the one he'd searched for all these years, but now wasn't the time. I also didn't want to distract him with that revelation when he was about to go to battle.

The look on my face was earnest, my tone pleading. "I know you don't have any reason to trust me, but could I ask you to just this once?"

Caelan studied me intently, his piercing hazel eyes searching for any hint of deceit. The tension in the tent was palpable, with only the crackling fire and the distant hum of the camp's activities punctuating the silence. After an interminably long time, he finally spoke.

"Leila, the stakes are high. You're asking me to trust you at a moment when any mistake can cost us dearly. But I sense sincerity in your eyes, and perhaps ... familiarity? There's something about you that's hard to ignore."

I swallowed but kept quiet.

He sighed and ran a hand through his silver hair. "I've been wrong before, and it's cost me. But sometimes, we have to trust our gut. I'll give you this chance, Leila. But remember, any treachery you inflict upon us will not only endanger us, but you as well."

I nodded, relieved by his decision but aware of the gravity of the situation. "I understand, Your Highness. I promise you won't regret this."

With an understanding nod, he turned back to the maps. "Alright, then. Positions need to be finalized, and our scouts need to be briefed. Let's get everything in place. We don't have much time."

∼

THE NEXT FEW hours were consumed by preparing for the upcoming battle. I coordinated with Valoria's scouts, ensuring they knew the importance of the flare's timing. Caelan, alongside his trusted generals, set about deploying troops and ensuring every contingency was accounted for and addressed.

As the night wore on, a sense of impending confrontation hovered in the air. Everyone could feel it—the oncoming storm that would decide the fate of Valoria. As I stood at my lookout point and watched the distant horizon for any signs of movement, I hoped that when dawn broke, we would stand victorious, after turning the tables on the Crimson Clan *and* Keldara.

As the moon rose to its zenith and cast a pale glow over the landscape, tension among the Valorian forces reached a crescendo. Every soldier and scout was on high alert, their senses tuned to any sign of the Crimson Clan.

I remained vigilant at my post. Though the cold night air bit my skin, I couldn't afford to shiver—not when so much depended on my precise attention to detail. Every shadow and rustle in the underbrush had to be noted, every possible threat assessed.

Caelan positioned his troops strategically, hidden away from prying eyes but ready to strike at a moment's notice. The camp appeared quiet, almost deserted to the untrained eye. But I knew better.

Then, it happened—a subtle shift in the wind, a faint echo of movement from the east. I strained my eyes and peered into the darkness. There it was again—a stealthy rustle, followed by the soft thud of footfalls on the forest floor. The Crimson Clan was approaching, unaware their presence had been detected.

My heart raced as I reached for the flare. This was the moment of truth. I ignited it and the bright light shot into the sky, bursting in a shower of sparks that illuminated the darkness. There was no turning back now.

The Crimson Clan continued on their path for several more minutes until they were surrounded. Then, the Valorian army attacked.

The sound of steel against steel rang out and commands were yelled from both sides. Magic filled the air as Valorian mages did battle from the vantage point of having the upper hand. The conflict erupted into a cacophony of chaos and power, a dance of flashing blades and arcane explosions. The Valorian mages chanted incantations that sent shockwaves through the ranks of the Crimson Clan.

I watched as the Valorian forces maintained their formations, each unit moving as one under the cover of their mages' power. The battlefield was a living, breathing entity of warcraft, and every soldier was a vital organ within it.

Despite being caught by surprise, the Crimson Clan was a formidable foe. They were warriors at heart. Even though they didn't have any magic, they were much stronger than the average human, thanks to their demon blood.

I watched from above as Ronan sped through the passageway on horseback. Silas and others followed suit as they charged for the heart of the battlefield ... where Prince Caelan fought. I watched in horror as Ronan aimed his double swords for the killing blow. Jumping down from my vantage point, I knocked a rider off their horse and slung my leg over the saddle.

With a hard yank on the reins, I pushed the horse to its limits and raced toward Caelan. Once I was close enough, I extended my hand toward Ronan and made a fist as I took hold of the blood running through his veins. He pulled his horse's reins and halted as his swords tumbled from useless hands. He groaned and wavered in the saddle.

It was now or never. If I wanted to protect Caelan, if I wanted to protect my people, I couldn't hide anymore.

Summoning the full force of my will, I squeezed my hand tighter and channeled the potent blood magic that ran through my veins. It required every ounce of concentration, for controlling the very life force of another was a perilous endeavor.

Ronan writhed atop his horse, his face contorting in agony as his blood turned against him, a marionette to my grim puppetry. His soldiers slowed and confusion etched their faces as their leader faltered. My intrusion into his body was an intimate violation of his formidable strength that left him vulnerable and exposed.

I couldn't hold him long, though. I hadn't practiced blood magic in many years due to my need to hide. But I managed to hold him long enough for the Valorians to capitalize on the distraction.

Caelan, ever the astute warrior, noticed the pause in

Ronan's assault and with a swift series of motions, disarmed another assailant before turning his attention to the debilitated leader of the Crimson Clan. He approached Ronan with his sword at the ready, his eyes not on his enemy but on me as recognition dawned within them.

"Leila?" he called out, his voice a mixture of disbelief and realization. "No ... *Lyanna*?"

I ignored him and yelled as I tightened my hold on Ronan. "Hurry!" But Silas was quicker, and he took advantage of Caelan's distraction to jump in front of Ronan to shield his friend and leader.

With a grunt I released my grip and Ronan tumbled off his horse. He landed with his face turned toward me; a face filled with pain and betrayal as he fixed his gaze on me and tried to stay conscious. "Why?" he muttered.

"Why?" I scoffed. "As if you don't know!" I growled. "Weren't you planning to sacrifice me to the demon fox?"

Ronan's eyes widened. As Ronan and I were in the center staring at one another, everything else seemed to fall away, even as the battle continued to rage around us. Silas and Caelan fought while the rest of Ronan's men protected their vulnerable leader against the Valorian army.

"Let me explain," he groaned, but I held up a hand to stop him.

My voice was cold. "No need. Mykal told me everything."

He frowned. "Mykal?" he asked in confusion and then realization dawned. "The commander of the Keldaran army?"

I nodded. "He told me everything. I won't fall for your lies anymore."

Just then, one of the Crimson Clan soldiers charged toward me with his sword drawn. I narrowed my gaze and waited until he got closer.

"No!" Ronan shouted. "Stop!"

But his soldier didn't listen. His attention was fixed solely on me—the threat against their leader. Once he got closer, I reached out my hand and gripped his blood, seizing him in his tracks. With a fling of my wrist, I tossed him across the battlefield.

Ronan's face paled as he witnessed my raw display of power and the truth that lay bare between us. Breathing heavily, I stood with my chin raised as the potent energy of my blood magic crackled like static around my fingertips.

His warriors hesitated and fear overtook their earlier fervor. They knew, as Ronan did, that the battlefield had shifted with my revelation. I was no mere pawn to be played—I was a queen on this chessboard of war, with powers they couldn't begin to comprehend.

Murmurs flooded through the ranks of Valorian soldiers at my display of power.

"She's the lost princess!"

"We found her!"

"The healer Leila is the princess!"

Ronan struggled to his knees with ragged breaths, his gaze never straying from mine. "Leila—Lyanna, *please*," he said, his voice strained. "You must listen to me. Mykal is the deceiver here, not me."

The urge to unleash another wave of blood magic was strong. I wanted to make him pay for his betrayal, for the manipulation, for making me a part of his schemes. But something held me back. A flicker of doubt? Or was it the last strand of the connection we once shared?

"Silence!" I commanded, my voice laced with power. "Your words are poison, Ronan. There's nothing you can say to untangle the web of lies you've woven."

Around us, the clash of steel and the cries of the fallen continued, a stark reminder of the chaos Ronan helped orchestrate. I turned my back to him, ready to join Caelan and put an end to this, but Ronan's next words halted me.

"Lyanna, the demon fox ... it's not what you think. I was trying to protect you—"

"Protect me?" I whirled around, my indignant anger flaring. "By marking me for a demon? You have a strange way of showing you care, Ronan."

He grimaced and had the grace to look ashamed. "That ... was an accident. I didn't mean to. I was caught up in the moment. I would never hurt you!"

I scoffed. "As if I'd believe *you*." I was about to turn back around when I saw a flicker of movement, then watched in horror as Caelan bypassed Silas and charged toward Ronan, who was still on his knees.

I don't know why I did what I did, but my actions turned the tide.

As Caelan lunged, my eyes widened and I yelled, "Ronan!"

He glanced over his shoulder in time to see Caelan swing his sword. Ducking, he rolled across the ground and popped back up to his feet, away from the bite of Caelan's sword.

I sat atop my horse in shock at what I just did. Why did I warn him? This was our opportunity to get rid of him once and for all! Deep down, I still had lingering feelings for him, no matter how much his betrayal stung.

The battle raged around me, but in that moment, everything slowed down. I was perched on the precipice of a truth I wasn't ready to accept. I warned Ronan because, despite everything, I couldn't bear to watch him die. Was it the remnants of what we shared, or was it the part of me that knew his death wouldn't end this war?

Caelan regrouped quickly, and his eyes darted between me and Ronan. A flash of hurt and betrayal crossed his features before he masked it with the stoic façade of a prince at war. "He is our enemy, Lyanna. He isn't who you think he is. You were the one who told me that."

"I—" I stuttered, unable to think clearly.

"I won't hurt him," Ronan said, gasping for air. "You said you didn't want me to hurt him, so I'll listen. I'll do as you say. I won't touch him. So it's up to you, Leila. Stop this or let him kill me."

Caelan sneered. "It would my pleasure."

"Caelan, *stop!*" I said loud enough for him to hear.

In a blink, a myriad of emotions flashed across his face. Chief among them were conflict, pain, and the weight of leadership that demanded decisive action. He slowly sheathed his sword and the sneer that touched his lips faded into a grim line of resolve.

"Retreat," Caelan demanded of Ronan. "Tell your men to retreat ... but you ... *stay.*"

Ronan looked up at me, his eyes pained as he nodded. "Retreat!" he yelled.

"Ronan!" Silas called out, but Ronan only pointed a glare his way.

"I said retreat!"

Slowly, the Crimson Clan warriors turned and headed back the way they came, until only Ronan and Silas remained.

Silas looked up at me in horror. "You ... *you* are Princess Lyanna?" he asked, even though he already knew the answer. When I nodded, he looked between me and Ronan. "You'll regret this, Princess."

"Is that a threat?" I growled.

Silas shook his head. "No. It's a promise." Without another word, Silas jumped back on his horse and galloped from the battlefield to safety, leaving Ronan as our hostage.

24

We returned to the Valorian camp in silence. When I slid off my horse, Caelan rushed to me and tenderly gripped my face, his eyes searching for some recognition and checking my body for injuries.

"It's you ... It's really you!" he murmured reverently. His eyes widened and glossed with unshed tears when I released the magic that hid the crescent moon mark on my forehead. "You were right in front of me this whole time and I never knew. How could I not know?" he asked himself.

I gripped his wrist, his hands still holding my face. "I was eleven the last time we saw each other, Caelan. There's no way you would have known me as I am now."

He brushed my hair back and caressed my face. "Still ..." he whispered. "I should have recognized you. I'm sorry ..." Suddenly, he released me as if I'd burned him. "Oh, gods, I'm so sorry, Lyanna!" Horror flashed across his face as he thought back to the arrows ... the torture ... everything he'd done to me.

"You didn't know," I said again.

He shook his head. "It doesn't matter. What I've done is unforgiveable." His eyes reflected his inner turmoil, revealing the struggle to reconcile his personal regrets and what he'd just learned. A war raged in him, one that mirrored the chaos that had only recently ceased on the battlefield.

"Caelan, stop," I urged, reaching out to steady his wavering focus. "Your actions were against an enemy you were unaware held a face from your past."

His jaw clenched and he looked away, unable to meet my gaze. Ashamed. "That doesn't excuse my actions. I can't—"

"Look at me," I interrupted, a gentle command that drew his tormented gaze back to mine. "You cannot undo the past. None of us can. But you can learn from it. We both can."

He remained silent for a moment, breathing deeply as he processed my words. The guards and soldiers around us gave us space, a quiet bubble amidst the camp's recovering bustle.

"I've been living with a ghost," he finally whispered. "A memory of a little girl I swore to protect. And now ..." His hand reached up as if to touch the crescent moon mark, but he stopped short as if he suddenly felt unworthy.

"And now that little girl is a woman, strong and alive," I said, my voice firm. "I don't need your protection, Caelan. The Lyanna you knew is gone. But in her place is someone who can stand with you, not behind you." I reached for his hands and squeezed them tightly.

After a few moments, he pulled me toward him in an embrace and held me as if I was the air he needed to breathe. "Don't ever disappear again ... okay?"

I nodded. "I promise."

"Caelan!" someone yelled from behind us. We spun around to see my brother fast approaching. He held a bright smile until he neared and caught sight of me. His eyes zeroed in on my crescent moon mark and he came to a halt, his eyes widening. "You're ..."

I smiled. "It's me, Marcel."

His expression darkened. "No. No. It can't be!"

"It is, Marcel," Caelan confirmed. "I witnessed her blood magic. Now I also understand how you cured me from the poison."

I nodded.

"You—you've been here all along and hid ... *from us*? The ones who loved you most?" Marcellus shouted in anger.

It was a reaction I hadn't expected.

"I'm sorry, Marcellus. I didn't mean to hurt you, but there were things I needed to find out before—"

"No!" He shook his head. "You're not my sister. Lyanna never would have done that!" With a dismissive glare, he stormed off in a fury.

I attempted to go after him, but Caelan stopped me. "Give him some time. He's awaited your return for ten long years, and during that time, your parents suffocated him for fear of losing him, too. He ... he believed you were somewhere in Asteria with memory loss, which is why you didn't return."

"So, he's resentful?"

Caelan nodded. "Possibly."

His words, though meant to provide clarity, only deepened the weight in my chest. It was one thing to anticipate a reunion and brace for all the complex tides of emotion that came with it, but it was quite another to witness a loved one's pain—pain I'd inadvertently caused.

"I need to explain," I insisted, the urgency of reconciliation pressing on my spirit.

Caelan gently released me. "You will, but not now. Let the shock pass. Let him see that you're truly here, truly part of our world again. Sometimes, presence is louder than any rushed explanation."

He was right, of course. Marcellus's pain was raw, and the complexities of my disappearance and sudden reappearance could not be unraveled in an instant. The wound was too fresh, and I was an unwelcome reminder of a decade of loss and anguish.

Turning back to face the camp, I knew the night's battle was only the first of many I would have to endure. The war was far from over, and personal battles often cut deeper than those fought with swords and magic.

"For now," Caelan took my hand again, "let's prepare to return home. Valoria eagerly awaits the return of its beloved princess."

With those words, I realized that my life as Leila, the healer of the Central Plains was over. I was now Princess Lyanna—the lost princess found.

ABOUT THE AUTHOR

Join my Facebook group, **Karina's Kick-Ass Reads!**

Reviews are very important to authors and help readers discover our books. Please take a moment to leave a review on **Amazon**. Thank you!

ALSO BY KARINA ESPINOSA

Mackenzie Grey: Origins Series (Completed)

SHIFT

CAGED

ALPHA

OMEGA

Mackenzie Grey: Trials Series (Completed)

From the Grave

Curse Breaker

Bound by Magic

Stolen Relics

Bloodlust

Mackenzie Grey: The Crown Series (Completed)

Queen of the Lycan

Blood of the Wolf

Return of the Alpha

The Joey Santana Series (Completed)

Cursed

Sinner

Legacy

Wicked

The Last Valkyrie Trilogy (Completed)

The Last Valkyrie

The Sword of Souls

The Rise of the Valkyries

From the Ashes Trilogy (Completed)

Phoenix Burn

Phoenix Rise

Dark Phoenix

Fated Fae Elementals Trilogy (Completed)

A Hint of Delirium

A Blaze of Fire

A Touch of Iron

Sevyn Rose Trilogy (In Progress)

Killer Wolf

Captured Wolf

Savage Wolf

ABOUT THE AUTHOR

Karina Espinosa is the Fantasy Author of the Mackenzie Grey novels, The Last Valkyrie, Joey Santana, and From the Ashes series. An avid reader throughout her life, the world of Fantasy easily became an obsession that turned into a passion for writing strong leading characters with authentic story arcs. When she isn't writing badass heroines, you can find this self-proclaimed nomad in her South Florida home binge watching the latest K-drama or traveling far and wide for the latest inspiration for her books.

For more information:
www.karinaespinosa.com